THE GRAVING DOCK

ALSO BY GABRIEL COHEN

Red Hook
Boombox

THE GRAVING DOCK

GABRIEL COHEN

THOMAS DUNNE BOOKS
ST. MARTIN'S MINOTAUR
NEW YORK

M+S

THOMAS DUNNE BOOKS.
An imprint of St. Martin's Press.

THE GRAVING DOCK. Copyright © 2007 by Gabriel Cohen. All rights reserved. Printed in the United States of America. No part of this book may be used or reproduced in any manner whatsoever without written permission except in the case of brief quotations embodied in critical articles or reviews. For information, address St. Martin's Press, 175 Fifth Avenue, New York, N.Y. 10010.

Design by Dylan Rosal Greif

www.thomasdunnebooks.com
www.minotaurbooks.com

Excerpt from "The River That Is East," from *Flower Herding on Mount Monadnock: Poems by Galway Kinnell.* Copyright © 1964, renewed 1992 by Galway Kinnell. Reprinted by permission of Houghton Mifflin Company. All rights reserved.

Library of Congress Cataloging-in-Publication Data

Cohen, Gabriel, 1961–
    The graving dock / Gabriel Cohen. — 1st U.S. ed.
        p. cm.
    ISBN-13: 978-0-312-36266-9
    ISBN-10: 0-312-36266-8
    1. Police—New York (State)—New York—Fiction. 2. Brooklyn (New York, N.Y.)—Fiction. 3. Boys—Crimes against—Fiction. I. Title.
    PS3603.O35G73 2007
    813'.6—dc22

2007024592

First Edition: November 2007

10 9 8 7 6 5 4 3 2 1

What is this river but the one
Which drags the things we love
Processions of debris like floating lamps
Toward the radiance in which they go out?

—GALWAY KINNELL, FROM "THE RIVER THAT IS EAST"

THE GRAVING DOCK

CHAPTER *one*

Out on the cold, blustery end of a Brooklyn pier, Herman Rios and Angel Oviedo had just caught a flounder when death literally drifted into their lives.

"What the hell is that?" said Herman as his friend reeled in the unhappy fish. Prior to this moment, they had never seen one of the bottom-dwelling creatures in its natural state.

Angel stared at the fish, which had both eyes on one side of its flat body. He dropped it on the concrete and backed away fast.

"Throw it back," urged Herman. "That *bastit* must've grew up near a nuclear power plant."

"Least I caught something," Angel said, glancing at his friend's empty bucket.

Herman shrugged. He bent down and rummaged through his tackle box until he found a new lure. The guy at the bait shop had sworn by it: The head was lead and the body was comprised of four little pieces of surgical tubing.

Angel stared out at where his line led down into the gray-green water. He was hoping for a few stripers, which were supposed to run well in the cold weather. After a while he grew tired of watching the filament and his gaze traveled beyond the sheltered cove. Red Hook was a humble neighborhood of warehouses and machine shops, but the waterfront offered a spectacular view of New York Harbor lying under a vast cloud-dappled plain of sky. Across the south stretched the spare, simple span of the Verrazano-Narrows Bridge. To the southwest, across the gleaming harbor, lay the wooded shoreline of Staten Island. The Statue of Liberty stood in the middle of the harbor; she seemed so close Angel almost believed he could chuck a rock and hit her green torch. Some anonymous island covered with low brick buildings sat in the water farther north, and then the view was dominated by the southern skyline of Manhattan, bold glass buildings reflecting back the morning sun. There was a huge recent hole there, but Angel preferred not to think about it.

He glanced at his line again—still quiet—and then something moving in along the edge of the cove caught his eye.

"You see that?" he asked his friend. "What you think that is?"

Herman squinted at an object bobbing along in the bright choppy water. His eyes grew big.

"It looks like some kind of *cwawfin.*"

Indeed it was, a homemade wooden box just four and a half feet long.

CHAPTER *two*

Twenty-four hours before he was summoned to peer down into that opened box, death was the last thing on Jack Leightner's mind. This was unusual: As a detective with the elite Brooklyn South Homicide Task Force, corpses were the focus of his every working day.

He had the weekend off, though, and he was far from New York City's steady influx of bodies. At the moment, his attention was riveted by another box, one whose dimensions were considerably smaller. Standing just inside the closet, he slipped the black velvet case out of his traveling bag and into his pants pocket, but it was too obvious there, so he took it out again and removed the ring. He felt like he was getting an ulcer.

"What are you doing in there?" asked his girlfriend, Michelle. She had flopped down on their new bed as soon as they'd checked in and unpacked.

"Nothing," Jack replied, slipping the ring into his pocket. "I'm just trying to figure out what to wear down to dinner." This was a silly excuse, as he only had two choices: one of the dark blue sports jackets he wore on the job, or the tweed jacket he saved for the occasional court appearance or NYPD retirement racket.

They had just arrived on the train from Grand Central. It had run along the sparkling Hudson River, through the last bright scraps of fall foliage, past the gray stone blocks of Sing Sing prison. The inn was only an hour and a half north of Manhattan, but it might as well have been on another planet. There was no rap music thumping in the streets of this quaint little town, no car alarms, no trash piled on the curbs. No NYPD vehicles blowing by to remind Jack of his latest case.

As he stepped back into the bedroom he wondered if Michelle might be suspicious, but she was busy reading a brochure. She lay on top of the frilly bedspread. That wasn't the right word: It was probably a *duvet*, or a *sham* or something; there was undoubtedly a Victorian name for it. That was the big keyword here, *Victorian*, and it seemed to mean that everything had to be wildly overdecorated and look like something you shouldn't sit on, or even touch. It wasn't Jack's style, but he hoped his girlfriend liked it.

Michelle Wilber was forty-one, with long black hair, slightly slumped shoulders, and wrinkles in the corners of her eyes. (Jack had never been the kind who chased after young women.) Right now she looked so good that his heart ached.

"I'll be right back," he said.

"Okay," she murmured, engrossed in her reading.

He stepped out into the hall and gently closed the door. The inn was supposed to be one of the oldest in the United States. The plank floors had been polished smooth by generations of guest feet. The narrow stairs down to the lobby were so ancient that they bowed. At least the place was well kept; he would have been very disappointed if he had brought Michelle to some kind of dump. (You could never really tell from an ad—the photo might show laughing couples lounging around a fancy pool, and then you'd arrive and find a little cracked kidney bean full of dead leaves.)

Behind the front desk the innkeeper was tapping away at a computer, one of the only objects in the whole place that wasn't topped by some porcelain knickknack. The woman was a brisk middle-aged blonde.

"Hello," Jack said. "I need to ask a little favor."

The woman peered through tortoiseshell half-glasses. She was several inches shorter than he was, but managed to give the impression that she was looking down at him. "Yes?"

Her smile struck him as brittle. Maybe that was because he had asked to change rooms earlier. It wasn't his fault. On the Internet, a view from one of the windows had showed a cozy little street packed with antiques shops. When he and Michelle actually showed up, though, a chambermaid had led them up to a room at the back, which faced out onto a parking lot and a drive-through bank. Maybe the innkeeper had heard his Brooklyn accent and assumed she could get away with it. Normally Jack might not have cared, but this was a special occasion and he was determined to do it right.

He cleared his throat, glanced at the stairs, and took the ring out of his pocket. "I need a little help with this," he said. "I'm gonna propose to my girlfriend at dinner tonight."

The innkeeper's smile suddenly grew a lot more genuine. "Isn't that wonderful!" she said. "What can we do?"

BY THE TIME JACK got back to the room, Michelle had kicked her shoes off and piled a couple of pillows under her wavy hair. There was a hole in the toe of one of her stockings and that made Jack feel better—he wasn't the only one unaccustomed to such upscale digs. He had prepared an excuse about getting something from the car, but she didn't even ask where he had been. Michelle was pretty self-sufficient. It was not that she was uninterested in what he did, but she trusted him—she only got on his case if he screwed up in some major way. He couldn't help comparing her to his ex-wife, who would probably have grilled him like a detective in an interview room.

He looked at his watch; they had the whole day to kill. He supposed they could scope out the antiques shops, but the thought made him itch.

He pressed a hand against his stomach. He had always prided himself on keeping in shape, not letting middle age turn him flabby, but he could feel a hint of a pot developing. "Hey—why don't we go get some of this country air everybody's always going on about?"

Michelle set down the brochure, smiled, and unbuttoned her blouse. "What's your hurry?"

AFTER, THEY TOOK A walk, setting off along a two-lane blacktop that led out into the countryside. A couple of days after Thanksgiving the weather had taken a plunge into winter and the air was nippy, but after a few minutes of hiking Jack was warm enough to unzip his jacket. The busy tourist kernel of the town gave way to some grand, dilapidated old estates, and then the view opened up across stubbly farm fields dotted with an occasional cow. Crows cawed up in bare branches; other than that there was an almost eerie silence, broken only by their own footsteps and an occasional passing car.

Jack wished they had come in spring, when there would be flowers and stuff to look at, or in the fall during peak foliage days, but Michelle was not put off by the stark views. She found things to comment on, pointing out an interesting weathervane or farm silo. Jack was an observant sort himself, but he focused on different things, like how isolated some of these country houses were, how easy it would be to break in. How owning a gun might make some sense out here, rather than in the city where every time somebody fired one of the damned things they ran the risk of popping an innocent—or not-so-innocent—bystander.

"Couldn't you see us living in a place like that?" Michelle said, pointing at a little farmhouse.

"I don't know," he said, not wanting to dampen her good cheer. He *did* know: He'd probably go nuts after a few months in a quiet place like this. If he took a job with a police force out here, he'd probably spend his time investigating teenagers' break-ins of summer homes. A good murder would probably only come along every five years.

A scruffy little brown-and-white dog trotted out of a yard and started following them. Jack bent down and scratched its ears. "Go home, pooch," he said, his breath puffing white in the still country air, but the dog set off with him when he moved on.

By the time he and Michelle reached the next town, they were both hungry; even the little dog looked like it could use a snack. The village seemed rather run-down and not at all touristy. There were no cute little cafes or even convenience stores. It soon became apparent that there was not a single commercial dining establishment in the whole place. Every once in a while a car whizzed through, headed somewhere else. Finally, Jack saw a gaunt old woman step out onto her front porch.

"Excuse me," he called up. "Is there someplace to get a bite to eat around here?"

"Well," she drawled, "there's some nice places about three miles up the road that way." She pointed toward their starting point.

Jack turned to Michelle. "Sorry, honey."

Michelle just grinned.

That was one of the things he loved about her: She was such a good sport. She had proved that in the most dramatic way imaginable, just after they had gotten together this past summer, when he had taken a late-night call, left her bed, set off to meet an informant for a case he was working on—and taken a bullet in the chest. She could easily have bailed out, and he wouldn't have blamed her—they barely knew each other—but she had rushed to the hospital, visited him every day, helped him with his physical therapy when he finally came home. In the middle of all that, September 11 happened, and they spent several days huddled together in front of the TV. It seemed as if they had lived a lifetime in that terrible month.

Jack shrugged. "I guess we'd better head back, then."

A few yards away, the little dog sat on its haunches looking up at him with what seemed like a Brooklyn expression. *Whadda-yagonnado?*

TWO MILES INTO THE return trip, even the dog was drooping. Jack wondered if he'd have to start carrying the thing.

"You okay?" Michelle asked.

Jack was tired—he was still recovering from his bullet wound—but he nodded and kept walking.

Finally, they reached the dog's yard and it perked up and trotted off. *Adios, amigos.*

By the time they made it back to town, chilled and faint with hunger, even Michelle's good spirits were wearing thin. They found a luncheonette on the main street and settled into a booth.

"I'm gonna order one of everything," Michelle said.

Jack scratched the side of his mouth. "Let's save some room for dinner." After the mix-up with the rooms and the long, hungry walk, his hoped-for perfect day had already gone a bit off the rails. It wasn't so much that Michelle would expect a fairy-tale proposal—it was more that he was determined to do things better than when he had gotten engaged to his first wife. He had been in his early twenties and Louise had gotten pregnant and there hadn't even been a proposal, really, just a sort of somber discussion and an agreement that marriage seemed like the right thing to do.

―――――――――

"I'M HUNGRY AGAIN," MICHELLE said three hours later as they prepared to head down to the inn's fancy dining room. "It must be the country air. Or maybe the good loving." She smiled and gave her dress a tug in front of the mirror.

The moment of truth had arrived. Jack chewed an antacid as he started putting on a necktie.

"C'mon," Michelle said. "We're out in the country—you don't need to dress up."

"You sure?" Jack was an expert at many things—crime scene investigation, ballistics, even forensic entomology—but fashion was not one of them. This made him an anomaly among NYPD detectives, who loved to put on the style.

"Of course," Michelle said. "This is our chance to relax a little."

Down in the dining room the ceilings were low, with dark wood beams from when the place had been a tavern during the Revolutionary War. The flickering oil lamps didn't give off much light, but enough to show that every man in the place was wearing a tie.

Jack frowned, but Michelle squeezed his arm. "You look great."

He gave his name to a portly older woman at the entrance to the dining room and made sure he made eye contact—*I'm the guy who's gonna propose tonight.* She smiled and led them to a nice corner table. Jack held Michelle's chair out for her and then he sat down.

A short girl in a frilly apron approached. Her teeth were covered with braces and she looked like she might still be in high school. "Can I take your beverage order?" she said cheerily, stretching her mouth around the words.

"I feel like something fun," Michelle said. "Can I get a Cosmopolitan?" This was a drink she had learned about on nights out with the women from her office in Manhattan. The company rented out plates and tablecloths for parties.

"And you, sir?"

"I'm okay for now." He didn't want alcohol to interfere with his upcoming speech.

The leather-bound menu weighed about two pounds. The appetizers cost more than the entrées in most places he was used to. He tried not to raise his eyebrows. It wasn't that he was cheap, but he had grown up poor in Red Hook, Brooklyn, to parents who thought take-out chow mein was a great extravagance. He rested a hand on top of Michelle's. "Order whatever you want."

"The Caesar salad looks good."

Jack gave her a worried look. "You can't have a salad for dinner." What kind of story would that make when they were old and sitting around on a porch somewhere?

Michelle looked beautiful, her skin glowing in the candlelight. *I don't have a single doubt about this woman*, Jack marveled.

He glanced at a middle-aged couple two tables away. They were the only black people he had seen since he had gotten off the train. They were more formally dressed than anyone else in the room. The guy sat as straight as if there were a board in the back of his jacket. He looked about as comfortable here as Jack was, but he had probably never allowed himself to consider skipping the tie.

Jack made it through the dinner. He managed to order something, and even to eat something, and to make small talk about how the sweater-vested bartender looked like he might have fought in the Revolutionary War himself. He kept reaching down to his pants pocket and then remembering that he had surrendered the ring to the innkeeper, who was going to pass it on to the chef, who was going to hide it in Michelle's dessert.

A busboy cleared their entrée plates. "Hoo," said Michelle, who had finally settled on linguini with shrimp. "I'm stuffed."

Jack tried not to frown. "Have a little dessert. How about the chocolate mousse? You love chocolate."

Michelle sighed. "I'm fine. Thank you, honey. This was such a beautiful dinner."

"Get the mousse," Jack said. "I'll help you eat it." He wished he had just held on to the damned ring.

Michelle took a sip of her wine. "All right—but only if you'll help."

After the waitress took their order, Jack sat back and wiped some sweat off his upper lip. He was known as the Homicide Task Force's most dogged veteran, a guy who didn't mind tackling the most difficult, evidence-starved cases. Proposing made such challenges seem like a walk in the park.

Even though he and Michelle had known each other for only a short time, they had gone through so much together, and he was sure she wouldn't say no. Almost sure. His armpits were sweating profusely and he was glad his jacket was still on.

The waitress swept out of the kitchen bearing a silver tray. With a flourish she set down the mousse and two little glasses of port. "Compliments of the chef."

Jack tried to smile as he nodded his thanks, but he wondered if the port was overkill. Michelle gave no sign of suspicion, just picked up her spoon and scooped up a tiny dab of whipped cream. After a minute, another. At this rate, it might take an hour to reach the ring. Jack wanted to help, but what would happen if *he* accidentally scooped it up?

"You okay?" Michelle asked.

"Huh?" he said. "Of course. It's just a little hot in here."

Thankfully, once Michelle hit the chocolate she began to take more of an interest in the dessert. She finished a big spoonful and closed her eyes in rapture. "Oh my God. This is amazing."

Jack glanced over at the bar. The waitress was beaming at him and the bartender gave him a thumbs-up. The room was packed now and he wondered how the other diners would react when he got down on one knee.

Michelle licked some mousse off her finger and gave him a sultry look. "Don't you want some?"

"It's okay. I'm good."

She smiled again. "You certainly are." She dipped the spoon in, dipped the spoon . . .

His chest got tighter with every dip. Absurdly, he wondered which knee to get down on. He tried not to stare at Michelle's parfait glass. Another spoonful. Another. And then . . . she scraped the spoon along the bottom of the empty glass.

He stared openly now, in shock. He had spent two months' pay on the ring, like you were supposed to. He'd run the gauntlet of the jewelry stores up on Forty-seventh Street, the Diamond District, *the horror*—salesmen practically diving over their counters, as if he had worn a sign on his head: SCHMUCK LOOKING FOR ENGAGEMENT RING . . . And he had finally found just the right one.

Vanished.

CHAPTER *three*

Specks of glass glittered in the asphalt as Jack drove deep into the heart of Red Hook. Past vacant lots, low factories, modest row houses; past dead weeds rising out of sidewalk cracks. He drove through the quiet, run-down streets but also through the remembered world of his childhood, when these streets had swarmed with sailors and shipbuilders and longshoremen, back before the boom years of the Brooklyn docks had irrevocably gone bust. In those days the place had been packed with bars, movie theaters, groceries, and clothing stores; now you had to leave the neighborhood to shop or to see a show. There was talk of a revival but the place still felt like a ghost town.

He pulled over for a moment, took out his cell phone, and dialed the inn, his second call of the morning.

"Did you find it yet?"

"I'm sorry, sir," the innkeeper said. "I promise you we're doing the best we can." She didn't sound particularly sorry, but at least she had given up on her argument that the inn was not responsible. (She had stuck to that claim until he had finally done what he hated to do: pull out his badge when off duty.)

"It's not replaceable," he said. Not strictly true, but he couldn't face another shopping trip.

"Sir, I told you," she said. "We're doing the best we can, and if there's any problem, I'm sure our insurance will take care of it."

Jack just snorted and signed off. No insurance was going to compensate him for watching his romantic weekend go up in smoke, or for the Oscar-worthy performance he had had to pull off for the rest the night, pretending to Michelle that everything was okay.

He stopped in to a bodega for a cup of coffee. He was tempted to pick up a pack of smokes, but his long hospital stay had gotten him off the nicotine; it would be stupid to start up again. He took a sip of the thick Puerto Rican java and got back in the car.

He surveyed the sidewalks idly as he drove past: a couple of kids goofing around at a bus stop, swinging their backpacks at each other; a big battleship of a woman nattering away on a little cell phone. As he neared Coffey Street, his stomach clenched. Just two blocks down, in a dank warehouse basement, his world had almost ended. He flashed on a moment from that crazy summer night: police scanners crackling, paramedics shouting as they stretchered him up and out. He'd lain on his back watching streetlights slide by overhead like bright full moons and he had believed that he was about to die . . .

The anxiety ebbed as he drove on. "I'll understand if you'd rather not take the case," his boss had said to him this morning. "I can give it to Santiago or Reinhorn, but I figure you know the neighborhood best." Normally Brooklyn South Homicide used an impartial rotation, with each of the detectives catching new cases in turn, but Detective Sergeant Stephen Tanney was making an exception. Was it a test, Jack wondered, an opportunity for his boss to find out if his recovery was complete?

He drove another block, then turned toward the harbor, down a cobbled street bordered by anonymous little factories and machine shops. Down at the end, he parked behind a couple of patrol cars, a detective's Grand Marquis, and the Crime Scene wagon. Being back in Red Hook gave him the willies, no doubt about it, but he was eager to put recent events behind him and to immerse himself in a case.

As he stepped out into the cold, damp air, his nose filled with the smell of some industrial solvent, a metallic scent, like spray paint, probably coming from one of the factories lining the street. He strode down the old cobblestones, then veered into a little waterfront park. A lawn led down to a small bay, which opened out onto the gray expanse of New York Harbor. Once upon a time this had been the site of the wooden Coffey Pier, where he and his childhood pals had dived laughing out into the water (wearing underpants because none of their parents could afford swim trunks), but that pier had long since rotted away. Recently it had been rebuilt in metal and concrete.

The base of the pier and a stretch of rocky coastline were cordoned off with yellow Crime Scene tape. Beyond that flimsy barrier the inevitable crowd of local spectators had already mushroomed up, wearing the baggy jeans and hooded sweatshirts of the city's poor. They cracked nervous jokes and stamped their feet to stay warm. "Yo, *CSI!*" they shouted, though they were actually looking at a couple of jumpsuited technicians from the Medical Examiner's office. (Thanks to the hit TV show, public interest had moved away from homicide detectives and settled on the Crime Scene teams, which was fine with Jack—he wasn't looking for glory.)

He moved through the crowd, badged the young uniform guarding the perimeter, and ducked under the tape. Down at the water's edge several cops were gathered around some sort of wooden object, but first he set out across the sloping lawn toward a clump of the city workers who dealt with the dead. Usually they'd be standing around relaxed, shooting the shit, but they seemed tense now and Jack could tell that something unusual was going on.

He felt warmer when he joined the huddle, and it wasn't just the added protection from the wind. After a too-long medical leave, he was back in his element.

A short Dominican man with ramrod posture and a near-bald pate nodded hello: Anselmo Alvarez. The supervisor of the Crime Scene crew turned to introduce the man next to him, whose fancy wool coat and Italian leather shoes said *detective.* "This is Tommy Balfa from the Seven-six squad."

As a member of the task force Jack's mission was to team up with local detectives, who caught all sorts of cases and didn't necessarily have much experience with homicides. He reached out to shake hands. The man looked to be around forty-five, with a handsome, rugged face. He wore thin, elegant leather gloves, and gripped Jack's hand a little too hard. If this was some thirties movie, Jack thought, Balfa would have been cast as the gigolo.

Jack squared his shoulders. "What do we have?"

Instead of answering, Balfa led them down to the water's edge, where a coffin-shaped wooden object lay on a fringe of stony beach. The box looked custom made. The lid was open, facing away.

"Is the photographer finished?" Jack asked. Nothing could be moved until a Crime Scene tech took pictures of the entire area. If there had been a murder and the perp was caught, it might be years before the case went to trial, and then this scene so vivid before his eyes would exist only as a series of photos to be pinned on a court-room wall.

Alvarez nodded.

Jack moved around and stared down into the box. Inside, resting on a gray wool blanket, lay the body of a Caucasian boy, perhaps ten years old. In thirteen years with the task force Jack had seen a number of juvenile corpses, and many in far worse shape, but he still winced. This was something you never got inured to, especially if you had a kid of your own—or if you had a brother who had died young.

There was no obvious cause of death. The first thing Jack noticed was something written on the boy's forehead with what looked like red Magic Marker: the letters *G.I.* The child was fully clothed, in blue jeans, sneakers, and a cheap plaid shirt buttoned to the neck—something you might buy from a discount department store. Eyes closed, skin pale and slightly blue, arms resting at his sides. Cheap bowl haircut.

Jack took out a notebook. The sight of the kid was deeply disturbing, but he needed to focus on what was in front of him, not his emotional response. His mind began working furiously, questions popping. Did *G.I.* mean some kind of Army connection, and was the kid lying on an Army blanket? Who had built the floating box, and where had it gone into the water in the first place?

First, though, he was concerned about how the tabloids would run with such a story. Most homicides offered little novelty—they were the result of skirmishes over narcotics turf, domestic disputes, petty acts of revenge. The press loved an unusual angle. (He could vividly recall the time in 1982 when he had stepped into a bodega in the middle of a midnight-to-eight and seen the infamous *Post* cover, HEADLESS BODY IN TOPLESS BAR.) And now? They would nickname the victim "Coffin Boy" or something equally ghoulish. His race would matter, too. Black or Hispanic kids bought it all the time and barely made a paragraph on some inside page, but a white kid? Forget it—the story might well go national.

Jack called out to a uniformed sergeant. "We need to get those spectators moved all the way out of the park. And block all entrances. No press." He wanted a few minutes to focus before things got out of hand. He turned to Alvarez. "You have a cause of death?"

The Dominican shook his head. "I don't see any wounds or evidence of trauma or strangulation. We'll have to take him back and do an autopsy." He glanced down at the pager clipped to his belt. "Excuse me, gentlemen."

Jack turned to the local detective. "Do you have any witnesses who saw how this thing got here?"

Balfa nodded toward the pier. "I've got a uniform holding them out there."

"Who are they?"

The detective lowered his voice. "Coupl'a 'Rican greaseballs. I can't believe it: They called Nine-one-one and then actually stuck around."

Jack was not surprised by the man's casual racism—he had been a cop too long—but he was not thrilled about it, either. He figured that somebody who spoke to him about greaseballs might well talk about kikes when he wasn't around. He didn't say anything, though—the nature of his job was that he probably wouldn't be paired up with the man for long.

He followed the detective out. The new pier was much fancier than the old one, but it was already showing subtle signs of decay. The trash cans were just rusting metal drums, but someone had taken the precaution of chaining them to the light poles. Out above the harbor, the sun was locked behind a white haze, making it hard to distinguish where the sky ended and the water began. To the northwest loomed the Manhattan skyline, with its gaping new absence. Even though Jack had had months to get used to the fact, it still seemed impossible that the towers were missing. He turned away.

The cove was bounded by a modern brick bunker on the right and an old warehouse on the left. Graffiti covered the sides of the latter building: *Red Hook Rules* and *S.A.D.* He wondered if the latter was some kid's initials, or just a general commentary on what had become of the neighborhood.

After interviewing the two wind-chilled young Hispanic men— who had stayed because one of them had a brother on the job and he wanted to do his civic duty—Jack and his new partner talked to some of the onlookers, but none of them had been present when the coffin washed ashore.

THE TWO DETECTIVES WENT for lunch at the edge of Red Hook, near the Gowanus Expressway. The highway had severely damaged the Hook, separating it from the rest of Brooklyn. Belmontes Sandwich Shop was one of the few remnants of the old neighborhood—it had been around for eighty years and had survived thanks to four generations of Belmontes. The front window held a collection of American flags and faded plastic flowers. The paneled walls inside sported signed photos of celebrities, including Frank Sinatra. (Jack had seen such photos so many places around New York that he wondered how Ol' Blue Eyes had found any time to sing—it seemed that he had spent most of his days eating pizza and getting cheap haircuts.)

He had little appetite this afternoon, but Tommy Balfa stepped up to the counter, manned by crusty men in white T-shirts and little paper hats, and ordered the house special: an Italian hero featuring roast beef, fried eggplant, and fresh mozzarella.

Jack ordered another cup of coffee. One of the countermen, a burly man with a Tasmanian Devil tattoo on his arm, looked up and his eyes widened. "Hey," he said, "didn't you used to be Jackie Leightner?"

"I still am."

"I'm Richie Pepitone," the man said. "I used to play ball with Petey."

Jack nodded politely but his face tightened. His younger brother had been killed when they were just teenagers. The counterman looked like he was eager to chew the fat about old times, but Jack moved away toward the register. The old times had not been such good times, so why dwell on them?

There were no chairs in Belmontes, so the detectives sat out front in Balfa's immaculate blue Grand Marquis. He turned the engine on and Jack was grateful for the heat pouring out of the dashboard vents.

Balfa cleared his throat. "So you know the neighborhood, huh?"

Jack shrugged. "I grew up here." It seemed to him that the other detective's look grew slightly cagey, but he might have imagined it.

Balfa popped a can of Coke and set it on the dash. He unwrapped his sandwich and ate hungrily.

"You been with the Seven-six long?" Jack said, making conversation.

Balfa shook his head. "I just got here a few months ago."

"Where were you before that?"

"Narcotics. East New York."

Narcotics had always seemed like a shitty detail to Jack. It was pointless, like shoveling sand from one end of a beach to the other. No matter how many skels you arrested, it didn't do anything to solve the problem. People on the bottom end of the totem pole wanted a little shot of pleasure in their crappy lives. Ultimately, you would need to do something about why they were unhappy in the first place—and how could the police address that? They were mostly there to keep the poor from bugging the taxpayers: off the street, out of sight. At least in Homicide the moral issues were simpler. *Killing people: bad.*

"Did you like it?" he asked.

Balfa's eyes gleamed. "I loved it."

Jack scratched the side of his mouth. Some cops got into a cowboy lifestyle in Narcotics, thrived on the danger. Some got themselves in trouble. "Why'd you leave?"

Balfa snorted. "My wife couldn't take it. Said she was gonna pack up and split if I didn't get into something safer."

Jack let the subject drop. He could smell the fried eggplant as Balfa chewed his sandwich. Every couple of minutes the detective checked the rearview and side mirrors; Jack wondered if this was a habit from his days with Narcotics. The man seemed preoccupied, and Jack wondered if he was thinking about their case. "What do you make of it?" he asked. It was time to size up his new partner's abilities.

"Huh?" Balfa paused in midbite.

"This case. You got some ideas?"

Balfa looked down at the remains of his sandwich. He wrapped them up carefully and wiped his hands. He shrugged. "I guess we need to check Missing Persons, see if anybody's lost a kid."

"What else?"

"I dunno. If the coffin was store-bought, we could've checked on sales records, but that thing looked homemade."

Jack waited in vain for more. He was disappointed by the detective's lack of curiosity. What was the coffin doing in the water in the first place? If it was meant to be a burial at sea, why hadn't the thing been weighted down? Did the person who launched it *want* it to be found? Had it been put into the water from somewhere else on shore, or from a vessel? What could be determined from the forensic evidence, like the origins of the blanket, or the hardware used to make the box?

"What do *you* make of it?" Balfa asked.

Jack sipped his coffee and glanced out through the windshield. A couple of firemen from the engine company down the street were coming up the block with their usual cocky athlete's gait. They looked younger than the usual guys, though, and a sadness seeped into his chest—this house had lost seven members on September 11.

Jack turned to his new partner. "This is all speculation, obviously, but I can see several different scenarios. The simplest one is that somebody's kid dies of natural causes. He can't afford a regular burial, so he builds the box and launches it out. I guess some city statute would apply, but that wouldn't make it much of an NYPD problem. On the other hand, I can't see some bereaved parent writing on his own kid's forehead with a Magic Marker, no matter how screwed up he was with grief . . . If this is a homicide, then I wonder if he knew the boy. We'll see if the M.E. finds signs of prior physical abuse."

"Why do you say 'he'?"

"What do you mean?"

"You keep saying that the perp was a *he*. Maybe it was a *she*. Or even a *they*."

Jack nodded. "You're right. Anything's possible."

Balfa took out a cigarette and lit up. "Who knows? Maybe this is one of those devil worship things."

Jack stared at him, but couldn't tell if the detective was serious or not. Back in the eighties there had been a big hubbub about Satanic Ritual Abuse, but that had turned out to be a hysterical urban myth, without a single documented case. The sad fact was that in the overwhelming majority of child murders, the perp was not a sinister stranger, but someone known to the victim. "I don't think so," Jack said dryly. "Let's stick to the evidence. The box looks pretty well made, which suggests that the perp—or perps—has some familiarity with carpentry. I wonder where he built the thing, and how he would have transported it without drawing attention. Hopefully, we'll get a tip about suspicious activity.

"I'd guess that our guy has some kind of personal connection to the water. Lives near it, works on it . . . A burial at sea is not gonna occur to your average city resident. Our witnesses say that the box floated in from the north. We'll have to talk to the Charlie Unit"— the Harbor squad—"and see what they say about tides and currents."

He looked over at Balfa, expecting the detective to be a little chastened by all of the points he had failed to consider, but the detective was just staring out through his side window again, as if he had something more important to think about.

CHAPTER *four*

J ack found Gary Daskivitch in the dumpy little lounge in the Seven-six precinct house. Half a meatball sub sat on the cigarette-scarred Formica table in front of the huge detective. The other half seemed to be inside his cavernous mouth. He grinned when Jack walked in. "Hey, the cavalry returns! Are you back on the job?"

Jack nodded, then went over and fed some change into the soda machine. He listened in vain for the accompanying clunk.

Daskivitch stood up. "Here," he said, elbowing Jack out of the way. He rocked the big box back as easily as if he were throwing a little English on a pinball machine. *Kachunk.* He tossed Jack his ginger ale. "You on that weird case that floated in this morning?"

Jack shrugged. "Only if it's a homicide. We'll have to let the M.E. call it." He liked the young detective; the crewcut bear had been teamed with him on two prior cases and Jack had done his best to indoctrinate the kid into the art of homicide investigation. Despite the fact that Daskivitch didn't look like the brightest crayon in the box, he had been the perfect student: eager to learn, a quick study, thankful for the knowledge. Jack had started to consider himself something of a mentor to the young detective, but now he owed the bigger debt of gratitude. It was Daskivitch and his wife, after all, who had set him up on his first date with Michelle, and it was Daskivitch who had done his best to keep Jack's spirits up during his long hospital stay.

He shut the door. "What's the story with this Balfa guy?"

Daskivitch set his sandwich down again and wiped his hands on a fistful of paper towels. He frowned. "I don't know. He hasn't been here long—I guess the verdict is still out. He keeps to himself. Not much of a team player, I guess you could say." He shrugged, evidently deciding not to badmouth a colleague. "He's all right, I guess."

Jack nodded thoughtfully. Not much of a recommendation. "How long has he been on the job?" A lot of cops started early and got out as soon as their twenty was up. Sometimes they lost interest as they neared that pension.

Daskivitch swallowed the last of his sub. "I think he's got about ten years."

Jack frowned: So much for that theory. Ah well . . . maybe his new partner was simply not a very good detective. In the old days, cops got promoted on the basis of their achievements, but the department had changed and now people could move up based on all sorts of political bullshit.

"You want any help?" Daskivitch asked eagerly.

"I don't know." Jack watched the big detective's face fall, like a kid disappointed in his Christmas presents. "I'd be glad to work with you again, Gary, but you might wanna think before you get involved in this one."

Daskivitch sank back in his chair. "Why?"

Jack leaned back against a wall. "Well, for one thing, the press might get all over this. Then we'll have every kind of pressure to get results."

Daskivitch shrugged. "I don't mind a tough job."

Jack nodded. "I know you don't. But if you get tangled in a press case, it can really jam up your career. I don't care much, myself—I've got my twenty, and I've got my rank." (Out of some six thousand detectives in the NYPD, Jack was one of only a couple of hundred who had reached the top rank of First Grade.) "You've got your whole career ahead of you."

Daskivitch brightened. "Yeah, but if I helped break a case like that, it would do me a world of good."

Jack shook his head. "It's not just the career thing. These jobs can do a real number on you. Up here." He tapped his temple.

Daskivitch waited, sensing that a tale was on the way. For cops, it was all about the stories. The Department offered all sorts of technical courses, but the real training happened like this: one cop talking to another, reliving a case.

Jack rubbed a hand over his face. "You ever hear about Baby Annie?"

Daskivitch shook his head.

Jack sighed. "Back when I was a rookie on patrol in Bay Ridge, one morning we got an anonymous call. A couple of the guys went to check it out: In a vacant lot, they found a cardboard TV box. Inside it was a little girl, D.C.D.S." *Deceased, Confirmed Dead at Scene.* "She was tied up. She was malnourished, and she'd been seriously abused." He fell silent for a moment, remembering; he could picture the girl as clearly as the day he'd seen her. "We worked double shifts for weeks. Nobody worried about overtime."

There were all sorts of less-than-noble reasons why detectives wanted to close cases. There was pressure to keep the stats up. There was the salary increase that a promotion could provide. There was an intellectual pleasure in solving puzzles, and the satisfaction of proving that you were smarter than the bad guys. But a case like Baby Annie's reduced the job to its starkest Biblical form: You just wanted to catch and punish the sick bastard who could do such a thing. You wanted to avenge the child.

"We had no ID," Jack continued. "No evidence, nothing . . . We got a thousand tips, but none of them led anywhere."

Daskivitch's boyish face had taken on a rare somber look. "Why was she called Baby Annie? Did you find out who she was?"

Jack shook his head. "We couldn't stand calling her Baby Doe; we thought she deserved some kind of a name. We kept that case open for years, hoping somebody would give us a real tip; you know, try to plea down some other case, make a deathbed confession . . ."

On TV, detectives solved every case by the end of the hour, but in real life, Jack knew, about a third of New York City's homicides went uncleared. And those were just the *known* murders—there were plenty of crimes that never got solved because the police never even found out about them.

He sighed. "After a while we took up a collection at the precinct and we bought that little girl a headstone and gave her a proper burial . . . We didn't know when she was born, or when she died, exactly, so we put the only date on the headstone that we knew for sure: the day we found her. The lead detective retired years ago, but he's still working on the case, hoping something will turn up . . . He's never gotten over it."

He straightened up. "Anyhow, think about it before you get involved." He realized that he was trying to protect the young detective from the hard realities of life in the same way that he had tried to protect his own son.

Both gestures were probably equally futile.

A CHILD IN A box. In other quarters the situation would have called for mourning, or for prayer. In this meeting, though, the focus was Departmental politics, even if nobody wanted to spell it out.

They sat in the small, cramped office of Balfa's boss, Detective Sergeant Larry Riordan. The thin, mournful-looking man presided behind his desk, rubbing his jaw with a characteristic pained expression. Above him rested one of the chief reasons for his pain: a big board marked with a box for each case. The victim's name was written in black if the case was open, and then changed to red if the detectives managed to close it. A squad supervisor's job was to provide the bean counters down at One Police Plaza with as many red boxes as possible, and he was reminded of that fact with stressful frequency. Even so, Riordan was a veteran of street work who did his best to protect his team from the vagaries of the paper cops, which was more than Jack could say for his own boss, who had dropped by for this confab. Sergeant Stephen Tanney was only thirty-seven, with a full head of curly red hair and an immaculate mustache. The man was relatively new to the homicide task force; so far he seemed most interested in pleasing the higher-ups.

Riordan opened with a question for Jack. "What do you make of this?"

Jack sat forward and rested his forearms on his knees. "I think we should press hard now, so we'll have a good jump on things by the time the M.E. finishes the autopsy. I'd be glad to stay on tonight and see what I can find out."

"Hold on," Tanney said. He always reminded Jack of a tame actor doing his best to play a tough guy. "Let's not start talking overtime before we even know what this is." If the M.E. ruled out unnatural causes, the local precinct would still have the case, but the homicide task force would be off the hook.

It's a dead child, Jack wanted to say. *Stop worrying about your goddamn budget and do the right thing.* He held his tongue, though. He had had conflicts with his boss before, and was reminded of a sign in his local hardware store: PRESS BUTTON TO REGISTER A COMPLAINT. The button was mounted on top of a mousetrap. "We did our best to secure the scene," he said, "but I think I spotted a guy from the *Daily News.*" He watched as the little career-impact calculator in Tanney's brain clicked away. Press interest meant public interest, which meant Department interest, which meant that jobs might be on the line.

Tanney frowned. "All right. Why don't we send some uniforms out, do a waterfront canvass? I'll see if we can get some manpower from the next shift, and of course we'll run the kid through Missing Persons . . ." He turned to his fellow sergeant. "Can you spare some people?"

Riordan nodded. He turned to his own detective, who ultimately owned the case. "What do you think, Tom?"

Balfa just shrugged. "Sure. Let's find out who the little bugger was."

AFTER HIS DAY TOUR was over—and after his boss went home for the day—Jack dropped into One Police Plaza in Manhattan and volunteered several hours of his own time, checking computer databases to see if he could discover the boy's identity. He had his work cut out for him: At any given time, nationally, there were at least a thousand unidentified dead children.

CHAPTER *five*

A t home, Jack stopped in the hallway to listen for signs of activity from his landlord upstairs. The man was eighty-six, a recent widower, and he had suffered a stroke during the past summer.

Jack heard a door open, and a moment later a pleasant young Jamaican woman came downstairs buttoning up her winter coat. Mr. Gardner's home-care nurse.

"How's he doing?" Jack asked.

The woman smiled. "Feisty as ever. He says he wants to take me to Atlantic City."

Jack grinned. "You can't keep a good man down."

The woman raised her eyebrows. "How about you?"

"I'm not ready for any marathons, but I'm getting stronger every day."

She nodded. "Good, good." She pulled on a hand-knitted purple hat. "You take care of each other now. And stay out of trouble."

The house was in Midwood, at the center of the immense concrete and asphalt plain that was Brooklyn. It was a quiet neighborhood, populated largely by Hasidic Jews. They were unexciting neighbors, but that suited Jack fine: He got all the excitement he could want at work.

After the nurse left, he slowly mounted the stairs to say hello. The hallway was musty, and the stairs were carpeted in Astroturf. Mr. Gardner was a great fixer-upper, but he worked with found materials.

Jack paused on the landing to catch his breath. He thought of his second week in the hospital, when he had begun his physical therapy. The bullet had passed through his lung and a fragment had lodged in one of his vertebrae—its heat had shocked his spinal cord, causing temporary paralysis from his chest down. As that started wearing off, he had spent a morning just trying to raise his foot enough to step up onto a little fake curb.

The TV was on so loud inside Mr. G's apartment that the old man couldn't hear Jack's knock. He was always watching: ball games, game shows, old war movies in the middle of the night . . .

Jack went in and found him in his usual spot, sitting in an old duct-taped recliner in front of his ancient TV. The room smelled of mothballs, mildewed carpet, and the old man's faintly sour skin. Mr. Gardner looked up through blocky old eyeglasses as thick as the bottoms of Coke bottles. His gaunt face broke open in a gap-toothed smile—it drooped on the right, on account of the stroke, but not much. Jack had always thought of him as "the old man," and himself as very vigorous in comparison, but his convalescence had done a lot to balance out that difference, and he felt closer to his landlord than ever.

"Jackie! How ya doon?"

Jack shrugged off the question. He glanced at the TV. A game show.

The thought of him sitting in front of the TV all day depressed Jack. The last time he had visited, they watched a talk show in which a squat woman with huge tits had gotten into a threesome with two mooks with mullet haircuts, and they all argued about which one had fathered her baby. Why was it that if you wanted to watch TV in the daytime, the networks assumed you were a moron?

Mr. G clicked again.

Jack gestured at a pair of newscasters smugly jawing in front of a picture of a man in a turban. "They catch him yet?"

Mr. G frowned. "Bin Laden? No. I don't know what they're waitin' for."

"You mind if I turn this off for a second?"

Mr. G shook his head, a bit nervously. These days in late 2001, everybody in the City had turned into a news junkie, afraid of another terrorist attack. It was only in the past couple of weeks that the acrid smell of smoke from Ground Zero had finally stopped drifting across the river. It had been a hell of a few months, for Mr. Gardner as well as for Jack. The old man had lived in the house for ages, anchored by his familiar routines, and he was shaken by any kind of change. That was why Jack himself was anxious now.

"I wanted to ask you something."

Mr. G peered up at him.

He scratched at an imaginary spot on his pants leg. "You know Michelle, that woman I've been seeing these past few months?"

Mr. G nodded slowly. The old man was a great landlord and a friend, but he was wary as an old peasant, determined that nobody was going to put anything over on him.

Jack cleared his throat. "I was wondering how you'd feel if she moved in with me."

Mr. G scowled. "Whadda ya mean, shack up with ya?" The man never went to church, but carried strong remnants of his Catholic upbringing.

Jack smiled. "Not exactly. Can you keep a secret?"

Mr. G nodded uncertainly.

"I'm gonna ask if she'll make an honest man out of me. I got the ring and everything." Jack winced, remembering; he'd *had* the ring, anyhow.

Mr. G stared for a moment longer, and then grinned as widely as his impaired facial muscles would allow. "Good for you, kid!" He fumbled for the lever at the side of his chair, and managed to tilt it back a bit. "That goddamned nurse doesn't let me take my real medicine." He reached down under the footrest and pulled out a dusty bottle of Seagrams 7. "Go in the kitchen and grab us a couple of glasses."

DOWNSTAIRS, LATER, JACK SANK into a hot bath. For most of his life he had been a brisk-shower kind of a guy, but after he got out of the hospital Michelle had pampered him a bit, and turned him on to the luxury of a good soak. It went well with his general appreciation of cleanliness, and with the job—Lord knows there were plenty of days when he wanted to scrub some unpleasantness off his skin, or out of his head.

The image of the boy in the box came to mind and his face tightened. He told himself not to get emotional. He had seen many disturbing things in his years with the homicide squad, and he had learned to compartmentalize, to avoid taking these bad images home with him. Otherwise he would never have been able to function.

Still, memories from the day rose up. *The way the boy's plaid shirt was buttoned so neatly at the neck.* Whoever had put him in the box like that had had some sort of feeling for the kid. The child's face was fixed in Jack's mind; he had asked the Crime Scene photographer to take a Polaroid that he could use for ID purposes.

Ideally, he should have been able to look in one central Missing Persons database, but he'd had to scroll through a welter of different lists. There were several national ones, but many places kept their information local, or segregated by branch of service. There were state police databases, sheriff's lists, and private sites maintained by volunteers . . . They made for a haphazard, disjointed hodgepodge, and searching through them was a miserable experience. They conveyed more sadness than hope, image after image of lost souls smiling out from baby pictures, graduation photos, wedding albums . . .

He had asked a computer tech to scan the Polaroid, and then they had used Photoshop to give the kid open eyes and make him look less grim. They had posted the photos to another type of Web site, ones that law enforcement used to spread images of unidentified bodies. The whole thing was like a gruesome parody of computer dating: people searching for loved ones, cops and coroners hoping to identify the dead.

Both types of database had been enhanced by a technological development: the science of facial reconstruction. For the missing, forensic anthropologists used computer imaging to guess how people might look after years in limbo. For the unidentified, they created images of what the victims might have looked like before they were reduced to bone. In both cases, there was a grating uncanniness to the images: The missing looked perversely cheerful, while the unidentified tended to look like Neanderthals in some museum of natural history. Both types took a personal toll on Jack Leightner. He couldn't help wondering what his brother would have looked like if he hadn't been killed, and he was reminded of the shoddy embalming job his father had been given when *he* died.

He closed his eyes. *Let it go for now.* Steam was building up in the bathroom, and soon a sheen of sweat formed on his face. He leaned back and sighed, finally beginning to relax. This bath thing was a great idea and he wondered why he hadn't discovered it sooner. He smiled a little: Soon Michelle would probably be getting him into bubble soap and scented candles . . .

He thought he heard the front door open, but then realized that it was just one of the old house's clanking radiators. He knew

Michelle was working late, but she had said that she would probably come by.

His heart lifted when he finally heard her footsteps in the hall. She knocked gently on the bathroom door. "Jack?"

"Come on in," he said.

She entered, sat on the closed toilet seat, and smiled. "You look mighty comfy."

"I'm just having a little soak," he said, as if some sheepishness was called for. He sucked in his gut; he had always prided himself on keeping a trim physique, but between his convalescence and Michelle's good cooking, he had put on several pounds.

"Did you eat?" he said. "There's some leftovers in the fridge—I made dinner for Mister Gardner."

"You cooked?" she said, eyebrows raised.

He shrugged. "I heated. Are you hungry?"

"I'm fine. We ordered Chinese at the office."

"Was it a particularly rough day?"

"Just busy. Why?"

He frowned, lying there in the bath. "I don't know. You look kind of dirty."

It took her a second to catch on, and then she grinned. "Let me guess: You know just how to get me clean."

He shrugged again, modestly.

While Michelle took off her work clothes and hung them on the back of the bathroom door, Jack thought of the first time they had made love when he got out of the hospital. He had felt very weak, and would have been satisfied just watching her disrobe, but then she had helped him out of his own clothes. She had climbed up over him, and he raised his head: Through the curtain of her hair, he saw her breasts hanging like lovely fruit over his frail chest. He had squeezed his eyes shut—not in pain, for once, after weeks of pain—but in a strong suffusing pleasure . . .

"*Hello*," Michelle said now, interrupting his reverie. She looked down between his legs and then gave him a sultry smile. "Who's your little friend? I mean, your *big* friend . . ."

She lowered herself gingerly into the water and slid down to hook her legs around his. Thank God for roomy old bathtubs. She soaped her hands. He inhaled sharply as she touched him, and then his breath came short and quick. After a minute, he reached out, grabbed her wrists, and pulled her toward him. She gasped as he slid up into her, and he held her there on his lap. She wrapped her arms around him and rested her chin on his shoulder. It felt different to be together in the water like this. It felt damn good.

Slowly he started to move, rising up into her, breathing hard. She didn't have her diaphragm in, and he knew they couldn't do much more without taking a huge risk, but his whole body was full of a powerful sweet light.

After another minute, he sighed and withdrew. All of that unreleased sexual energy was bound up in a wave of love, and he was tempted to bag his elaborate proposal schemes and just ask her to marry him right then and there.

She started shampooing her hair, and he noticed that the water was growing cool, and soon such mundane details brought him back to earth. He sat and contemplated her. He felt like he was *addicted* to her, and it wasn't just the sex. It was the sound of her key in the lock when she came over, it was the feel of her lower back as he stroked his palm across it just before they fell asleep, it was the pure comfort he could feel just holding her in his arms as they watched some dopey TV show. He wanted these good feelings available all the time. *Married.* It was a miracle—he had never thought he'd want that again, not after the long, slow decline with his ex-wife, the bickering, the loss of desire, the petty, daily drip of dissatisfaction like a leaky faucet that neither of them could ever quite get around to fixing. After all these years, Michelle had shown him that his heart still worked for something more than just keeping him alive.

"Do you miss not having kids?" he asked suddenly.

Michelle went silent. She had been married before, too, but her husband had died of emphysema. She had never bugged Jack about having children, but he had seen a wistful look come over her face when they passed some young family on the street.

After a moment, she shrugged. "Sometimes. Though I guess it's not completely too late . . ."

Jack nodded cautiously. He already had a son—it was a mark of the seriousness of this new relationship that he was willing to consider the subject again. But first things first: He needed to find out if she would marry him.

He stood up and reached for a towel. "What are you doing next Saturday?" That was his next day off that coincided with her weekends. If she was free—and if he got the ring back in time—he hoped to give the proposal another shot.

CHAPTER *six*

Michelle Wilber finished her bath with a shower, letting the hot water pound against shoulder muscles tense from a long day of working her office phone. She was still reeling from Jack's question about kids, but she decided to put off thinking about it until later.

When she pulled the curtain aside and emerged with a towel piled high on her head, she found him standing next to the sink. He was brushing his teeth, and he turned to her with a frothy grin.

"*Well*," he mumbled, "if it isn't Cleopatra herself."

She turned sideways and stuck her arms out stiffly, like a figure in an Egyptian painting.

Jack grinned. He was very appreciative of any little humor on her part; she sensed that his first wife had not exactly been a barrel of laughs.

He rinsed his teeth and then stared into the open medicine cabinet.

"Something wrong?" she asked.

"Did you put the dental floss somewhere? I usually keep it right next to the toothpaste."

"I don't know," she said. "I just stuck it back in."

He seemed to wrestle with himself for a moment, but he couldn't resist making a comment. "It's not a big deal, or anything . . . It's just that, it's easier if you keep things in some kind of order. Medicines on one shelf. Dental stuff on another."

She had noticed something: When she moved his socks to a new drawer, or even just shifted the location of the kitchen trashcan, he seemed surprisingly put out. Long ago he had set the place up in a way that was comfortable for him. She kidded him about it, but she figured that maybe he needed order at home to counter the terrible *dis*order he saw in his work (not to mention his chaotic early home life as the child of an alcoholic). Still, he had to concede that most of her changes were for the better. It wasn't that she was some sort of Suzie Homemaker—she had her own busy career outside the house—but making her surroundings pleasing was deeply important to her. She had an appreciation of life outside the job that he seemed to sorely lack. He loved his work, but she brought him closer to the rest of the world.

She gave him a wry look, then moved around him to pick up her own toothbrush. "Wanna hear a good joke?"

He didn't answer.

"Knock knock."

He made a face.

"Come on," she said. "Just play along."

He crossed his arms. "Who's there?"

"Control freak—now you're supposed to say 'Control freak who?'"

He got the joke, and laughed, but grew serious again. "Are you saying that I'm a control freak?"

Michelle smiled. "I'm just teasing. You're very neat—and very cute."

LATER, AFTER THEY HAD gotten into bed and finished what they had started, Michelle could tell by Jack's breathing that he was drifting away.

"'Gastrointestinal,'" she said suddenly.

A muffled noise from his pillow. "What?"

"Your mystery," she said. "I thought of another possibility." He had told her about his case, and his guess that the initials on his latest corpse's forehead stood for the military term *General Issue*. He had spared her any details about who the victim was; he generally didn't discuss his work with anyone except a fellow cop.

She rolled over, thinking. "Or how about 'glycemic index'? That's what you check when you have diabetes . . ." She mused on, enjoying herself. (For him, this was work, but for her it was just a strange new parlor game.) She remembered something she had read about computers. "What about 'graphic user interface'? No, wait, that would be G.*U*.I."

"'Gary, Indiana,'" he said quietly.

She had to think for a moment. Just as she came up with something, she was disappointed to hear a subtle snore. "'Geographical Institute,'" she murmured into the dark.

She closed her eyes, but sleep wouldn't come. After a few minutes she rolled over and looked at the faintly glowing hands of the alarm clock: It was almost midnight. She lay back carefully, trying not wake Jack, and stared for a while at the dark ceiling, thinking about the way he had raised the subject of kids, and then just as quickly let it drop . . . It was pretty obvious that he had talked about her childlessness as if it was a done deal.

In truth, she *was* close to the final age limit for having kids, but she rarely panicked about it, unlike many single women she knew, and that was because she had mixed feelings about the subject. She liked kids well enough—and loved her little nieces and nephews dearly—but when she saw the harried, sleepless looks of the young mothers she knew, the way that kids seemed to take so much romance out of life, sometimes she wondered if the tradeoffs were worth it. On her infrequent visits to her parents down in suburban Philadelphia, her mother always laid a big guilt trip on her, as if she was abnormal, or—at the very least—selfish and inconsiderate.

Jack, on the other hand . . . He already had a son, Ben, a shy, gangly kid in his early twenties. She could understand if he didn't want to go through diapers and all that baby stuff again, but still—if a major door was going to be closed in her life, she wanted to be the one to shut it.

CHAPTER *seven*

W e get some floaters," said Sergeant Mike Pacelli, "but they don't usually come in boxes."

He hit the starter switch and Jack was glad when the little blue NYPD launch stopped swaying and surged away from the Harbor Unit dock. Black clouds puffed out of the stern, and the smell of salt water was overtaken by a strong odor of diesel fuel. The engine was loud, and the deck rumbled beneath Jack's feet. Both men fell silent as the boat veered out into New York Harbor, toward the Statue of Liberty.

Jack shoved his hands deep into his coat pockets. He stood in an enclosed cabin, but the wind on the water brought the temperature way down; he wondered how long it would take for the boat to warm up.

The launch plowed across the pewter surface. There was a powerful sense of freedom to this mode of transport: While Jack spent half his time struggling through the City's tangled traffic, this was like driving out across a huge, empty parking lot. You could drive in circles, do figure-eights, whatever you wanted . . .

He glanced at his old Academy classmate, calm but authoritative behind the wheel. Pacelli—born and raised on the Jersey shore— had never shown much interest in the City; he was just happy that the five boroughs were largely surrounded by water. He didn't care that the "Charlie Unit" didn't even have investigators, as long as he could get paid for working on a boat. Pacelli had a potbelly now, his hair was graying, and his face was weathered by long exposure to sun and wind, but with his dark Ray-Bans and cocky grin it was easy to picture him as a teenager speeding past a beach in a little powerboat, trying to impress some girl.

Jack smiled back. "This is a pretty sweet detail," he said, speaking loudly over the noise of the engine.

Pacelli nodded. "I couldn't take street patrol. Out here, you don't have to deal with any of that 'he-hit-me, no-she-hit-me' crap." He paused to listen to a dispatcher's voice crackling out of the radio mounted next to the wheel, then decided it was something he could ignore. He fell silent for a minute, then turned to Jack with an awkward expression.

Jack tightened up inside: He knew what the man was about to ask.

"How are you feeling these days?"

Jack shrugged, doing his best to act casual. "Fine. Better than the Jets—you see the game last night?" He didn't like talking about his shooting or recovery. Back in the hospital, he had noticed something strange. Like any wounded cop, he had received many visitors, from the mayor and the commissioner on down. His colleagues would drop by, hand off some magazines or a fruit basket, say they had to run, and run. It took him a while to figure it out: All cops wanted to believe that they were invulnerable, magically protected by the badge. Seeing a wounded coworker put the lie to that belief. Now he just wanted to put the shooting behind him, to blend back in and resume the work he loved.

He was glad to change the subject. "Tell me about the bodies."

Pacelli moved the throttle forward to pick up speed. "We don't find them much in winter. In the cold weather they tend to sink and stay down, and they don't come up until the spring."

Jack nodded. When the water warmed up, bacteria released gases in the corpses and they rose to the surface, usually around mid-April. It was known as Floater Week. There was a strange poetry to it, all those cold submerged bodies rising up: the drunken boaters, the bridge jumpers, the victims of mob hits (who often escaped their concrete shoes or chains as their bodies softened and frayed). Somebody had once called death "that bourne from which no traveler returns," but every spring, there they came, not to be denied, all lifting toward the light like watery Pentecostals on Judgment Day.

On shore to the right, block after block of huge beige warehouses slid by, the old Brooklyn Army Terminal; it had once processed most of the troops headed off to World War II. Up ahead came the piers and brick warehouses of Red Hook, where Jack was raised. The waterfront there was dominated by a few ship-loading cranes and the huge conical metal silo of the old Revere sugar factory. (At one point the factory had been owned by an associate of Ferdinand Marcos of the Philippines, and Jack knew a local who liked to joke that the abandoned silo was filled with Imelda's discarded shoes.)

The bow of the NYPD launch pounded up and down and threw sheets of spray as it encountered an occasional wake. During the summer, the harbor would have been crowded with speedboats, sailboats, even Jet-Skis and kayaks, but there were few vessels out in this chilly weather: mainly ferries and tugs, or tankers just arrived from the ocean, which opened out just beyond the Verrazano Bridge to the south. The ships rested on the water like majestic animals on some African plain.

"Is this the end of the season for private boats?"

Pacelli nodded. "Pretty much. By mid-January most people take their craft out of the water, because we start to get ice out here."

Jack stared out the broad windows of the cabin. If the coffin had not been unloaded from some small boat, it had probably been launched from shore. *Where* was the question—if he knew that, he would know where to look for witnesses.

Pacelli turned away from his constant scanning of the water ahead. "Have you gotten a preliminary report from the M.E. yet?"

Jack nodded. "It seems that the kid was poisoned, by injection."

Pacelli got a little wide-eyed. "Do you think it could be a terrorist thing? Like this goddamn anthrax that's going around?"

Jack shrugged. Since the World Trade Center attack, jittery New Yorkers were picturing terrorism everywhere: in accidents, in subway delays, even traffic jams. The fact was, though, that poisoners usually wanted their crimes hidden. Poison was a rather old-fashioned MO. For centuries it had been a favored means to surreptitiously get rid of a spouse or to speed up an inheritance, but recent advances in forensic toxicology and pathology had rendered it increasingly rare.

"Actually, it was *fentanyl*," Jack said. "I'm glad it was that."

"Why?"

"It's a powerful opiate-based anesthetic. That means the kid probably didn't suffer much. With some other poisons, like strychnine or antimony, you get a violent, agonizing death, but a fentanyl overdose puts you under pretty fast."

Pacelli looked impressed. "You really know your stuff."

Jack waved away the compliment. "What can I say? You're out here saving live people, while I'm just checking out a bunch of stiffs."

There were another couple of reasons why he was thankful about the case. The M.E. had reported no signs of physical or sexual abuse. And the tabloids were still so dominated by every detail of the Trade Center attack that the story of the waterborne coffin had received surprisingly little play.

"Any idea who the victim is?"

Jack shook his head. "I haven't found him in any Missing Persons reports. And we've checked with every school in the city." He sighed. "You wouldn't think a kid could just disappear and nobody would give a damn. Pretty soon we'll have to set up a hotline and put a photo in the papers, but I'm not looking forward to that; we'll get calls from every nut job in the Tristate area."

"You're working with a guy from the Seven-six on this?"

Jack nodded. "He's organizing a team of uniforms to canvass along the waterfront, to ask if anybody saw that box go in the water. That's why I want your help. Obviously, we can't cover every mile of the shoreline—we need some idea where to focus."

He heard a clanking and looked across the bow; the launch was nearing a buoy, a scaffolded metal tower bobbing in the water like a punch-drunk boxer. Pacelli steered to the right, following the rules of this watery road. He brought the launch around the southern end of Red Hook and into narrow Buttermilk Channel, which separated Brooklyn from a low, flat island covered with redbrick barracks. Some old Coast Guard base. It was just a quarter-mile from the Brooklyn shore, but so quiet and removed from the hubbub of New York life that nobody paid it any mind.

Jack stared at it, thunderstruck. How could he have missed something so obvious?

The name of the place was Governors Island. *G.I.*

"What's the matter?" Pacelli said.

Jack filled him in.

Pacelli shook his head. "Sorry, but I doubt that's your answer. The island has been pretty much closed down since the Coast Guard gave up their base there in the mid-nineties. The public's not allowed at all. There are still a few security guards and a little firehouse, to keep an eye on things, but there's only one ferry for transportation; it goes to and from Manhattan just a couple of times a day. There'd be no reason for it to carry a kid, and definitely not a coffin. You can talk to whoever's in charge over there these days, but it's basically off-limits."

Jack frowned. It didn't sound promising, but he made a mental note to ask Tommy Balfa to contact whoever was running the island's security.

Pacelli veered to the left, around a blackened chunk of wood.

"You get a lot of stuff floating around out here?"

Pacelli nodded. "The most common thing is wood from old piers, but we get just about everything you could imagine: plastic bags, crack vials, Styrofoam coolers, Coney Island whitefish . . ."

Jack smiled at this childhood slang for floating condoms.

As Pacelli neared the Red Hook pier where the coffin had first been spotted, he cut the engine. The boat swung like a hammock at the mercy of the water, and the cabin began to strike Jack as very small and airless.

"You okay?"

Jack swallowed uneasily.

Pacelli grinned. "Waves getting to ya, huh? Here's what you do: Just think of cold pork chops smothered in maple syrup. Or fried eggs floating in oil . . ."

Jack grimaced and his old friend laughed. "Sorry. Tell you what: Why don't we just cruise along?"

Jack gripped a handrail and nodded.

Pacelli restarted the engine and turned north again. They motored through the channel and out into the open harbor, just a short distance from the thicket of skyscrapers rising from the southern tip of Manhattan. The absence of the Twin Towers was like a slap in the face. Beyond the remaining skyscrapers, over on the west side of the island, teams of volunteers were hard at work, sifting through twisted mountains of wreckage and rubble, by an unimaginable degree the biggest crime scene the city had ever known.

Pacelli saw where Jack was looking, and shook his head. "Man, I sure hope they catch that Bin Laden bastard. I'd like to personally string him up by the balls." He turned the boat to the right, into the broad opening of the East River.

"Tell me how the water works," Jack said. He knew plenty about homicide and the intricate workings of the city streets, but this was unknown territory. His job was hardly a solo venture, like it was in the movies—to a large extent, a detective was only as good as the network of helpers he or she had built up over time: confidential informants, friends at the DMV and phone company, old colleagues with specialized knowledge . . .

Pacelli squared his shoulders, eager to show off his expertise. "First of all, if the box was dumped into the harbor, it would probably have landed out on the south shore of Long Island."

"How do you know?"

"The DEP did a study a few years back. They dropped thousands of little plastic bottles all over the harbor and the rivers, and then tracked where they ended up."

"Well, we have a couple of witnesses who said it was moving from the north."

"Okay, it would've probably come down the East River here."

"How do these currents work?"

"First of all, you know that this isn't really a river, right?"

Jack made a face, as if he had suddenly been called on back in grade school. "What do you mean?"

"Technically, it's a tidal strait that connects the harbor with the Long Island Sound. If it was a river, your problem would be simple, 'cause it would only flow one way, and it would be easy to determine the speed and movement of the box. But this is a very complicated body of water. The tides are semidiurnal, which means the damned thing changes direction four times a day . . . not to mention the slack tides in between, when it just sits there. Then you've got your currents, which sometimes run in the opposite direction from the surface water. Throw in the air currents, which also influence the way something's gonna move, and it's a goddamned circus."

The light outside the windows dimmed; Jack looked out and saw that the launch was slipping into a realm of shadow beneath the grand old stone towers of the Brooklyn Bridge. Beyond rose the blue metal span of the Manhattan Bridge, and the ugly industrial lattices of the Williamsburg Bridge beyond that.

"How long is the river, or strait, or whatever?"

"Sixteen miles," Pacelli answered. "Times two, when you count both shorelines."

Jack winced. "That's a lot of ground to cover."

Pacelli smiled. "Yeah, but I've got good news. Look upriver."

Jack squinted ahead. "I can't see very far. There's a crook in it."

Pacelli nodded. "That's the good news." He pulled out a chart. "See, the river bends like a sock here. The heel's right up ahead there on the Brooklyn side, and it's got a little bay dipping off of it. That's the old Navy Yard Basin." Pacelli pointed to a small cut in the shore just above it. "That's the Wallabout Channel." He moved his finger along the upper portion of the river. "When stuff enters the river from up here, it tends to wash back onto the shoreline nearby, or else float down into the Wallabout, which acts like a catch basin."

Jack considered the chart. "So our box probably entered the water somewhere below that channel. That'll narrow our search a lot."

Pacelli nodded again. "And you can narrow it down a lot more, because you've got the Navy Yard here, a big power plant right on the shore here . . . There's not much publicly accessible shoreline."

Jack's beeper went off. "Hold on," he told his colleague, and used his cell phone to contact the task force office.

A minute later he hung up, shaking his head, puzzled.

"The M.E. just called my boss: They got some new test results. The kid was definitely poisoned, but now it turns out that he would have died soon anyway. He had very advanced leukemia."

CHAPTER *eight*

J ack sat in his car, thankful to be back on solid ground. He squinted down at Tommy Balfa's card as he punched the detective's number into his cell phone. He had to admit that the device often made his job easier, but he rarely used it when he was off duty. For one thing, the tiny keys made his not-particularly-large hands feel like clumsy sausages. For another, he hated the way the phones had ruined the distinction between private and public space, and the way they conveyed such a ridiculous sense of self-importance, as though every little action was worthy of being broadcast. *I'm waiting for the bus. I'm getting on the bus. I'm on the bus.* They made him cranky.

Balfa answered, but the connection crackled.

"Can you meet me at your squad room?" Jack asked.

"I'm out on a job, but I can be there in fifteen."

"I'll wait for you," Jack said. He was already in the neighborhood; he figured he'd kill the time by buying a muffin or something to settle his stomach.

He walked over to a pastry shop on Court Street and bought a *sfogliatelle*, a seashell-shaped Italian pastry, and then strolled down a quiet side street, enjoying the faint taste of orange rind mixed in with the filling's ricotta cheese.

He considered the latest findings in the case. Yes, the boy in the box had been a homicide, but now it seemed like maybe a mercy killing. He shrugged: That was better than finding out the kid had been abused, but he was still eager to catch whoever had administered the drug. If it had been some loving parent who had done it to put their child out of agony, that was one thing, but the business with the homemade coffin and the writing on the kid's forehead definitely indicated a perp with a few screws loose. It wasn't his job to determine that mental status—he would find the killer, and let the shrinks sort it out.

The next step would be to fax the kid's photo to hospitals in the Tristate area, see if he had been treated there. (If he wasn't local, though, the search might get tough: There were seventy-five hundred hospitals nationwide.)

As Jack turned a corner three blocks from the station house, he noticed a little white Honda Civic double-parked fifty yards down. Before he got any closer, the passenger door opened and Tommy Balfa stepped out. The detective bent down and said something in through the window, then turned and hurried away. Jack wondered why the car hadn't just dropped Balfa off in front of the station house. It pulled out into the street and a few seconds later passed Jack by. The window was sliding up, but he caught a glimpse of an attractive young redhead in the driver's seat.

BALFA WAS ALREADY BEHIND his desk when Jack walked into the squad room. "How ya doin'?" the detective said.

"I'm good," Jack answered. "You out working on our case?"

"Actually," Balfa said calmly, "I was finishing up another thing. I had to meet with a C.I."

Jack didn't say anything, but he was looking down at the detective's wedding ring and thinking, *Yeah, right: some confidential informant.*

"Anybody I might know?"

Balfa just smiled. "If I told you who he was, then he wouldn't be confidential."

Jack shrugged. *Whatever.* Balfa was certainly not the first married cop to be catching a little nookie on the side. He had more important things to worry about than this particular precinct detective. "Did you contact your Narcotics guys about the fentanyl?"

Balfa was rummaging around for something in his desk drawer; he barely looked up. "Didn't get around to it yet."

Jack blinked, surprised by the detective's nonchalance. "Did you find out who's running security over at Governors Island?"

Balfa pinched his bottom lip. "Not yet. Sorry. I had to finish up this other thing."

Jack frowned. Back at the end of the eighties, the Seventy-sixth precinct had seen its fair share of murders, but those stats had dropped precipitously over the following ten years. Murders were rare here now—especially murders of children. Even though he had a backlog of his own cases, he had spent hours of unpaid OT trying to discover the kid's identity. And here Balfa was, dicking around, without a care in the world . . .

He thought of a sign some wag had posted on a wall back at Brooklyn South Homicide: IF OUR RESTAURANT DOES NOT MEET YOUR EXPECTATIONS, PLEASE LOWER YOUR EXPECTATIONS.

It could have been Balfa's motto.

CHAPTER *nine*

J ack is swimming. He feels like a fish and he's swimming; he's free to glide along and everything's blue, and friendly rays of sun slant down and Petey is swimming, too. Petey is younger but he's a better athlete, so he can swim deeper and farther. This is Jack's brother, whom he loves so much it causes a sweet pain in his heart.

He comes up for air and he knows the place: It's the Red Hook public pool and it's full of kids shouting and families laughing and little babies learning how to dogpaddle. And he dives back into the blue and discovers that he can breathe underwater now and he glides forward, looking to tell Petey the good news.

Only he doesn't see his brother, and there's a voice coming down into the water from the loudspeakers, and he bursts up and the lifeguards are shouting "Everybody out! Everybody out!" They're pointing at the sky, which is filling with dark thunderclouds. And everybody's rising, spouting up, and clambering out over the sides. The pool is huge, bigger than a football field, but there's only a few people left in it. Now no one. But Petey still hasn't come out. Now everyone is gone—the families, the lifeguards, the little shouting kids—everyone but Jack, and he runs along the vast concrete plaza that surrounds the pool, which is quiet as the grave now under the lowering sky, and he's peering down into the water, trying to locate his brother, who is missing.

He woke, gasping.

"You okay?" mumbled Michelle.

"I'm fine," he answered, and she rolled back over into sleep.

Jack lay waiting for his heart rate to return to normal.

One night after he and Michelle had first grown close, he told her something he had hardly told anyone: The story of how his brother had been killed when they were both kids, how he had been powerless to save him, how the killers had never been caught. She asked if that was why he had become a cop. He had shrugged it off, said he'd never thought much about it.

He thought about it now.

What particularly bothered him was that he had not even succeeded in identifying the boy in the box, let alone figuring out who had killed him. The kid was not in any national missing children database, or in the FBI's fingerprint database (hardly surprising, considering his age). All queries to area hospitals had come up empty so far, as had checks with schools and social services agencies throughout New York, New Jersey, and Connecticut. A national search was a daunting prospect, and would require considerable resources. The problem was that nobody was making a fuss about this particular kid.

The worst part was that dead bodies kept coming in to the Kings County morgue; if it filled up, and the child was still unidentified and unclaimed, his small body would end up buried out on Hart Island, in an anonymous grave in Potter's Field. Jack was determined not to let that happen.

THE MORNING WAS NIPPY and his breath clouded up as he climbed out of his car on Mermaid Avenue. The ocean and the Coney Island boardwalk were just two blocks to the south, and usually the whole area smelled of salt water and fried grease, but those odors were muted in these winter months.

In the Brooklyn South Homicide office, things were business-as-usual: The bright fluorescent-lit space was filled with desks piled with paperwork, and the other four detectives of Jack's team were hunkering down behind the piles, like drivers settling in for a demolition derby. Amid the usual wanted posters, union notices, and department paperwork, two computer-printed banners ran across the back wall. *He who is not pursued escapes. Socrates.* And, *If a man is burdened with the blood of another, let him be a fugitive unto death. Let no one help him. Proverbs 28:17.*

Jack signed in to the command log. "Please tell me there's some coffee left," he muttered as he headed for the makeshift little kitchen in the back storeroom.

He didn't get that far. Sergeant Tanney stuck his curly head out of his office. "Leightner, I've got a fresh one for you."

Jack winced. "Can't you give me a couple more days on the Red Hook thing?"

Tanney shook his head. "This one's gonna be big, and I need you on it."

Jack sighed, but didn't argue. As new jobs came in, the detectives caught them in turn. They could go "off the chart" for four days to focus exclusively on a fresh job, but unless the case was high priority, after that they went back into the rotation. He had worked the job involving the boy in the box as hard and as thoroughly as he could, and would continue to do so in every free minute, but this new case would have to take precedence. (He just hoped that Tommy Balfa would show a little initiative.)

Five minutes later he and Hermelinda Vargas, another detective from his team, were speeding north toward the Seventy-eighth precinct.

———

MIGHTY STATUES OF REARING horses flanked the entrance to Prospect Park's southernmost corner. The inner roadway that circled the park was closed to cars between the morning and evening rush hours, but Jack steered around the metal barrier.

Like Coney Island—and the harbor—the park provided the residents of Brooklyn with some respite from the miles of asphalt, concrete, and brick that covered the rest of the borough. The park had been designed by the same guy who created Central Park, and had similarly elegant features, but this place was not overrun with tourists; as befitted Brooklyn, it was a lot more low-key.

Jack steered the unmarked Chevy along the park drive. To his left, bordering a small lake, honey-colored cattails swayed in the bright morning sun. Geese waddled along the shore, while out on the water hundreds of white seagulls rested, all facing the same direction, into the wind. In warm weather the park provided a refreshing blast of green, but now everything was brown and gray: the ground bare, the trees stripped to their stark branches.

Somewhere in this wooded landscape, two bodies lay sprawled on the rotting leaves. More than a decade ago, that fact would have set Jack's heart thumping. He had hardly been a rookie back then, with years of experience on patrol and as a precinct detective, but Homicide was a whole new challenge. Now he was just going to another day at work.

His colleague, who had come along to provide a little extra support for what was sure to turn into a press case (a white jogger killed in a public park), was similarly calm. Hermelinda Vargas—whom everyone called Linda—was a short, self-assertive woman. After work, when the team went out for a beer, men would hone in on her because of her soccer-ball-sized breasts. When they caught a blast of her withering sarcasm, they would usually retreat. Hermelinda was fiercely in love with her husband, a scrawny little electrician. She liked to say that she had become a cop because it was her destiny: Her first name meant "shield of power."

Now she sipped a cup of coffee and checked out the passing scenery. Though the park drive was closed to cars, that didn't mean that it saw no traffic. First the detectives passed a blond jogger in a trim sweatsuit, her tight ponytail tossing in a circle above her head. A hundred yards on they zipped by an inexperienced Rollerblader lurching forward, arms thrust out, and then a pack of bicyclists in sleek pro gear, their goggles and aerodynamic helmets making them look like a swarm of space aliens. These signs of activity were good for the case: Though the shootings had happened in the park's interior woodlands, the perp would have had to cross the loop to get there, and maybe some of these weekday athletes had seen him do it.

Their earnest progress around the park made Jack think of the extra few pounds at his own waist. He lived only a mile or two away—maybe he could take up a little jogging during his time off. It would be good to get out into nature a little, watch the seasons change. He resolved to stop by a sporting goods store and pick up some appropriate running clothes.

His partner swiveled as they passed a jogger in a Spandex outfit. "Jesus, did you see that guy's tights? Come on, people: Leave a little to the imagination." Vargas didn't say much, but when she did, she prided herself on talking like one of the guys.

Jack decided to buy some old-fashioned baggy sweatpants.

They were getting close now, as they swooped past some of the park's genteel landmarks: an Adirondack-style gazebo on the lake, a turn-of-the-century covered pavilion . . . Soon they came upon the Boathouse, an elegant white building with huge arched windows and a red-tiled roof. It faced onto a serene little lagoon, an offshoot of the lake, separated from it by a graceful stone bridge. A Chinese bride in yards of white taffeta sat by the shore as a photographer snapped pictures. Jack wondered how the woman kept from shivering in her sleeveless dress, but evidently it was worth the discomfort. Chinese wedding parties loved this spot: With the bridge in the background, the sparkling water, the willow trees, it made an ideal calendar-style image for the wedding album.

Jack stared at the lagoon. Ever since the fiasco at the inn upstate he had been agonizing about a spot for his next proposal. Why not here? He could suggest a little stroll with Michelle, lead her up onto the bridge . . . Thank God the inn had finally found the ring, miraculously unmangled, inside the garbage disposal (or so they claimed).

"I think this is the turnoff," Vargas said.

Jack veered onto the Center Drive, which led into the heart of the park. As they left the loop road behind, the cheery tone changed. The woods became quiet, nearly devoid of people, and various lonely paths led off into the underbrush. A subtle air of menace crept in, as if they were entering a fairy-tale forest.

A hundred yards ahead, a group of NYPD vehicles was clustered like a bunch of big flashing beetles. Jack parked far away, so he wouldn't risk getting blocked in. The sound of his closing door seemed to echo in the woods. Ahead he heard an occasional crackle of radios, but the area was otherwise still, the quiet broken only by the scuffing of his shoes on the asphalt, an unseen dog barking in the distance, a squirrel skittering through the dead leaves. He breathed deep: The air held a mulchy, piney smell.

Beyond the vehicles, to the right, some yellow Crime Scene tape stretched across the turnoff for a secluded path. Jack and Vargas badged the uniform standing guard, and got the familiar nod of respect. *Ladies and gentlemen, the cavalry has arrived.*

THERE WAS A PHOTOGRAPHER at work here, too, but his subject was the dark opposite of the happy view near the Boathouse.

The crime scene was about two hundred yards up the path, which twisted and turned so that it lost all sightlines with the road and then descended into a quiet hollow between two ridges. A wire fence ran along the left side, and a steep hillside rose along the other: It made a perfect spot for a mugging, because the victim had nowhere to run. People tended to misjudge the center of the park; Jack had often seen odd loners wandering its interior paths. Even the nature didn't look so bucolic here: Jack noticed a tree—hit by lightning?— that had crashed down and split its neighbor in half, and another one with an ugly tumor glommed around its trunk.

A group of detectives, uniforms, and pathologists from the M.E.'s office stood, hands in coat pockets, outside a perimeter marked with more yellow tape. They were waiting for the Crime Scene team, in their paper jumpsuits, to finish photographing and collecting evidence. In the middle of the scene, two bodies were splayed out along the path. The nearest one was Caucasian, probably in his forties, wearing a high-tech silver-and-blue running outfit. The second, lying on his back with his head pointed up the path, was a squat African-American teenager engulfed in a bulbous down jacket.

"Aw shit," Vargas said dryly. "Someone done killed the Michelin Tire Man."

One of the uniforms looked startled by this gallows humor, but Anselmo Alvarez smiled as he ducked out under the tape. The Crime Scene supervisor lifted one of Vargas's gloved hands to his lips. "Hermelinda," he said, pronouncing the name flawlessly. "We have to stop meeting like this."

Jack shook hands with a rail-thin detective in a camel-colored coat: Richie Halpern, one of the Seven-eight's senior detectives. The man's rough pink skin and shock of white hair reminded him of a lab rat.

"Your case?"

Halpern nodded.

"Any IDs yet?"

"They found an empty wallet next to the white guy. He's a doctor over at Methodist; lives near Seventh Avenue."

"And the other one?"

"Unknown."

Alvarez signaled to the pathologists, who moved inside the perimeter for a preliminary examination of the bodies. They would check for rigor mortis and use rectal thermometers to help determine the time of death, take samples from the red pools under each body, bag the extremities of the victims to preserve trace evidence.

While the detectives waited their turn, they shot the shit, traded news about colleagues, inquired about each other's families . . . Jack stood to the side, contemplating the bodies. Even from yards away, he could see a couple of the bullet holes. They were not very dramatic, but years of experience had taught him that gunshot wounds were often quite modest.

He knew all about bullets. He had seen them pried out of floors, out of walls, out of armchairs, toys, briefcases, books, TVs, even a Thanksgiving turkey. He knew their sizes, velocities, trajectories, how they rebounded off brick or metal. Over and over he had seen what they could do to human flesh. It was only recently, though, that he had literally absorbed the knowledge. Underneath his shirt now, between his solar plexus and his right nipple, was a scar the size of a dime. (A quarter, if he was feeling dramatic.) The burning metal had passed through his lung and a fragment had lodged in one of his vertebrae. That piece was still inside him, too difficult to remove—a doctor had shown him the ghostly white spot on his X-ray.

The greatest damage was not physical. When his son, Ben, was small the boy had gone through a brief obsession with cuts and scrapes and Band-Aids. At the heart of it was the kid's uneasy discovery that his body was vulnerable. The effect of a bullet was a thousand times greater: It was an invasion and a violation. It was an obscenity. It changed everything. Before Jack's shooting, he had been unaware of his belief in an invisible membrane that protected him from the world. He only realized it after a bullet shredded that thin parchment.

He glanced at his fellow detectives, chatting blithely. To them, corpses were remote objects, unrelated to their own bodies. They didn't know how easy it could be to cross the line.

Alvarez finally gave the go-ahead. "Keep to the asphalt," he cautioned; he didn't want any extra shoeprints on the mulch beside the path.

The Caucasian was curled in a fetal position. When Alvarez gently pushed him onto his back, the body moved easily—the low temperatures might have inhibited rigor mortis, or perhaps it hadn't had time to set in yet. The man looked older than Jack had first guessed, a handsome guy who kept himself in shape. Alvarez moved the hands aside; the doctor had been clutching at a bullet wound in his chest, and there was another one at the top of his right thigh. Jack noted a pair of headphones around the neck; he pulled out a ballpoint pen and used it to draw the cord away from the body. It was not attached to any device.

The other body, the one in the down jacket, lay stretched out. He wore a stocking do-rag, half pulled down over his face. In his bare left hand he clutched a semiautomatic pistol, a Mac-9; it smelled of cordite. Jack noted a hole in the chest of the down jacket: a glimpse of white feathers soaked with red. Under the brown nylon of the kid's do-rag, Jack noticed the glint of a little silver cuff on the right ear. Peering into the kid's slackly open mouth, he noted a gold cap on one of the front teeth. Kids were sometimes smart enough to bring throw-away clothes when they did a crime, but they tended to hang on to their jewelry. *Ah, vanitas . . .* He made a mental memo to run these identifiers through a computer database when he returned to the task force office.

He knelt down between the bodies, steadying himself with his fingertips pressed against the cold asphalt. The sweet, metallic odor of blood rose up to him and he shivered, blinked. Saw a basement room in Red Hook, a bullet-ravaged man lying on a concrete floor a few feet away, gasping out his last few breaths . . .

Hermelinda Vargas turned to one of the pathologists. "How many wounds do we have?"

"Just the three you see, I think." It was often possible to miss a hole, given the rough conditions out of doors; the autopsy would tell for sure.

Jack pulled himself out of his momentary mental lapse— thankfully the others didn't seem to have noticed. He stood up and checked out the blood spatter on the asphalt and the leaves. The way it had broken up into small drops indicated the force of the gunshots; they were elongated, with tails that pointed away from the source. What was surprising was that both sets pointed in the same direction, up the trail.

Jack pointed to the headphone cord. "Did you find a Walkman or anything?"

The pathologist shook his head.

Jack turned to Alvarez. "We've got more casings than wounds, huh?"

The Crime Scene man nodded at the five little plastic stands his team had set up next to ejected cartridge casings. "Yeah. And it looks like they all came from a Nine." All five had been found on the left side of the path, from the kid with the gun's perspective, which was odd, because semiautomatic casings normally ejected six to eight feet *to the right* behind the shooter.

Jack and his detective colleagues spent another ten minutes quizzing the pathologists and the Crime Scene crew. Then he turned to the local detective, to show deference to the owner of the case. "What do you think?"

Halpern glanced up and down the path. "This is looking pretty screwy. At first you think, okay, this is a mugging gone bad. But there's only one gun here, so how did the kid get hit? In theory, I guess he could have killed the other guy and then turned the gun on himself, but there's no burn marks or stippling on the wounds." That indicated that the gunshots had come from a distance of more than eighteen inches.

Linda Vargas scratched her nose. "I don't mean to get all *politically correct* here, gentlemen, but let's not jump to conclusions about who's the perp."

Halpern frowned. "What do you mean?"

"Look, just because we've got a black kid wearing a do-rag, let's not assume he was the one who brought the gun to the party. Who knows? Maybe this doc was some kind of *Death Wish* urban vigilante type, out looking for trouble . . ."

Halpern was clearly making an effort not to look skeptical. "How would that work? The kid's the one with the gun."

Vargas nodded. "Okay, but let's say the doc shot the kid, and then the kid managed to get the gun away from him, and fired back before he went down for the count." She turned to Jack.

He shrugged. "It's possible. But look at this outfit." He pointed at the doctor's skintight running gear. "There's nowhere to conceal a piece. I doubt he would just roam around carrying it in the open."

Vargas nodded thoughtfully. "You've got a point there."

Jack frowned. "The missing Walkman is what bothers me. I mean, maybe somebody came along after the shooting and snatched it up, but who'd want to get involved in something this bad?" He called out to Anselmo Alvarez. "Can we get an on-site residue analysis on these guys? Just the hands . . ."

Alvarez nodded and had his men go back to their truck and pull the necessary equipment. When a gun was fired, primer residues usually landed on the shooter's skin and clothing. Normally, tests would be conducted in a lab, but new technology had made it possible to check for them at the scene.

Jack took another look around the bodies. "The spatter doesn't feel right. I think there was another shooter."

A few minutes later Alvarez came over, shaking his head. "Well, well, well: It looks like *neither* of our friends here fired a gun today."

All three detectives reacted the same way: They turned to scan the empty woods. The real shooter was out there, somewhere else.

Jack turned back to the scene. "Here's the way I see it. I don't want to discount the possibility that our doctor could have started things, but let's begin with a likelier scenario. Our jogger comes up the path and there's two perps waiting for him, maybe up on that ridge. One of them, Mr. Michelin here, runs out in front. The shooter takes up a position behind the vic to box him in. They ask for his wallet and his Walkman. Maybe he tries to be brave, thinks he's gonna pull some macho stunt. That's when everything goes haywire." He turned to his task force colleague. "Remind you of anything?"

Linda Vargas laughed.

CHAPTER *ten*

"Wait, back up a minute," said Jack's son, Ben, at dinner that evening. "What did the splatter thing tell you?"

The young man had barely touched his dinner, a meal Michelle had gone to a fair amount of trouble to make, but she didn't mind. Ben looked more animated than she had ever seen him. He was a tall, gangly kid, and he was usually quiet and withdrawn. (Or maybe he was just shy about the remnants of acne that still spotted his narrow face.) Even though he lived in Brooklyn, it was rare that he came by Jack's apartment.

Jack finished chewing a bite of chicken. She was surprised by his robust appetite, after such a gruesome day. "It's *spatter*," he said. "That's the way blood sprays out from a gunshot or other wound."

Michelle considered asking if they could finish this particular conversation after dinner, but she refrained. Not only because Ben seemed to be getting along with his father, but because it was one of the few times she had ever heard Jack talk so openly about his work.

He reached out and moved the salt and pepper shakers in front of him. "It's a simple matter of geometry. If two people face each other and they shoot, the spatter's gonna go in opposite directions." He made a couple of little explosive gestures with his fingers to demonstrate. "The weird thing here, though, was that it faced the same way for both. Let's say one guy shoots the other guy first . . ." He marshaled the shakers like toy soldiers. "Now, somehow, the second guy would have to move all the way around the first guy before *he* got popped." He shrugged. "Not impossible, mind you, but not very likely."

He looked up at his son. "You ever hear of Occam's Razor?"

Ben shook his head.

"Occam was some old guy, a monk or something. He said that if you've got two or more theories, the simplest one that accounts for all the evidence is usually your best bet. To put it another way, if you hear hoofbeats, think *horses*, not *zebras*." He straightened up. "Of course, you've still gotta stay open to all possibilities, 'cause believe me, we see the wackiest sh—, er, *stuff*."

Michelle smiled at this self-censorship, as if Jack's son was still eight years old.

"Anyhow," he continued, "I'm thinking there was another shooter."

Ben frowned. "But why would he shoot both of them: the jogger *and* the mugger?"

Jack grinned. "That's where the wacky part comes in. The situation reminded me of this case we had over in the Seven-five last year. Two punks tried to jack an Escalade. One stood on the driver's side, and the other on the passenger's. The driver tried to get away, so one of the homies reached up and shot at him through the window. Two problems, though: He couldn't see very well 'cause the window was so high, and he pulled off the shot gangster-style." Jack pantomimed holding a gun sideways, then shook his head. "It's the curse of the movies. We get all these thugs imitating the crap they see in some dumb flick."

"Why was the sideways thing a problem?" Michelle asked. She wasn't much impressed by all the talk of guns and violence—not nearly as impressed as Ben seemed to be—but she was happy to help the conversation along.

Jack snorted. "These kids think it looks good, but try aiming a gun when you hold it like that. And with a semiautomatic with a light trigger pull, there's even less control."

Ben was wide-eyed. "What happened?"

Michelle pressed her fingertips to her mouth, interested now, despite herself. "Don't tell me: The shot went out the other window and killed the partner?"

Jack nodded. "Another criminal genius bites the dust." He grinned. "It's what we call a public service homicide."

Ben leaned forward. "So you think something like that happened in the park?"

Jack shrugged. "It's a theory." He set down his napkin and stood up. "I'll go get the coffee and dessert."

Ben looked surprised. Perhaps his father had not been so domestic in the old family home, Michelle thought.

Jack stopped halfway across the room and turned back to his son. "Don't go talking about this case with your friends. They'll tell someone else, and then someone else will hear about it, and the next thing you know, it'll show up in the *Daily News*. And that would be bad news for your old man, *capisce?*"

Ben nodded solemnly; he seemed impressed by the trust his father was placing in him.

As soon as Jack was out of earshot, the kid turned to Michelle. "Wow! I think that's the most he's told me about his work since . . . *ever*. Usually I ask him how it's going and he never wants to talk about it." He shook his head, then smiled. "You must be having a good effect on him."

Michelle smiled modestly, but she was pleased. Pleased most of all that this rare family dinner was going so well. She liked Jack's son. Their first meeting had taken place under the most awful circumstances: the night Jack had been shot. There was the usual emergency room craziness, plus panicked cops milling everywhere, and then the commissioner and his entourage showing up. Michelle had just met Ben and was trying to explain why she was there even though she had only known his father for a couple weeks when Jack's ex-wife showed up, with some kind of boyfriend in tow, and things got even more awkward.

At first Ben had closed ranks with his mother, given Michelle short shrift, which was understandable, but she had stuck around, and eventually, after the first dicey days in Intensive Care, the ex had seen that someone new was in Jack's life and backed off. Soon all the press and Departmental frenzy died down and it was just Michelle and Ben, every day, making sure Jack got something decent to eat, that the nurses were taking good care of him. The son's initial confusion and hostility had slowly given way to a shy kindness, and they had become friends, bonding over crappy snacks from the hospital vending machines and gossip from celebrity magazines.

Jack emerged from the kitchen looking puzzled. "Should I bring forks or spoons for the dessert?"

Michelle smiled. The man was one of the NYPD's more senior and capable detectives, but in many ways he still seemed like a boy. All men were boys at heart, at least all the ones she'd spent time with. There was that familiar befuddlement over the workings of the simplest things, that need for praise and reinforcement, those quick resorts to anger or petulance.

All you could do was look on and shake your head.

CHAPTER *eleven*

Later that night, Jack made love with Michelle. Or tried to, at any rate. He propped himself above her, watching her closed eyelids move and twitch. She had disappeared into a deep interior landscape, as if she was searching for her orgasm on some far horizon only she could see. He tried to help her move toward it, but tonight he couldn't tell how much he was contributing.

Men struck him as pretty simple sexual machines. If you were with someone you found attractive, especially someone you loved, the only difficult part was trying to hold back from feeling too good. Women, on the other hand, could be like foreign cars, requiring subtle diagnostics and maneuvers.

Finally, Michelle moaned a bit, and he took that as his own permission to finish, but he wasn't sure that she was satisfied.

He rolled away, lay silent as his breathing slowed. She was an indistinct form in the darkness next to him. He shrugged to himself. Okay, so maybe it wasn't the best sex they'd ever had, but they'd have plenty of opportunities to improve on it.

He glanced at the clock on the bedside table. Six hours until he'd have to go back to work, but he didn't feel sleepy yet.

His mind drifted back over the day's tour.

After checking out the bodies in the park, the detectives had split up. Halpern had stayed behind to organize a canvass for witnesses, while Jack and Vargas had gone off to notify the doctor's wife. That was certainly one of the worst parts of the job, but Jack had done it many times and he knew not to worry about it until he got there. As he drove back out onto the loop drive, it didn't take long for the somber atmosphere of the crime scene to dissipate. The joggers continued on their merry rounds, cocooned in their headphones, oblivious to the tragedy that had unfolded earlier, just yards away; the little swarm of bicyclists zipped by again, continuing in its orbits around the park. The moral, as always, was simple and blunt: For the victims of homicide, life was blotted out in seconds, but for everybody else, it flowed right on.

When Jack reached the west side of the park, his ruminations about the bodies in the woods suddenly gave way. A concrete bandshell went past, empty and forlorn in the winter cold, but in his mind's eye he saw a big zydeco band on stage, a happy crowd spread out in front. A warm summer evening, people clapping along, little kids running through the throng . . . and there he was, dancing with Michelle, on their first date, the first time he had cut a rug in years . . . He decided that he would definitely propose to her in the park. The fact that the Boathouse was just several hundred yards from the morning's crime scene didn't faze him. This was New York City: How could you possibly avoid places where someone had died?

Michelle was silent in the bed next to him; he wondered if she was asleep.

He went back to retracing the day. Just beyond the park he and Vargas had pulled up in front of a fancy brownstone. He could remember a time when Park Slope had been a run-down, shabby neighborhood where few people wanted to live, but now the streets were packed with yuppies and their baby strollers, and brownstones were selling for millions. The doctor had found himself a prime one, just a few blocks from the hospital where he worked.

A pretty but harried-looking young blonde answered the bell, one little kid scampering in the hallway behind her, another on the way, by the looks of her belly, which was only half-covered by a pink T-shirt. The child—a boy with a pixie face under a head of wild blond hair—hid behind one of his mother's legs and peered around wide-eyed at the strange people who had just shown up at his door. Jack and Vargas exchanged a quick somber glance. (He remembered when his colleague had joined the task force, the only woman in his team. Some of the guys had tried to foist off death notifications on her, remarking how women were so much more "sensitive" about such things, but she made it clear that she was having none of it. "If you're not good at it," she had said, "you need to *get* good.")

The young wife let them in, and they sat with her in a fancy front parlor, with its elegant old moldings and its dusty chandelier, and Jack did his best to be gentle.

"No," the wife said at first, shaking her head, a weird kind of smile contorting her mouth. "He'll be back in a few minutes. He just went for a jog."

And then he had pulled out the driver's license from the wallet, and she held it up in front of her face, staring at it, and he watched her world implode.

A flurry of emotions rippled across her face. Who knew what was going on inside? Maybe she felt guilty because she had argued with her husband just before he left the house. Maybe their marriage was not going well, and there was some quick dart of relief. Or maybe she loved him with everything she had. You never knew for sure. All you knew was that you were watching someone's whole planned future suddenly disappear in front of them, as if they had been driving and ignored a warning sign: BRIDGE OUT.

Homicide detectives frequently said that their job was to stand up for victims who could never speak for themselves. Jack felt that sometimes—as he did for the boy who had floated ashore in Red Hook just days earlier—but he also knew that the dead were beyond help. No justice would ever bring them back. He could never restore this woman's husband to her, could never even restore her shattered sense of safety. As he watched her crumple into herself in the armchair in front of him, though, he knew that he would do anything in his power to catch the man's killer. He could at least get the perp off the street so this wouldn't happen to somebody else. And maybe he could help this woman feel in some small way that the world had not surrendered to chaos.

Suddenly he felt very tired.

"Jack?"

He roused himself from his sad reverie. Evidently he wasn't the only one lying here awake.

"Yeah?"

Michelle's quiet voice rose up into the dark next to him. "Remember, the other day, when we were in the bath and you asked me about kids?"

He sighed. The shift was jarring, and this new subject was too big to bring up now, so late. After dinner he had made a plan for a walk in the park with Michelle, just three days away. He wanted to get through the marriage proposal, to get that settled. Then they could worry about if and when to have a kid . . .

He reached out and stroked Michelle's shoulder. "I remember. No offense, but would it be okay if we talked about it some other time?"

CHAPTER *twelve*

In the happy horseshit land of TV cop shows, murders were committed by villains who cleverly plotted every step of their crimes, from luring victims to disposing of bodies.

In real life, homicides usually happened in jagged, unpredictable outbursts. A domestic squabble flared into sudden violence. A street diss provoked a macho response. Once the bodies hit the ground, the perps had a rude awakening: It was a lot easier to pull a trigger than to deal with the aftermath. How to dispose of a large, heavy body in the middle of one of the biggest, most crowded cities in the world? You could rarely bury the thing, in this world of concrete. If you did the killing solo, just moving the corpse presented a major physical difficulty.

In this case, even though the crime had happened in the relative isolation of the woods, the shooter would have been suddenly confronted with *two* bodies. Getting them out of the park past all of the joggers and bikers would have been nearly impossible, and the perp couldn't risk the time to bury them in the frozen ground. So he had staged a false scenario. The ruse had failed, but the detectives still had one unidentified body on their hands.

Not for long.

Since there had been no anthrax mailings or subway bomb threats that day, the next morning's tabloids actually had room for news of the killings. Just hours after they hit the stands, Jack received a call from a colleague in Flatbush. Detective George Billing's cigarette-rough voice: "I heard you were working that thing in Prospect Park and I got a tip for ya. Last night I pulled in this kid named Pudgie Dibell for trying to move some coke outside a bodega over here. He already has a sheet, so he's looking to make a deal. He claims he overheard two kids from the Trumbull Houses talking two nights ago. They said they were planning to go over to Prospect Park and *get paid*. 'Park Slope makes, Trumbull takes,' that kinda noise."

Jack leaned forward, resting his elbows on his desk. "Did he give good descriptions? The body I've got is a short, stout kid with one gold tooth and a silver cuff, right ear."

"That sounds right. James Ausbury. I know the kid—I've collared him a number of times myself: purse snatching, GTA . . ."

"And the other one?"

"Street name: T-Mo. Real name's Tryell Vincent. That one's a tough nut: violent assault, weapons charges, attempted homicide. I've been trying to put him away for years, but he's slicker than weasel shit. You wanna pull him in?"

Jack stood quickly. "I'm on my way."

"WAS IT HIM?" MICHELLE asked two days later as they settled into Jack's car. "Was he the shooter?"

Jack put on his seat belt, then turned to Michelle and raised his eyebrows theatrically. "Do you want me to jump to the ending, or would you rather hear the story?"

She raised her hands. "Sorry, Mr. Columbo. Tell it your way."

Jack was surprised to be telling the story any way at all. With his ex-wife, he had kept all talk about work to a minimum. Most cops did. He saw the ugly side of human behavior every day, and he didn't want to bring that home. You had to build a containment wall. Or at least he had thought he needed to. It had hardly protected his marriage. Had done the opposite, really—this was one of Louise's big gripes, that he didn't talk enough. Maybe he had a chance now to do things differently, after fifteen years alone . . .

He waited as a Hasidic family—a mother in her prim blond wig, three little girls in identical plaid skirts—crossed in front of the car. His hand drifted to his jacket pocket where he had stashed the ring. The sun was bright, and he tilted the visor down. An inch of snow had fallen the previous night, but now a freakishly warm day had already melted it, sending sparkling beads of light dripping off the eaves of Midwood's suburban houses. He turned onto Coney Island Avenue: a long, incredibly drab boulevard of car supply stores, Pakistani phone card shops, and taxi drivers' quick-eats joints. The avenue bisected nearly the whole of Brooklyn, from Brighton Beach all the way to his current destination: Prospect Park.

He stopped at a light next to a huge brick yeshiva, a religious school. Michelle glanced at it and frowned. "I hope this doesn't sound offensive, but why does Jewish religious architecture have to be so ugly?"

Jack chuckled. It was true. The Christians had their soaring cathedrals, the Muslims their airy mosques, but his people seemed to favor a dull and heavy sort of building, inspired, seemingly, by mausoleums . . . or matzoh balls.

He paused to remember where he had been interrupted. In truth, he was glad to be able to tell the story, not just because doing so opened up a promise of a new way of being with a woman, but because it helped him take his mind off his fast-approaching new proposal.

"*So*," he said. "Tryell Vincent. Definitely a bad guy." The suspect, twenty-two, had the lean, mean look of a predator, one of the small pool of aggressive offenders who committed a hugely disproportionate number of the city's violent crimes. Vincent was just under six feet tall, well muscled, with a strange dent on the right side of his head, evidence perhaps of some childhood accident or abuse. He had worn a fancy down jacket, another angry marshmallow. He slouched back in the hard chair of the interview room as if it were a lounger, legs spread out before him, hands clasped comfortably in his lap.

"He knew all about gaming the system," Jack continued. "He showed up with a sharp lawyer. The guy could have refused to talk at all—it's a constitutional right—but they were going out of their way to pretend to cooperate."

"Why?"

"He wanted to present his alibi. He claimed he'd spent the night before the shooting and the next day taking care of his invalid aunt. Who just happens to be a prominent member of the local church."

"Did she back him up?"

"*Oh yeah*. Said they had watched TV together, that he made her breakfast the next morning. The detective I was working with wanted to throw up—he had watched this guy skate away from major charges too many times."

"So what did you do?"

Jack shrugged. "We had to let him go." He pictured Vincent standing up and saying, "It's been real nice talkin' with y'all." The look on his face said *Fuck you, Five-Ohs. I beat you before, and I beat you again.* Then he strolled out of the interview room, right hand tucked down between his legs, practically cupping his balls. Jack's blood pressure rose again just thinking about it. The kid had likely just killed two human beings—including his own friend—yet he didn't seem to have a care in the world.

"And he got away scot-free?"

Jack put on a fake offended look. "Hey, who you talking to here?

I spent hours working to find a hole in the alibi. I checked his ATM card to see if he made any withdrawals that would place him away from the aunt's house, checked if he bought a fare card at a subway vending machine, checked to make sure he hadn't had any run-ins with the local police . . . and then I got ahold of his cell phone records." He grinned. "Turns out he called his aunt early on the morning of the shootings."

Michelle raised her eyebrows. "How did he explain that?"

Jack shook his head. "I didn't give him the chance; he and his lawyer would have just come up with some slick explanation. Instead, I went back to the aunt and read her the riot act about perjury. And then I asked why her nephew would need to phone her if he was right there in the kitchen, making scrambled eggs."

"Did she admit she had lied?"

"Not at first. She thought about it a minute, then said that she had asked him to call her phone to make sure it was working. *Just a little test . . .*"

"How could you prove that wasn't true?"

"I pulled the phone record out of my pocket and asked her how a simple test could possibly take eleven minutes. I told her that her nephew was going upstate, and she was going with him."

"What did she do?"

Jack grinned again. "She thought about it for another thirty seconds, and then she looked up at me and said, 'Would it be okay if I feed my cats before I testify?'"

HE PULLED UP ON the edge of the park, got out, and opened the trunk.

"What are you doing?" Michelle called back over the roof of the car.

He lifted out the cooler he had stashed there earlier in the day. "Just a little picnic." Champagne, cheese, crackers, strawberries. If everything worked out right, it would turn into a celebration.

Several stretch limos were parked along the avenue, and he soon saw why. As he and Michelle headed into the park, they overtook a Chinese wedding party. The young men looked like models in their white tuxedoes and gelled black hair. The young women in their taffeta gowns were a bunch of bright flowers levitating along the asphalt path. As they all crossed the loop drive and then descended toward the Boathouse, Jack saw another wedding party posed stiffly along the edge of the little lake, and then another. Brides and grooms everywhere—it was like the punchline of a joke. Someday, he and his new wife would remember the site of their engagement and laugh.

"Do you want me to take a turn carrying that?" Michelle asked, nodding down at the cooler.

Jack shook his head. "I'm good."

She smiled. "Yes, you are."

It was their little joke.

The afternoon sun sparkled on the water and the sky was bright blue, with just a few puffy clouds. It was warm enough out that for once the Chinese bridesmaids didn't have to suffer in their sleeveless gowns. Across the way, the little bridge arched across the water; beneath it, a family of ducks sailed into the lagoon.

"Why don't we walk around?" Jack said. He wanted to get away from the other people, to find his own perfect spot. Once again, he wondered which knee he should get down on. He swallowed. All of a sudden, he was nervous again. *What are you thinking?* he asked himself. *This woman has only known you for a few months. What makes you think she's gonna say yes—a beautiful woman like her, a geezer like you?*

Then he thought back to the end of their initial date, that first sweet, powerful kiss at the end of the night. And he thought back to the first time Michelle had spent the night. The connection had been so strong, stronger than anything he had ever felt with his first wife. And Michelle had stuck by him after the shooting; they had lived through 9/11 together . . . Sometimes you just *knew*. He was being nervous, was all, floating these doubts. She would definitely say yes.

They walked around the edge of the lagoon, breathing in the fresh winter air. The exertion was making Michelle's cheeks rosy, and she looked so beautiful that his heart almost couldn't take it. The path turned up toward the bridge. *Remember this*, Jack told himself. *Fix it in your memory.* If there was one thing life had taught him, it was that sadness was easy to recognize and carry around. You had to make a special effort to appreciate the fleeting moments when it was replaced by joy.

He took Michelle's hand as they reached the bridge. Everything was right: the weather, the location, the sunlight making the Boathouse across the way look like some fantasy Italian villa. The champagne would now be perfectly chilled, and the wedding parties in their bright outfits even made a perfect backdrop for what he was about to say. It was all coming together just the way he had planned.

He set the cooler down and hitched up his right pants leg. He was about to bend his knee when his beeper went off.

CHAPTER *thirteen*

The water was a military color, like the barrel of a big gun or the side of a battleship. The winter sun burned a scintillating path across it, dead ahead to the northern end of Governors Island; it was so bright that Jack had to avert his eyes.

Despite the relatively warm day, it was chilly out on the water and he turned up the collar of his coat. He noticed a charred wooden beam drifting like an alligator on the harbor currents, and he thought of the wooden box and what he had seen inside. Then he thought of a moment, decades ago, when he had stood on the deck of a huge Navy ship bound for Europe. It was nighttime, and the ocean was an endless moonlit plain, and he was having a smoke with an old lifer and shooting the shit. Idly, he asked what a man should do if he fell overboard in the middle of the ocean, if nobody saw him go. "Way the hell out here, there's no point trying to swim," the old sailor replied. "Just swig down some water and kiss the world good-bye."

Jack looked up and the island was already filling the view. The trip over from the southern tip of Manhattan had taken only seven minutes. As the ferry neared its destination, he scanned the land ahead. It was completely flat and just above sea level. This end reminded him of the ritzy New England college his son had attended at a ridiculously high expense: a group of brick barracks with white cupolas and white-framed windows. Straight ahead, a big American flag snapped in the breeze above the landing slip. The rumble of engines beneath Jack's feet changed tone as the ferry edged in. Despite the fact that he had grown up less than a mile away, this afternoon would mark the first time that he had ever visited this shore.

Some kind of rent-a-cop was waiting for him. The man sat in a golf cart parked next to a fat black cannon. He looked to be about forty, and his face was pale, as if he was descending into one of the latter stages of shock.

"Thank you for coming," the man said, extending a hand. "My name is Michael Durkin. I'm a supervisor for the private security company that's been looking after the island since the Coast Guard left." He put the cart in gear and drove east along a neat lane past some brick buildings near the water's edge. The harbor and the Manhattan skyline ruled the view to the north.

"I'm sorry about your day off," the man said as they turned toward the interior of the island.

Jack thought of his interrupted proposal, of Michelle having to take the goddamn *subway* home, but he just shrugged. If he had wanted to live the way other people did, with a clear line between private life and work, he should never have become a cop. That was simply the way things were, and he wasn't about to start complaining now.

He focused on his surroundings. He noticed that the street signs were blue, and bore Coast Guard insignia. An old fort rose up on the right, its massive stone walls topped by a grassy berm; Jack vaguely remembered something about the island's long history of protecting the harbor from foreign invasion. Its lawns were trim, its trees noble, its barracks dignified, but it suffered faint signs of decay that would never have been allowed on any active base: chipping paint, cracked sidewalks . . .

"It must be pretty hard to keep things up around here," Jack said.

The security man just nodded; his mind was clearly on other matters. He offered Jack a cigarette, then stuck the pack back in the pocket of his gray uniform shirt.

They got out of the cart on the edge of a stately quadrangle of big yellow woodframed houses, with square-columned front porches. A sign read NOLAN PARK. Durkin nodded toward the homes. "These were officers' quarters. They were two-family homes, with basements—but you'll see that for yourself."

Paths of brick set in a herringbone pattern bisected the quad, which was decorated with more black cannons. Wind sighed in the old chestnut trees lining it, and some dead leaves scraped across its walkways, but the place was otherwise eerily quiet. No car horns blaring, no radios thumping, no general city noise at all. The only other sounds came from off-island: a faint thropping of a helicopter overhead, the clang of a buoy out in the channel separating the island from Brooklyn, which was visible between the houses in the easternmost row. Jack almost flinched when the ferry suddenly blasted its horn behind him.

He spotted a couple of vans parked in front of one of the houses at the southeast end of the quad, along with an unmarked car that had an official look.

THEY WERE MET AT the door by a brisk, businesslike young man with a clipboard. He wore a blue jacket with FBI shoulder patches.

"I'll need to see some ID," the Feeb said.

Jack badged him, and the agent made a notation in his log.

"This way," Durkin said.

Jack stepped with him into a quiet hallway. The front rooms on either side were barren, nearly stripped of furniture, but he noticed a couple signs of former habitation: a plastic-covered couch that might have been too bulky or too tacky to move, a toddler's Big Wheel tricycle tipped over and abandoned in a corner. The place was illuminated only by whatever natural light made it past the faded curtains. It seemed colder inside the house, and faintly damp.

Another Feeb passed them brusquely in the hall. Jack waited until the man was out of earshot, then turned to Durkin.

"What's up with the feds? Who's got jurisdiction here?"

Durkin shrugged. "Any day now the island's supposed to be turned over to New York, but it's still federal property."

Jack frowned. He didn't like feds, didn't like them at all. They tended to be arrogant, secretive, and contemptuous of cops. Anyone who thought that all law enforcement was on the same team had only to read the papers to see how September 11 had exposed the true rivalries and competition.

They left the hallway and entered a bare white kitchen, where they were met by a Crime Scene tech, federal issue. "I'm going to need for you to put these on," she said, handing Jack a paper jumpsuit and a pair of booties.

Durkin grimaced. "I'll wait for you here."

Jack couldn't blame the man for not wanting to revisit the crime scene. He was used to looking at dead bodies, but for civilians the sight cut through all the bullshit they put up to avoid thinking about how fragile life really was; it bypassed the mind and went straight to some deep animal place of vulnerability and fear.

Attired in the jumpsuit, he descended into the basement, one big low-ceilinged room, wood-paneled, with a pool table and a wet bar. It was windowless; several battery-powered floodlights lit the place for a swarm of technicians. The place smelled bad.

"Are you Leightner?"

Jack turned to find a heavyset, bespectacled black man approaching, reaching out a meaty hand. Another blue-windbreakered Feeb.

"I'm Ray Hillhouse," the man said. "Thanks for coming."

The guy seemed surprisingly open and low-key; he reminded Jack of a cheery TV weatherman.

"I came across one of the memos you sent out about your Red Hook case," Hillhouse continued. "You'll see immediately why I thought of you."

The FBI man led Jack across the musty blue wall-to-wall carpet, around the pool table, over to the wet bar. Next to it lay the body.

Like every homicide crime scene, this was a storm of activity with a terrible quiet eye at its core. All of the crackling walkie-talkies and gruff banter, the photography and fingerprinting, the note-taking and speculation—it all faded into the background when Jack looked down at the victim, who had dropped into a somber realm beyond all action and noise.

He was a male Caucasian, a bulky older man, clothed in the same gray uniform as Michael Durkin, only the victim's pants and shirt were stained with blood. He lay on his side, forlorn, like a slaughtered animal. A possible murder weapon lay just a couple of feet from his crew-cut head: the heavy end of a pool cue, also stained with blood.

Jack glanced beyond the body to a half-open closet door. A number of opened cans and boxes were jumbled inside, and seemed to be the source of a rancid smell. Another olfactory note competed for attention: unwashed body.

Hillhouse hitched up his pants. "Seems like our perp spent some time down here. And he wasn't too big on hygiene—though he didn't really have much choice. The island's water system is off; they can't keep it running all the time just for a few firemen and maintenance people."

Jack noticed what seemed to be a makeshift bed behind the wet bar: a pile of heavy gray blankets. He thought of the lining of the floating box that had brought the dead boy to Red Hook. He had mentioned it in his memo—was this what had flagged the attention of the FBI agent? He slowly moved around the body and then knelt down. No, here was the giveaway, brazen as a neon sign: the letters *G.I.* were inscribed in red across the fallen security guard's forehead.

THE ESSENCE OF THE job was to go back in time, to project yourself through that still eye of the storm, and to come out into another whirl of activity, the one that had put the body there in the first place. In this case, it looked pretty simple to reconstruct.

"Yesterday," said Agent Hillhouse, "the security firm that runs things here got a call from your colleague Balfa asking them if they had noticed any unusual activity. This guard—his name is Barry Reynolds—made the rounds, driving all over, rattling doorknobs. The last anybody heard from him, he called in on his walkie to say that he hadn't found anything out of the ordinary. That was around four-thirty yesterday afternoon. And then he went off the radar. He wasn't found until this morning."

Jack frowned. "Why did it take so long?"

"First of all, he didn't specify his location in that last call. Second, there are only a handful of people here overnight these days, and so there was only a tiny search party."

Jack shrugged. "Okay, but this place isn't very big."

"It looks small from the water, but there are more than a hundred and seventy acres. And there was housing for four thousand people here before the Coast Guard left. There were a lot of places to look."

"How'd they find him?"

"They just walked around, calling him on his walkie. It's so quiet here that Durkin actually heard the sound of it coming up out of the basement." Hillhouse stepped aside to let a couple of techs pass, then turned back to Jack. "Hey, speaking of your guy Balfa, is he coming out?"

Jack shook his head. "It's his day off, too, and he's out in New Jersey or someplace." Catching some more nookie, no doubt. Jack frowned as he thought of their recent phone conversation. Most detectives would have been thrilled to hear of such a potential break in a case, but Balfa had just seemed preoccupied with his own business, as usual. He'd actually had the gall to say, "I'm sure you can handle things."

"All right," Hillhouse said, pushing his glasses higher up on his nose. "So our man Reynolds is walking around Nolan Park. Maybe he finds a door unlocked, or he hears something suspicious. He comes into the house, pokes around, decides to check the basement. He comes down, shining his light"—the FBI man nodded toward a flashlight lying on the floor a couple of yards away.

Jack picked up the story. "Someone's waiting for him in the darkness, but they don't meet right away, or else he probably would've ended up near the bottom of the stairs. He comes across the room, and the perp is hiding. Maybe he's down behind the bar here, or in the closet. Reynolds makes it all the way across the room, and he discovers the perp. He challenges him. The perp grabs the pool cue, or maybe he was already holding it, waiting . . ."

The FBI man frowned. "His choice of a weapon is odd."

"Why?"

Hillhouse walked over behind the bar. "Look at this."

Jack came around and saw what he was pointing to: a small bottle of gun oil, a bore brush, and a couple of cleaning patches. He bent down: The scent of oil was strong, and the cleaning patches were damp.

Jack's eyebrows went up. He thought for a moment. "If he used a gun, the sound might've given him away. And once somebody knew he was here, he'd be screwed. Where you gonna run to? Speaking of which, I assume you guys have searched the place pretty well?"

Hillhouse nodded. "Of course. We brought over a dog team this morning. The freshest trail led over the side of the esplanade behind the house, right to the water."

"He kept a boat there?"

"Doubtful. It would have been spotted in daylight. We're thinking an inflatable raft, like a Zodiac. Maybe he took it out of the water, stashed it under the porch . . ."

Jack nodded. He liked the way the FBI man focused on the possibilities, the way he obviously cared about his work. Why couldn't this man be his partner, instead of a lump like Tommy Balfa?

"There's something else you should see." Hillhouse led Jack around the other side of the pool table. Several more blankets had been shoved underneath. "We pulled this stuff out," the agent said, pointing at a number of items spread on the carpet: a couple of comic books, a little portable video game player, some empty candy wrappers, a pile of child-sized clothes. Jack crouched to examine the evidence. Maybe this was where the boy in the box had spent his final hours. The candy and the entertainment indicated that the perp had showed at least some concern for the child's mental and emotional state. The boy had not been bound . . . was it possible he had come here willingly—that he might even have seen this as an exciting last adventure?

"Look over there," Hillhouse said, pointing at the floor nearby. Jack saw a toiletries kit. Next to it rested a half dozen bottles of prescription medicines and painkillers—and a hypodermic needle and a tiny unmarked bottle of some liquid. The fentanyl that had sent the boy into his final sleep?

He checked out the far corner of the room, an improvised workspace. A couple of screwdrivers, a putty knife, some emptied tubes of sealant. No hammer, no saw. Anselmo Alvarez had observed that the floating coffin had been put together without any nails, and now Jack understood why. The sound of hammering or sawing would have been too risky. Which meant that the perp had pre-cut the wood, then carried it over and screwed it together on the island.

Which meant that he had committed the homicide with full premeditation—this was no accidental overdose.

After a minute, Jack stood up and glanced around the room again. It was a treasure trove of potential clues: fingerprints, blood, hair and fiber samples, traceable purchased products, maybe dirt or pollen carried to the island on the perp's or child's clothing . . . Thank God he finally had something to work with.

Moving slowly, he made one final circuit.

"What are you looking for?" the FBI man asked.

Jack scratched his cheek. "I think it's safe to say that our perp left in a hurry. He abandoned food and clothes; he didn't get rid of the kid's stuff, didn't make much of an effort to cover his tracks. It would be nice to think that he's just some nut who committed one mercy killing and one defensive attack when he got trapped. It would be nice to think that this will be the end of it."

Hillhouse nodded thoughtfully. "But you're concerned that he took the gun?"

Jack shook his head. "Who knows? Maybe he just sees that as a means of self-defense. He hasn't used it yet, as far as we know. No, there's something that worries me more."

The FBI man's glasses had slipped down his nose again; he stared over the top of them. "What's that?"

Jack grimaced. "He took the Magic Marker."

RAY HILLHOUSE GOT CALLED away by one of the Crime Scene techs. Jack spent a few more minutes poking around the basement, and then he went up to the kitchen for some fresh air. He found Michael Durkin sitting on a kitchen counter, slumped against a cabinet.

"You all right?" he asked.

The security man winced.

"Tell you what," Jack said. "Why don't you show me the water-front, so I can see where the perpetrator might've escaped to?"

Durkin slid down the counter until his feet reached the floor.

THE SECURITY MAN LIT a cigarette and drew in a deep lungful of smoke. "Quite a view, huh?"

Jack nodded. The two men stood on an asphalt esplanade just behind the house. It stretched off around the island in both directions.

"I grew up right over there." Jack pointed across the channel. The Red Hook side was dominated by the loading cranes of the container port, and multicolored stacks of the massive containers were piled next to them like a child's giant toy blocks. "I've never seen it from here, though. It's weird: It's kind of like the first time a barber holds up a mirror and you see the back of your head." He turned around, leaned against a railing, and faced back toward the island. "This is quite a place."

The security man nodded. "It used to be a whole self-contained world. They had a school, a bowling alley, swimming pools, churches, markets. They even had a seven-hundred seat Loews movie theater." He pressed his hands down on the railing and stared across the water. "You know the Talking Heads?"

"The TV news creeps?"

Durkin shook his head. "No, the band. From a while back."

Jack nodded. "Oh . . . *right*. With that cute blonde, *Debby* something? . . ."

Despite his sad mood, Durkin managed a smile. "*Whatever*. The point is, they had a song that said, 'Heaven is a place, where nothing ever happens.' I think about that sometimes, driving my little golf cart around this island." He squinted, even though the sun was at his back. He cleared his throat, but remained silent.

Jack glanced at him. "Hey, Michael? Is there something you haven't told me about this situation?"

The security man rubbed a hand over his face. He looked away for a moment. When he turned back, pain was etched all over his face. "Um, well, *yeah*. That man in there, Barry Reynolds . . . he's my father-in-law." He sighed. "I'm the one who got him the job. He used to be a cop. Not in the city, but over there in Jersey. Newark. He put in his twenty, and then he retired, and then . . . like a lot of retired cops, he didn't know what to do with himself. He was the kind of guy who always liked a good drink at the end of the day, but he started really . . . pretty soon it wasn't just a beer now and then. He seemed real depressed. My wife started getting worried about him. I did, too. I talked him into going to some meetings, AA and all, and it seemed like it was working. The thing is, I don't know if you've been to Newark recently, but it's a hard luck town. Lots of bars, cheap liquor stores. A tough place to stay sober . . ."

The security supervisor cleared his throat again and watched a tugboat muscle a long flat barge against the current. "Anyway, I had this job out here, and I figured I could do him a favor. I brought him on board, so to speak. It seemed like the perfect place for somebody who was trying to dry out. No liquor stores, no bars, absolutely nowhere to buy a drink." Durkin's voice broke. "I really liked the guy. And I wanted to help him. This was perfect. There was no way he could get himself in trouble."

CHAPTER *fourteen*

That night, Jack's bed was a raft. He floated on a sea of memories: Michael Durkin's miserable, guilt-wracked face; the view of Brooklyn from Governors Island; being ten years old and jumping off a pier in Red Hook, laughing with his brother Peter. But Petey was gone forever . . .

Michelle reached out in the dark and laid her hand on his shoulder, reminding him that he was not alone; they were on the raft together. He turned to her, caressed the side of her face. She hadn't just stuck with him after the shooting—she had brought him back to life even before it, after all of those years when he had pretty much given up on love.

He leaned over and kissed her. He pulled the covers down off her body, slowly ran his hand over her flat warm stomach, over the round hill of a breast. Her nipple hardened under his palm. He eased her panties off of her hips. Soon he was inside her, diving in a warm blue sea, no memories now, just this eternal present moment.

This time, everything felt right.

She cried out; he joined her; they *were* the sea.

"THERE ARE ONLY TWO kinds of problems in this world," pronounced Detective Sergeant Stephen Tanney early the next morning. "There are the *my problems*, and then there are the *not my problems*. This is definitely the second kind."

Jack sat up straight and clasped his hands in his lap; that helped keep him from strangling his boss. "But it relates directly to the Red Hook case."

The sergeant's office felt close and stuffy, especially with three people in it. Lieutenant Frank Cardulli, the head of the Homicide Task Force, was sitting in, listening to what his subordinates had to say. He was a stout, mustachioed fireplug of a man who had been in charge of the task force for years. Unlike Tanney, he inspired great confidence in his team.

Tanney frowned. "Aside from the fact that this has nothing to do with our task force jurisdiction, this isn't even a *New York City* matter."

A groan formed in Jack's throat and he did the best he could to hold it back. "We're talking about someone who committed two homicides."

Tanney shook his head. "We're talking about some nut bird who was holed up on federal property. If it wasn't for some fluke water current, this whole mess would never have had anything to do with Brooklyn."

Jack clasped his hands tighter. So typical. Yes, the new Compstat program was helping the NYPD target and deal with the areas of highest crime, and yes, crime rates across the city had plummeted. But it was hard to believe that the Department's ultimate aim was reducing crime itself. The goal, as always, was making the stats look good. If the easiest way to do that was simply to move the crime elsewhere, so be it. If it could all be shifted out of state, the top dogs would have been perfectly happy. Who gave a shit what was happening in New Jersey or Connecticut? No Department jobs were riding on *those* stats.

Jack stared down at the floor. *Count to ten,* he told himself. "What we have here," he said slowly and deliberately, "is someone who has killed two separate innocent people, including a child. And he did so in a way that's likely to blow up in the media, as soon as some smart reporter makes the connection."

Tanney snorted. "Give it a rest, Leightner. How many times do you think I'm gonna fall for that one? This new shit happened on federal property. It's not our worry."

Jack turned to Lieutenant Cardulli. "What do you think?"

The lieutenant leaned back in his chair and steepled his hands together. He deliberated for a moment, then leaned forward. "Well, I certainly agree with you that if we've got some wackjob running around out there, he's gotta be stopped. But the sergeant is right: This is a federal case. And even if the city did have jurisdiction over the island, it would be a Manhattan thing." He stood up and sighed. "We've got plenty to do without worrying about cases that aren't even ours." Jack started to protest, but Cardulli raised a palm. "I'm not saying you shouldn't continue to work on this, but we can't pull you out of the rotation. If you need some extra resources to work the Brooklyn side of it, I'll do my best to help out."

Jack nodded wearily. Like his elderly landlord was fond of saying about just about every problem, from potholes to bouts of the flu: "Whadda ya gonna do? Ya can't fight City Hall."

THE HOMICIDE TASK FORCE was like a crew of fishermen, only they didn't even have to cast their hooks: Cases kept flopping over the side of the boat. You never knew what each day's catch would bring.

There had been times when they flew in so fast that the detectives could barely keep up. Back in 1990, soon after Jack joined up, the precincts of Brooklyn South had seen two hundred and sixty murders. He remembered one crazy tour when the first call came just five minutes after his team punched in. Another came an hour later, then another. By the end of the shift, five fresh homicides had piled up, and the detectives could only stare at each other, amazed.

By this last month of 2001, the yearly count looked like it might reach only about ninety. Some attributed the drop in deadly crime to the waning of the crack epidemic, or changing demographics. Others pointed to the effectiveness of the Compstat approach. One thing was sure: No matter what, the commissioner and the mayor would claim the bulk of the credit.

And whatever happened, homicide never quite went out of style. People were not happy with each other, and they expressed their frustration with guns, with SUVs, with baseball bats, with electric carving knives, with their bare hands.

During the next three days, Jack and his team worked a couple of particularly pointless cases. First came a grim job out in Flatbush, a cocaine addict who had drowned her two young children in the bathtub. Then there was a middle-aged man in Canarsie who shot his friend and neighbor of thirty-five years in a dispute over dog poop on a lawn. There were no mysteries involved, other than the fundamental one: Why were people dropped on this earth, only to put each other to such sad or stupid ends?

CHAPTER *fifteen*

It was a bad hair day from the get-go.

Jack emerged from his house into a cold, drizzly winter morning.

Then his car engine refused to turn over, which meant that he had to do something he always did his best to avoid: ride the subway. A detective prided himself on getting around in a respectable ride; taking the subway felt like showing up on a donkey.

He almost burned his tongue trying to sip a takeout coffee as he walked to the station. When the train came, there was only one available seat, next to a young blonde with a severe but beautiful face. A piece of newspaper lay on the empty seat. Jack bent to brush it away, but the woman shook her head. "You should not sit there," she said in a thick Russian accent. "It's *steecky.*" He shrugged and moved over to grasp a pole. Out of the corner of his eye, he watched the blonde. Russians were common on the Q line, which ran to Brighton Beach; they went back and forth from the City, laden with shopping bags, living their mysterious, impenetrable lives. (Jack's own parents had come from that part of the world, but it was hard to feel any common ground with these newer immigrants.) He heard a burst of metallic disco music; the blonde dug a cell phone out of her purse. (Unfortunately, the train ran above ground out to

Coney Island, which meant a constant babble of one-sided conversations.) The call seemed very important to the young woman: She gripped the phone tightly and spoke urgently, but Jack couldn't tell if she was about to smile or burst into tears.

Directly in front of him sat two girls wearing elaborate hairdos and huge hoop earrings. One of them conducted an endless monologue. "He was like, 'Where you goin', bitch?,' and I was like, 'Who you talkin' to? You must'a got me confused with someone who gonna put up with your shit' . . . " Across the way, a young woman in a velour tracksuit sat popping her gum in a bovine daze. Waiting for the next loud pop set Jack's teeth on edge.

Rush hour in NYC. At each stop, people pushed in and out of the train like amoebas in a science film. Jack found a seat, but then stood up to offer it to a pregnant woman, then had to scrunch into a corner when a tattooed teenager wearing incredibly baggy, low-slung pants entered the car pushing a mountain bike. Jack took a deep breath and tried to stay calm, offering thanks that he didn't have to do this every day.

He wasn't the only one who looked uptight, especially when—between stations—the elevated train suddenly jerked to a stop. He heard a siren somewhere below, and then another one. His fellow passengers glanced at each other uneasily; these days, every alarm felt like the herald of a new terrorist attack. The speakers overhead emitted a staticky, urgent-sounding, totally garbled message, which did nothing for everyone's peace of mind. The gum-popper suddenly cracked her gum in the middle of the grim silence that followed and people visibly flinched. Everybody exchanged sheepish looks when the train started up again; they were all thinking exactly the same thing: *Thank God. I'm actually gonna live to see another day.*

By the time Jack reached Coney Island and stepped out into the salty air, he breathed a big sigh of relief.

As soon as he arrived at work, Sergeant Tanney called him in to his office to inform him that the squad's schedule had been re-arranged: He would have to work Christmas Day.

"I'm already working Christmas Eve," Jack pointed out.

Tanney just shrugged. "Brady is gonna be out for his surgery all that week and I need to cover the tour. Besides, with a last name like Leightner, I wouldn't think that working Christmas would be all that much of a hardship for you."

For just about the entirety of his police career, Jack would have agreed. He was Jewish, and his wife had been Jewish, too. To them, as to most Jews, Christmas was a party to which they had not been invited. If you had to work, who cared? The holiday pay was nice, and then it was a relief when all the hoopla was over.

Now, though, things had changed. He was about to marry a Christian, a bona fide *shiksa.* He figured he and Michelle would probably work out some sort of compromise holiday, and the thought was not displeasing. When he went over to her place and saw her little pine tree with its precious heirloom ornaments, the kid in him, the one who had always felt shut out at Christmastime, felt a surprising flush of pleasure. He had been looking forward to spending the day with her, to watching her unwrap the presents he was going to buy for her, real soon.

"Is there a problem?" Tanney asked.

Jack suppressed a frown. He didn't want to explain his personal life to this stuffed-shirt, didn't want to have to demean himself by pleading. He shook his head. "No problem."

He would make it up to Michelle on New Year's Eve. He had already made the restaurant reservations at a fancy joint in Midtown. He would finally pop the question, and then she would certainly forgive him.

The third time is the charm . . .

He left the sergeant's office and settled down at his desk, only to find that there was still no word from FBI man Ray Hillhouse. He had been eagerly anticipating the forensics results from the crime scene on the island, but who knew? Maybe he'd never see them. The fed had been friendly, but that didn't mean that he wouldn't decide to hog the ball.

It was one frustration too many.

By the time he finally escaped the office and made it out to a crime scene, Jack was ready to punch a wall.

It was not the best of days to meet Tenzin Pemo.

THE DHAMMAPADA TIBETAN BUDDHIST Center was full of surprises.

First of all, Jack would have expected it to be somewhere close to Brooklyn's Chinatown, near Sunset Park, but it was housed in a gritty section of Flatbush, in an old brick building above a check-cashing joint. The place *looked* like the real deal—a big room decorated with bright paintings of fantastical deities; an altar presided over by a fat, smiling gold statue; a smell of incense—but Jack checked out the members milling around and not one of them looked remotely Asian. They looked, in fact, like the kind of upscale bohemian white people he might find in a Park Slope coffee bar.

When told that the director was named Tenzin Pemo, he was still holding out for a wizened Tibetan man, but someone led him to a back office and introduced him to a small, stout Caucasian woman. (She did look rather mannish, though, with her close-cropped hair and her square, homely features. Jack couldn't help wondering if she had taken up religion because she had never gotten any other offers.) The woman wore overlapping robes of winey red and orangey yellow, though one shoulder was left bare. Did she go around like that all winter long?

He didn't know anything about Buddhism. He supposed that in its own setting, in Tibet or India or wherever, it would seem like a normal everyday religion, but the way it had been adopted by white people here reminded him of the Hare Krishnas he used to see in Greenwich Village, kids from privileged families acting out against their parents, screwed-up and unmoored. Back in the sixties, he hadn't had the time or the luxury for hippie rebellion. He came from a poor working family, and he wanted desperately to escape Red Hook, and the fastest ticket out was to join the army, which he did. When he got back, he didn't have much patience for flower children.

He had to admit that this woman didn't have that fuzzy stoned look. She gazed at him with complete attention, and projected a calm authority, sitting firmly in her desk chair, hands folded in her lap.

In thirteen years with Homicide, he had seen many different reactions to the news of a death. Grief, horror, panic, evasion, fear, revulsion, anxiety, relief, even joy. He had watched relatives or friends sob, shout, faint, curse, tremble uncontrollably, avoid all eye contact, even laugh hysterically. But he had never seen anyone as poised as this, at least no one who was not deep in shock.

Shock would have been appropriate. At eleven-thirty the previous evening, a young monk from the center had been killed just a few yards down the street. Several witnesses had watched the whole thing from their apartment windows. A group of adolescent boys from the nearby projects had come upon the gangly, bald-headed young man as he was locking the center's street-level entrance. They started making fun of him because of the robes he wore below his army surplus parka. "Yo, faggot, nice dress." Experience had taught the detective that few things could be more dangerous than a pack of adolescent boys: They often had no sense of the consequence of their actions, couldn't conceive of death, and were so eager to hide their insecurities from their peers that they would go to terrible, tragic lengths to appear tough. In this case, the cackling and name-calling had escalated into trash throwing, and one glass bottle had caught the young monk in the back of the head.

Jack studied the woman in front of him. He took his time—it was his colleague Carl Santiago's case, and he was just along to help out. "So, are you a nun?" he asked.

The woman nodded. Very calm. Calmer than she should be if she had been close to the victim. Maybe the monk had been new to the center?

"How long did you know"—he glanced down at his notepad— "Andrew Steinberg?" The members of the center referred to the victim as Gen Kelsang Thubten. That seemed to be the style here: The clergy had an extra handle, like Brooklyn homeboys with their street names.

"He has been with our center for the past four years." Another surprise: The woman had a rather stuffy British accent.

"Would you say that you were close?"

"I would. He was one of my senior students before he was ordained, and we've worked together ever since."

"Would you say that you liked him?" It wasn't a professional question, really, but Jack found himself wanting to shake up the nun's unnerving composure, just on the off-chance that she had some hidden reason for staying so calm . . .

"I would say that I *loved* him," the nun replied evenly. "Almost like I love my own children."

Jack's eyes widened; he couldn't help it. "You have children?"

The woman smiled slightly, as though she was aware of his uncharitable assumptions, yet was not disturbed by them. "I used to be what you would call a housewife. I became a nun twelve years ago."

Jack's curiosity was piqued, but he didn't follow up—so far as he knew, this woman's former life had nothing to do with the matter at hand. He needed to get started with the usual drill: What was the victim's schedule; Had he had run-ins with neighborhood kids before? . . . Still, something didn't feel right. Just because the woman was a nun didn't mean she was free of any connection to her young colleague's death. Jack wanted to get underneath her serene exterior, to probe around a little.

He knew just how to ruffle her. "What's your real name?" he asked. Clearly she had invested a lot in her religious authority, and would bridle at having it challenged.

"Charlotte Colson," she replied without hesitation or irritation.

"Where were you at the time of the incident?"

"I was at home."

Jack had to admit that he had no reason to challenge her answer. Unless something unexpected popped up, he was pretty sure how the case would shake out: The kids who had done the crime would get nervous, and one of them would rat the others out.

He leaned back in his chair. "You seem very calm today."

The nun didn't stir. "I don't think that getting agitated will help the situation."

Jack's eyebrows went up again. "A little grief would be normal."

The woman seemed to wrestle a bit with her answer. "I don't . . . perhaps we have a way of dealing with things that might be a bit different than you're used to."

Jack glanced around the room. "What? This Buddhist thing? How's that different? Your friend's gonna come back in another life, or something?"

The woman seemed to consider a response, but she refrained. "I'm sure you didn't come here for a lecture on Buddhism."

Jack frowned. Maybe he hadn't gone to a fancy college, but he had completed his own rigorous course of study: Bloodstain Pattern Analysis, Toxicology, Forensic Psychology . . . and he could certainly detect a little intellectual condescension when it came his way.

"Try me," he said curtly.

The nun frowned. "You must be very busy."

"I've got time."

The nun considered him frankly. Then she looked away, as if

hoping that if she gave him a minute of silence, he might decide to go away. But he didn't. He had all day.

The nun finally spoke. "All right. Everybody suffers. But a great deal of our suffering comes from believing that things should never change. *I've gotten married, so my spouse should love me for the rest of my life. I need my parents, so they must never die* . . . We're continually shocked and disappointed when life doesn't go the way we think it should."

Jack sat back and waited to see where this was going.

"In reality," the nun continued, "everything is in a constant state of flux. The seasons change, plants and animals die. We'll all die, one way or another. I would think that in your job you must see how impermanent things actually are."

Jack shifted in his chair. "So, *what*: We're not supposed to feel sad when someone gets killed?"

"Of course we feel sad. Pain is inevitable in this world. How much we *suffer*, though—that's up to us."

Jack probed a corner of his eye with a fingertip. He was not impressed.

Tenzin Pemo rose to the challenge. She plucked a blue paperback book off of her desk. "Let me ask you a question, detective. Do you think this book has an independent existence outside your mind?"

He made a face. "Of course it does. My mind has nothing to do with it."

The nun set the book down in front of him. "How do you know it's real?"

Jack shrugged. "I just heard it thump onto the desk. I can pick it up. I can flip through the pages . . ."

The nun nodded. "Of course. You deal in evidence. You can *see* the book. You can *hear* it. You can *touch* it. But your whole experience of this book is coming to you through your senses, and exists only in your mind."

Jack snorted. "That's nuts. The book's sitting right there. If I drop dead right now, it'll still be there."

"How do you know?" The nun pulled her robe a little higher up on her bare shoulder. "Everything you 'know' is something that you learned about through your senses. I'll tell you what: Name one thing that you know about some other way."

Jack pondered the question. Every time he thought of something—classroom teachings, things he had heard about, evidence photos, proof he had seen for himself—he realized that they were all things he had perceived. "So, what are you saying?" he finally said. "This book *doesn't* exist?"

The nun shook her head. "That's not the issue here. The point is that our entire experience of the world exists only in our minds." She leaned forward. "Let me give you an example. Let's say you're sitting in the subway on your way to work. Can you imagine that?"

Jack nodded. Today he could imagine it all too well.

"Okay. Now let's say that someone sits down next to you, and they're talking loudly, or trimming their fingernails, or doing something you find very annoying."

Jack thought of the young woman popping her gum on the train this morning, and he smiled despite himself.

The nun steepled her hands together. "Now, you would likely say to yourself, 'Oh, look at this external problem that has suddenly intruded into my life.' You might try to tell the person to stop doing what they're doing, but this is New York City—you don't know if they're going to get angry with you, start a fight, maybe even pull out a gun. So you sit there in silence, getting angrier and angrier."

Jack crossed his arms. "All right, so what would *you* do?"

The nun shrugged. "I wouldn't have to *do* anything. Instead of seeing the person as an external problem I can't control, I could just think about the situation differently. I could say to myself, 'What a blessing! Here I am trying to develop more patience in my life, and here's a wonderful opportunity to practice!' Notice that the external situation didn't change at all; all that happened is that I changed my way of thinking about it."

Jack thought for a moment. "I guess I can buy that. But we're not talking about some jerk clipping their nails on the subway. This is a human being who was cold-bloodedly murdered. Are you saying that isn't a real problem?"

The nun leaned toward him. "I'm saying that if we can train our minds to deal with small difficulties, we can train them to deal with big ones."

Jack frowned. "So, what: You just don't care?"

"Of course I do. But I have to accept that this thing has happened. I could get angry at the children who did this, or I could crumple up in grief, but that wouldn't help Kelsang Thubten. Suffering is not something that exists out in the world. It's only in our minds. And that means that we can do something about it." The nun stood up. "Would you like a cup of coffee?"

"Actually," Jack said, "I would, but I wouldn't think you people would be allowed to drink the stuff. I mean, isn't it kind of a drug?"

The woman smiled sadly. "I'm a nun, not a saint." She went out.

Jack sat mulling over what he had just heard. He noticed a banner stretched across one wall of the small, tidy office. *If you can do something about the problem, you don't have to worry. If you can't do something about the problem, you don't have to worry. Either way, you don't have to worry.*

Easy to say. He thought of how Michelle was going to react when he told her he'd be working a double tour at Christmas. And he thought of the way his investigation into the boy in the box was getting bogged down at every turn. He had *plenty* to worry about.

He heard a sound behind him and turned to see Carl Santiago standing in the doorway. His colleague came in and sat on a chair in the corner. "So how did it go in here?"

Jack sighed. "I don't know. I just got a crash course in Buddhism." All of the petty aggravations of the day had added up to give him a headache. He leaned back and rubbed his tired eyes. "The nun seems pretty calm about this whole thing. *Too* calm, if you ask me."

"Uh, Jack . . ." Santiago said.

Jack ignored him. "I don't know, this all just seems like some blissed-out Hare Krishna crap . . ."

"*Jack*," Santiago said again.

Jack opened his eyes to find Tenzin Pemo standing in the doorway.

Calmly.

"Here's your coffee, detective. If there's anything else I can do to help you, please let me know."

CHAPTER *sixteen*

T hanks for showing me this," Jack told Ray Hillhouse as he handed back the forensic report. Ordinarily, the words would have rolled off his tongue with some difficulty—showing gratitude to a fed—but it was hard to begrudge this FBI man.

Hillhouse tucked the report back into an inside pocket of his trench coat; a brisk breeze was blowing up from the water, over the esplanade, whipping across Governors Island. The FBI man smiled. "It's *nice* to share."

Jack chuckled. "Maybe you didn't read the directive. The one that says that feds and cops are on opposite teams . . ."

Hillhouse wrinkled his broad nose. "I don't have time for that crap. My father was a detective with the Philly PD."

"What did he think when you went off to work for the FBI?"

Hillhouse shrugged. "He was proud of me. There weren't exactly a lot of black folks in the Bureau when I was coming up." He patted his coat pocket. "So what do you think?"

Jack rested his forearms on the railing and stared out at the Red Hook shore. It was one of his days off, but he was glad to be on the island. Michelle was at work. What else was he gonna do, watch TV? "This confirms at least one of my hunches. The stuff about industrial solvents and sawdust embedded in the clothes the guy left behind . . . Looking at that homemade coffin, I was thinking he maybe did some kind of carpentry-related work. I'm sorry we didn't get any hits on all those fingerprints, though. I guess we're not dealing with a career criminal—or at least one who's ever been caught."

Hillhouse pulled a package of pistachio nuts out of another coat pocket. "Want some?"

"Why not?" Jack took a small handful and started cracking them open. "I hate to say this, but I don't think we're dealing with a local. If he lived in the area, what was he doing camping out over here?"

Hillhouse nodded thoughtfully. "He could be from anywhere." The chill wind flapped his coattails and the FBI man grimaced. "You wanna take a little walk, warm up a little?"

Jack nodded and the two men set off between a couple of the officers' houses, across the Nolan Park quadrangle, into the interior of the island, dropping pistachio shells as they went. A ferry horn tooted somewhere out in the harbor, and then things returned to their normal deep silence.

"I've been based in downtown Manhattan for five years," the FBI man said. "But I never paid any attention to this place."

After lapsing into a couple of minutes of companionable silence, they came to a grass-filled moat in front of the old fort. A fierce stone eagle guarded an arched entry. They walked in, beyond the massive walls, and found themselves inside another quadrangle, surrounded on all sides by rows of white-columned brick buildings. A deserted little playground stood in the middle of the center lawn, with two forlorn metal ponies waiting for riders. Jack brushed away some peeling paint and sat down on one. "You know, what strikes me the most here is that this guy didn't just happen to pass by. If he didn't come over on the ferry—and that doesn't seem likely, considering all the crap he had with him—then he had to go to a lot of trouble to get here."

Hillhouse nodded. "And it's not exactly the most convenient place to hide out. No stores, no running water . . . He had to bring food, drinks, toilet paper . . ."

"So the question is, why go through all that trouble when he could have just holed up in some comfy little motel on the mainland?"

"Not only that," Hillhouse said, pulling a piece of paper out of yet another coat pocket. He unfolded it to reveal an aerial photo of the island. From above it had the shape of an ice cream cone, with the ferry slip at the top. "He could have hid out down near the southern end, which is apparently even more deserted than the rest of the place. So why would he want to be so close to the ferry, to the only place where people arrive every day? It was a lot riskier . . ."

Jack frowned. "I don't think it was the ferry. Maybe he wanted to be in Nolan Park."

Hillhouse nodded. "I've been thinking along the same lines. Maybe he had some personal connection to the place."

"Ex-Coastie?" Jack brightened. "Hey, do you think they had fingerprints on file?"

Hillhouse grinned. "We'll soon find out."

CHAPTER *seventeen*

Pulling on a Kevlar vest before an op always quickened the blood a little, but Jack, who had taken a bullet not long before, was glad that it covered most of his sweat-damp shirt.

The usual mundane atmosphere of the Seven-six squad room was stirred up by the excitement of the hunt. The detectives, wired on caffeine and adrenaline, were suiting up. Confronting an armed suspect was obviously one of the most dangerous parts of the job, so why did they look happy and excited as athletes in a locker room before a big game? Despite their decades of experience, they still didn't quite understand that taking a bullet was not like it was in the movies, where you just clutched your bloody shoulder and ran on. When no one was looking, Jack swallowed a couple of Tums to calm his stomach.

Linda Vargas popped a fresh clip into her Glock and then sat back and glanced around the busy room. The detective grinned. "I love the smell of fresh testosterone in the morning."

Tommy Balfa came in with a box of donuts and offered them around. The precinct detective was riding high. Of all people, he was the one who had found the next break in the case. (The Coast Guard connection had not done the trick—no fingerprint matches.) No, it was an anonymous call, followed up by Balfa, which had led to this special Saturday morning convocation.

Ray Hillhouse came in to join the team; Jack almost didn't recognize the man in jeans, sneakers, and a sweatshirt. Jack introduced him around, then invited Balfa over to brief him.

The precinct detective cast a somewhat wary eye on the stranger, but his excitement overcame his initial coldness. "I've been listening to the calls that came in over our hotline about the kid who washed up in Red Hook," he explained. He rolled his eyes. "Most of it was the usual aluminum-hat crazies, the lonelies, the conspiracy nuts . . . But there was one anonymous tip, a woman who said we should check out a guy named Darren Chapman who lives and works down in Vinegar Hill. I did a little legwork, and it turns out he's some kind of artist or sculptor or something. He works in wood and metal, stuff that could definitely match your forensic results. And he has a sheet: He was indicted for child abuse, though the case got thrown out of court on some technicality. He's divorced, but he's got a ten-year-old son."

Hillhouse raised his eyebrows, impressed. "This sounds pretty good. Does his boy match the description of your body?"

Balfa shook his head. "No—his kid's alive and well. At least, he showed up for school this week."

Hillhouse shrugged. "The guy still sounds promising. Have you talked to him?"

Sergeant Tanney swaggered over. He seemed the most pumped-up of all the team. The detectives had done the heavy lifting to find a suspect; now their supervisor was all set to tapdance in the spotlight. "We understand the man might be armed," he said, "so we're not taking any chances. We'll talk to him when he's face down, on the ground."

The sergeant asked for any final questions or comments, then actually said, "Let's move out," as if he was John Wayne in some old war flick.

FIFTEEN MINUTES LATER THE detectives were parked in two unmarked cars outside Darren Chapman's residence in Vinegar Hill, a tiny neighborhood of scruffy little houses sandwiched between the base of the Manhattan Bridge, a power plant, and the Navy Yard.

In the passenger seat of Jack's vehicle, Sergeant Tanney picked up his walkie. "You guys ready?" he asked Vargas and Hillhouse in the other car.

"Hold on a minute," Jack said.

The sergeant frowned. "What is it, Leightner?"

Jack turned to Tommy Balfa. "Have you got Chapman's home number?"

The detective pulled out a computer printout.

Jack took out his cell phone. The line rang five times before someone picked up.

Jack pitched his voice high and sharp. "You order Chinese food?"

"You've got the wrong number," said an irritated male voice on the other end.

Jack hung up. "Well," he told the others, *"somebody's* home."

THE DETECTIVES TOOK UP positions on both sides of the door, avoiding the potential line of fire. Jack glanced across at Sergeant Tanney, who was sweating profusely. Under other circumstances, Jack might have been amused, but this morning he could only sympathize. He kept swallowing nervously. He didn't remember much about the night he had been shot in Red Hook, but an image came to him now: Lying on a stark concrete basement floor, he had raised his head to see blood fountaining up out of his own chest . . .

He swallowed again and blinked the memory away; he needed all of his focus now. Next to him, Balfa and Hillhouse had a battering ram ready, in case they were denied access. Tanney carried a shotgun and the warrant that would guarantee them access. The other detectives had their guns out, pointed at the floor. The sergeant glanced at the team, then gave the high sign. He reached out and rang the bell.

The detectives heard some kind of muffled commotion inside, then someone shouting, "Hold him! Don't let him go!"

And then they heard a child's high-pitched squeal.

"Shit!" Tanney muttered. He turned to Balfa and Hillhouse. "Go!"

The two men stepped back, lifted the ram, and swung it at the door. The lock gave way and then they were through.

Jack came in right on their heels, found himself in an open loft space, frantically scanned from right to left—and couldn't believe his eyes. Something was rocketing toward them out of a back hallway, a low dark creature swathed in a strange white cloud.

Close on its heels ran a man dressed in sweatpants and a T-shirt, also covered in something white. He skidded to a halt when he saw the team of detectives crouched down, guns pointed. "Jesus!" he cried out, raising his hands; he was clutching something.

"Hold your fire!" Jack shouted at his teammates.

It wasn't a gun.

The creature, now recognizable as a big black Labrador, scampered across the room and disappeared behind a couch.

A boy appeared in the hallway. His jeans and T-shirt were wet and soapy. He saw the detectives and his eyes went wide. He edged over and took cover behind the man's leg.

Jack turned his attention back to the man's hand, and identified the big object there as a sponge.

They had been giving the dog a bath.

DARREN CHAPMAN MADE A face. "Let me guess. This woman who called you: Did she have a foreign accent?"

Tommy Balfa didn't respond—he wasn't going to give away the identity of a possible witness—but his crestfallen face answered the question.

They were all seated in a corner of the loft now, a living room area cobbled together out of couches and armchairs. Most of the big room was occupied by a number of abstract sculptures that looked to Jack as if the artist had taken a bunch of scraps from a woodshop floor and randomly glued them on top of one another. Aside from the sculptures, the room was incredibly cluttered: stacks of books on the floors, dirty coffee cups everywhere, tools lying on the broad plank floors. The thought of living in such a state of disorder made Jack's head spin.

The artist himself sat in the middle of the mess, still trembling from the shock of the invasion. He wasn't the only one who looked shaken up. All of the detectives knew how close they had come to pulling a trigger in a moment of high tension and confusion.

Sergeant Tanney turned to Linda Vargas and then nodded at the boy. "Why don't you take this young man into the kitchen and give him a drink of water?" *Question him separately*, was what he meant.

The kid looked scared. "Dad?" he said, voice quavering.

Chapman patted him on the shoulder. "It's okay, son. Go ahead with the nice lady."

The kid looked doubtful, but he let himself be led away.

Chapman rubbed a hand across his face. "That call—it must have been my wife. My *ex*-wife. We're divorced now, and everything's supposed to be settled, but Simone just can't let things end gracefully. She's nuts, if you want to know the truth."

Jack leaned forward. "Did she make the charge of child abuse?"

Chapman groaned. "Not *that* again. That charge was so ridiculous that the judge dismissed it before it even came to trial. My wife was just trying to block me from sharing custody."

Tommy Balfa pulled a sheet of paper out of his pocket. "Can you tell us where you were this past December seventeen and eighteen?" The day the security guard had been found on Governors Island, and the day before.

Chapman thought for a moment, and then started to stand up.

Tanney and Balfa jumped to their feet.

Chapman raised a hand to mollify them. "I just want to get a piece of paper."

"Sure," Tanney said. He nodded toward Balfa. *Go with him.*

The detective followed the man as he navigated between several sculptures, over to a desk at the far end of the room. Balfa watched tensely as Chapman rooted around. He found what he was looking for and carried it over to the sergeant. A postcard.

"I had a show at a museum in San Francisco. I was out there installing it all that week." He pointed to the bottom of the card. "Here's the number if you want to check."

Jack noticed that Balfa stayed on the other side of the room. All of his usual cockiness was gone. For the first time Jack actually felt some sympathy for the man.

Linda Vargas emerged from the back hallway with the boy in tow.

Tanney shot her a questioning glance.

Vargas shrugged and shook her head.

The boy edged over and stood next to his father, who put a protective arm around his waist and said, "Don't worry, everything's fine."

CHAPTER *eighteen*

W ho fixes the door?" Michelle said.

"What?" Jack stopped in the middle of eating his appetizer, which he was puzzled about to begin with. (What was the red sauce with the little flakes in it? Were you supposed to eat the lettuce, or was it just decoration?) The restaurant was a new Thai place in Carroll Gardens, all bare brick walls, nothing to absorb the din of a roomful of young customers chattering away on a Friday night.

Michelle leaned forward to be heard. "You said your team busted down the door. I'm just wondering how the poor guy gets it fixed."

Jack set down his fork and smiled.

"What?" Michelle said.

He shook his head. "Nothing." *What happened to the door?* It was such a civilian question. A cop would have been relieved that none of the detectives had been caught up in the horror of a wrongful shooting. A cop would have been concerned with whether Chapman wanted to press charges. Michelle was curious about the *door.*

"He'll get it fixed," he answered. "And the City will reimburse him—after about six months of paperwork."

He watched as she used her chopsticks to pick up a dumpling and deliver it neatly to her mouth. Personally, he didn't get the chopsticks thing. What was the point of performing acrobatics with knitting needles, when a good old fork could do the job?

"It must have been awful scary for that boy," Michelle observed.

He nodded. "I guess. But we had to get in there. For all we knew, the kid's father was about to do something awful to him."

It had been a legitimate mistake, and he couldn't fault Tommy Balfa. Any major investigation had its share of errors: false leads, blind alleys, incorrect deductions. Nobody was perfect; you just tried to keep the batting average as high as you could.

A busboy rushed over and swept away their plates. Jack glanced around. The place was packed, and the other diners all seemed to be about his son's age. The ones waiting for tables wore chic outfits, and clutched cell phones to their heads, or sipped martinis at the bar. They seemed so self-possessed, so cocky. These were the kind of kids you saw in downtown Manhattan—rich kids, they looked like to him. How had they ended up here, in *his* Brooklyn?

A beautiful young Thai woman glided up with their entrées. Jack stared down at his dish. "What's the brown stuff?"

"IT'S PEANUT SAUCE," MICHELLE said. "Try it—you'll like it." *He looks so dubious*, she thought. Like a child confronted with broccoli for the first time. "You've really never had Thai food before?"

He shook his head. "I've had lots of Chinese, though."

She smiled. Her boyfriend was incredibly worldly in one sense—he certainly knew the New York streets, knew bad guys, knew all about people who killed people—yet his universe was oddly narrow. He had never eaten Thai food, never heard of many popular musicians or famous films. He had almost no interest in national politics, or celebrity gossip, or even what he wore every day. He had been born just a mile or so from Manhattan, yet had grown up in Red

Hook—she got the sense that the place had been as provincial as some hick town.

She picked up her chopsticks again and dunked a little clump of jasmine rice into the garlic sauce on her plate. She smiled. "Wait till you see what I got you for Christmas."

He looked up eagerly. "What?"

She shook her head. "No, no, no—you have to wait until Santa drops it off."

He chuckled. "Santa, huh? Are you sure he makes deliveries to heathens like me?"

Michelle laid a hand on his. "You'll see. You just tiptoe downstairs on Christmas morning and I'm sure there'll be something in the stocking for you."

He frowned.

"What?" she said. "What's the matter?"

He pinched his lower lip. "Um . . . there's a little problem there. Tanney just told me I'm gonna have to work Christmas."

She pulled her hand away. "Why?"

He grimaced. "John Brady, one of the guys on my team, has to go into the hospital next week. He's getting surgery and I gotta cover for him." He pulled her hand back to the middle of the table. "Listen—I'll make it up to you. We'll have a great New Year's Eve. I've made the reservations, planned it all out. You're gonna love it."

She stared at him. "You made reservations? Where?"

He shrugged. "You'll see. Don't worry—you'll love it."

She frowned.

"What?" he said.

She picked up her chopsticks, toyed with them, set them down.

"What's the matter?"

She turned away. Over at the bar, two twenty-somethings were doing a little courting dance, flushed with what she figured was maybe second-date excitement.

"Are you mad at me?" he said. "Don't be mad. Let's enjoy the evening."

She turned back to him. "It's just . . . didn't you think I'd want some say in what we do for New Year's?"

He shifted uncomfortably, like a kid in the hot seat.

CHAPTER *nineteen*

H ey," said Tommy Balfa, looking up surprised as he entered the Seven-six detective squad room. "I wasn't expecting you today."

The squad room was quiet. Gary Daskivitch was out, as were the other detectives. Jack came over, holding a manila file, and dropped into a grubby molded-plastic chair next to Balfa's desk. He grinned. "I've got a whole new angle on our case."

"That's great," Balfa responded, without enthusiasm.

Jack figured that the detective was still chastened about the other day's bum lead. He lowered his voice. "I don't wanna harp on this, but don't worry about what happened on Thursday. We all make mistakes."

Balfa nodded, but now that Jack was sitting right across from him, he noticed that the detective didn't seem embarrassed or contrite. He just looked distracted again, jittery. Balfa glanced at the big old grade-school-style clock on the wall, then at his desk, then at the clock again.

"You got somewhere to be?"

Balfa ignored the question. "What's in the folder?"

Jack straightened up. "I've been thinking about our perp. He doesn't seem to have a regular place to stay around here, so where does he go, now that his little island nest is busted up?"

Balfa didn't venture a guess.

Once again, Jack was disappointed with the man's lack of interest, but he wasn't going to let it dampen his own excitement. "I asked Charlie Unit to let us know if they spotted any unusual activity around the waterfront. I did the same with the Coast Guard." He opened the folder and pulled out some reports. "Check it out: We seem to have a little rash of boat burglaries in the last few days, all after the incident on the island. And look what was taken: no valuables. Just food, blankets, crap like that." He smiled significantly. "When our man bolted, he had to leave a lot of that stuff behind . . ."

"Sounds interesting," Balfa said, but he was looking at his cell phone.

Jack stood up and walked over to a map of Brooklyn. "Have you got some pushpins? Let's plot these babies, see if we can narrow down where our man might be camping out these days."

Balfa glanced at the clock.

Jack sat down again. "What's going on?"

Balfa ran a hand over his mouth. "What do you mean?"

"You have something more important to do?"

Balfa frowned. "I don't know what you're talking about."

Jack looked around the squad room. He took a deep breath, trying to stay calm. "Do you resent my interference, is that it?"

Balfa didn't answer.

"I'm not your boss," Jack said. "I know you're not used to working with Homicide, so maybe I should have made that clearer. I'm just here to help. Most precinct detectives, frankly, are happy for the assist. But—bottom line—this is your case."

"All right," Balfa said. "So what's the problem?"

Jack stared at him. "You tell me. I gotta say: Sometimes I can't help thinking that you don't really give a shit."

Balfa raised his hands. "I don't know what you're talking about. Didn't I follow up on that lead just the other day?"

Jack nodded thoughtfully. "Yeah, you did. Like I said, nobody blames you for the way that turned out, either. But this is a case of a kid who got *killed*. Somehow that doesn't seem to be getting through to you."

Balfa made a face like he was wrestling with something. He sighed and sank back into his chair. "I've . . . look, I've been having some personal problems. Marital shit. I guess it's been stressing me out a little."

Jack sat back, too, trying to diffuse the tension. "All right. I can understand that. I'm just asking you to focus a little, to work with me here. Okay?"

Balfa nodded. And then he glanced at the clock. He stood up. "I have to make a quick run downtown. Why don't you start in on the mapping, and I'll be right back?"

Jack shrugged. "Why don't I go with you, and we can work out our next step?"

Balfa frowned. "I have to see my CI again about that other case. He gets real jittery, and he definitely won't talk if I'm not alone."

Jack stared. He doubted that the detective would actually have the stones to run off right now and hook up with his lover. No, the man seemed troubled somehow, like maybe something else was going on, something more stressful than an extramarital affair . . . "Okay then," was all he said. "I'll be here. See you in a few minutes."

Balfa grabbed his coat from a rack in the corner and left.

Jack looked down at his burglary reports, but he barely saw them. Something was definitely hinky. He had a pretty good bullshit meter, and right now the little needle was smacking against the high end of the red zone.

He stood up and hurried out of the squad room.

BALFA DROVE DOWN SACKETT Street. Instead of turning north on Clinton, toward downtown, he bore straight. Toward the waterfront.

"What are you up to?" Jack muttered as he followed in his car, two blocks behind. Though a spectacular sunset streaked the sky ahead—the last rays caught the bottom of a field of clouds like cotton wadding catching fire—the winter dusk was settling down fast. The good news was that there was still enough light so that he didn't have to turn on his headlights.

Traffic in Carroll Gardens was busy, the beginnings of rush hour, but Balfa continued on across the Brooklyn-Queens Expressway into quiet Red Hook. Following him here was going to be a lot harder, as cars were few and far between. Jack watched Balfa turn left onto Van Brunt Street. If he followed, the detective would surely spot the tail. He made a quick decision. From his childhood, he knew these streets well, and he would have to rely on that knowledge now, mixed with a little luck. He cut left on Columbia and picked up speed, hoping to catch up again with Balfa a few blocks down.

The gambit worked. Jack turned onto Summit Street, near the entrance for the Battery Tunnel, pulled over, and waited to see if Balfa would blow on by. And he did, continuing down Van Brunt toward the harbor. Jack gave him another two-block lead, then swung out after.

The detective drove almost all of the way to the water, then turned left on Beard, a street that ran past the old Todd Shipyards. When he was a child, Jack had come here often to watch the workers repair huge ships. The behemoths would be floated into one of two graving docks, which were like massive stone bathtubs, and then a gate would close and the water would be pumped out so that workers could have a rare opportunity to see what was normally hidden below the waterline. Then they could clean, weld, and repaint the rusty, barnacled hulls. With the constant clang of iron and steel and huge showers of sparks from the welding torches, the yards provided a grand free spectacle.

Now the shipyards were gone, and Beard Street was just a lonely, quiet street bounded by empty warehouses, derelict little homes, and vacant lots. A tail would surely be spotted here. Again, Jack cut over a couple of streets early and swung around in an attempt to catch up with Balfa a little farther on. A few blocks down, he hung a right, pulled over, and waited, but the other detective didn't reappear. Cursing under his breath, Jack got out of his car next to an ivy-choked chain-link fence. He was quickly chilled—he hadn't had time to pull his coat on, and a brisk wind swept down the deserted Red Hook street. He cautiously poked his head around the end of the fence and glanced down Beard; thank God the dark was settling in. A block back, Balfa had pulled up behind a parked car. He was too far away for Jack to make out what was going on.

He put the collar of his sports jacket up against the cold, and turned back around the other side of the block. He had grown up just four streets away, and childhood games had provided him with a knowledge of every nook and cranny. Stickball. Kick the Can. Ringolevio, where one team had to run and hide . . . He squeezed between two fences, ran down a little weed-filled path, and made it across the middle of the block. Panting, he paused to regain his breath, and then peeped out between two abandoned houses. (He half-expected someone to grab him and chant "Ringolevio-One-Two-Three!")

Fifteen yards up the cobbled street, Tommy Balfa stood next to the open window of a black SUV, talking to the driver. He turned to scan up and down the empty street, and then reached out as something was passed through the window. A bag or package of some sort—it was hard to make it out in the failing light.

As the other car pulled away into the deepening dusk, Balfa opened the back door of his own car and tucked the object behind his seat.

JACK WAS WAITING FOR the detective when he returned to the station house. Balfa didn't spot him when he pulled into an angled parking slot between two squad cars; didn't notice him until Jack yanked open the passenger-side door and slid into the front seat.

"You should have put it in the trunk," Jack said.

Balfa looked over, wide-eyed. "What? What are you talking about?"

Jack reached back between the seats.

Balfa grabbed his arm. "Fuck off, Leightner."

They were right in front of the station house. Cops were trotting up and down the stairs, walking down the sidewalk. What would they do if they saw two detectives tussling in the front seat of a parked car?

"Come on, Tommy," Jack said calmly. "You can let me see what's in there, or we can show your boss. It's up to you."

A young policewoman saw Balfa and gave a friendly wave. The detective considered his position for a moment, then released his grip on Jack's arm. He sat back stiffly. Jack reached down behind the seat. He pulled out a small, heavy gray plastic bag. Keeping one eye on the other detective, he opened it and glanced down. Stacks of money, wrapped with rubber bands. Big denominations.

"Usually," he said, "we give the informants the money. I don't think I've ever heard of it happening the other way around. Why don't you tell me what the hell you're mixed up with here?"

Balfa sank forward until his forehead rested against the wheel. "Fuck," he muttered. "Fuck, fuck, fuck."

CHAPTER *twenty*

I'll give the money back," Balfa said. "I'll turn these guys in." He was leaning forward, desperate, hands reaching out across the table.

The two detectives sat at the far back table of Ferdinando's Foccaceria, an old tin-ceilinged neighborhood restaurant just a couple of blocks away, at the edge of Carroll Gardens. In the early evening, before the dinner rush, the place was almost empty. Old photos of Naples hung on the walls, forlorn men standing next to fruit and vegetable stands, looking out from the beginning of the last century.

Jack crossed his arms, skeptical. "You'll turn *what* guys in?"

Balfa looked pale. "I'd rather not get into that right now."

Jack frowned. "Come on, man—I told you I'd hear you out, but I'm not in the mood for any more bullshit."

Balfa picked up his napkin and twisted it anxiously. "It's nothing really bad. I swear to you. No drugs, no violence, nothing like that. I'm just in kind of a *situation*. I'm gonna work it out." He leaned forward, face contorted. "I'm asking you for a break here, Jack, and I know that's a shitty position to put you in. But the money's not for me."

Jack scoffed. "Who's it for, then?"

The other detective seemed to crumple before his eyes. "I know you don't like me." Jack started to say something, but Balfa held up a hand. "You probably won't believe this, but normally I'm a good cop like you—everything by the book." He looked up. "Are you married?"

Jack just stared at him. "The money, Balfa. Who in the hell is it for?"

The other detective looked down at the table. "My wife and I, we used to have it really good. But now we've got a big problem."

Jack gave him a skeptical look. "What kind of problem?" He was thinking of the redhead he had seen dropping Balfa off near the station house, but the detective looked stricken, and when he spoke, his voice was raw.

"It's my daughter, Tiffany. She's nine. Three years ago she was diagnosed with non-Hodgkins lymphoma. It's a form of cancer. We got her some excellent treatment and it went into remission, but now it's back. Stage Four. The doctors have given her chemo, radiation, the works. They say there's nothing else they can do."

Jack stared at him. He wanted to ask why, if the man's own daughter had cancer, he couldn't have cared more about the boy who had drifted ashore in Red Hook, but now didn't seem to be a good time to press the point.

Balfa looked up at him, eyes filled with pain. "My daughter knows, that's the thing, she *knows*. And she's so fucking quiet about it. She sees that this is making things difficult between me and my wife, and so she just stays quiet. You wanna talk about hell on earth? You put yourself in my shoes, Jack. You try to look your own child in the face."

Jack frowned. "You've got health insurance from the job, obviously. What do you need the money for?"

Balfa sighed. "My wife and I heard about a new treatment. In Europe. Over here the FDA hasn't approved it yet, so the insurance bastards won't pay for it. We need to get her over there, give her this chance. I don't have squat for savings. I had no other way to do this, Jack, I swear to you."

Jack stared at the detective. He seemed so sincere, yet he had already lied a number of times. "You trying to jam me up, Tommy?"

"How do you mean?"

"Stand up," Jack said.

"What?"

"*Stand up.* I want you to go back to the bathroom. Leave the door unlocked. I'm gonna meet you there in thirty seconds."

"What are you talking about?"

"Do it."

Balfa looked confused, but he got up.

Jack sat for a moment. Then he got up and crossed over to the bathroom.

"Take off your jacket," he ordered.

"What?" Balfa said.

"Take off your jacket. This has IAB written all over it."

After a number of notorious scandals, the Serpico thing and a number of others, the NYPD had tightened ship. Of its 55,000 employees, 650 worked for the Internal Affairs Bureau. Every year, they conducted a thousand integrity tests. It could be a fake 911 call where you showed up and there were some drugs left out in the open, or a traffic incident where somebody would offer a bribe, or a more elaborate setup. They might rent out an apartment, say it belonged to some drug dealer, plant some cash, call you in with a fake tip, and watch you on hidden monitors. They conducted the tests in every precinct, and the subjects were selected at random. Highly decorated veteran cops were not exempt.

Balfa shook his head. "You've got it all wrong." He took off the jacket.

Jack patted him down.

No wire.

They returned to their table. Over by the espresso machine the waitress, a middle-aged woman with heavy orthopedic shoes and a seen-it-all face, was giving them a wry look.

Jack sat and stared at the other detective for a while. Balfa looked like he was about to collapse with anxiety.

Jack sighed. Ran a hand over his face. Sighed again.

"I made a mistake," Balfa said. "But I'm gonna straighten it out. I'm gonna fly right. Tell you what: You can even hold on to the money."

"No way," Jack said. That was the last thing he needed, to get directly implicated like that. "Who are these guys?" he asked. "What did you do for them?" Before Balfa could answer, he held up a hand. "Never mind. Don't tell me right now." Maybe it was best that he didn't know. For legal reasons, in case he ever got questioned under oath . . .

Balfa looked like he was about to cry. "Jack? What are you gonna do? Will you at least think about this a little? Don't even consider me; I'm just asking you to think about what'll become of my daughter . . . Just take a day or two to think about it. Will you do that for me?"

Jack scowled. "I don't need this. I don't need this at all." He looked away. "I'll think about it. I can tell you right now that I'm not gonna just let this slide, but maybe there's some way we can still get you out of this mess. It doesn't look very likely, but we'll see."

His beeper went off. He glanced down and read the message. It was Sergeant Tanney, probably wondering why he hadn't checked in. He stood up. "I have to go. I need to think about this." He pulled out a couple of dollar bills for the coffee. "Sit tight," he told Tommy Balfa. "Don't do anything stupid."

CHAPTER *twenty-one*

J ack looked up. Michelle had just said something to him, but he had no idea what it was.

"I'm sorry?" he said.

She gestured down at the dinner table, at the dinner she had prepared for them, chicken and a salad and wine. "I said, 'Is something wrong with the food?'"

"Of course not," he said. "It's delicious." As if to demonstrate, he cut off a piece of chicken breast, dabbed it into the gravy, and popped it into his mouth. And then he was drifting away again. Was it Internal Affairs, he wondered? It didn't make sense. The setup, if it was a setup, was just too unclear, too muddy for a random test; they couldn't have known that he would follow Balfa. Something was definitely wrong, though. The detective had lied before, about where he was going, about his "informant." This new tale about the sick daughter—Jack supposed it was within the realm of possibility, but it could easily be more of the same, bullshit piled on top of bullshit. He frowned at the notion: Would the guy actually have the gall to make up a fatal illness for his own daughter?

"Jack?"

He looked up. Michelle was staring at him again.

"Is something wrong?"

"No," he said. "It's a work thing."

"What happened?"

He started cutting the rest of his chicken into small, neat pieces. It was one thing to joke about some case that was all wrapped up, turn it into a dinnertime story, but this was too personal, too fucked-up. "It's nothing," he said. "Just a problem I'm having with a detective in Carroll Gardens. It's fine," he added, though it was anything but.

He considered his options. He could sit tight, mind his own business, hope that IAB was not looking his way, but there was no way he was gonna do that. If he was gonna turn a blind eye to bad business, why bother being a cop in the first place?

He could take it to Balfa's boss, spell out everything he had seen, let the chips fall where they might. Maybe, like Sergeant Tanney had said, there were just two kinds of problems in the world: my problems, and *not my problems*. Maybe he should just set this in someone else's lap, let them deal with it. That didn't feel like much of an option, either. Right out of the Academy, every rookie learned that the crime-fighter's code coexisted with a fundamental law: The Blue Wall. You stood up for your brothers. You didn't rat anybody out. File under Life's Little Ironies: It was the same way that criminals looked at things.

You were supposed to fight the bad guys, and never jam a comrade up—sometimes the two rules smacked up against each other, and then what did you do?

For Jack, his first moment of disillusionment had come with his very first assignment, out in the Sixty-eighth precinct. They had put him on nights, in a radio car with an older, cynical cop—a hairbag, as the cop slang put it—a drinker named John Flannery. Jack had been eager to work the streets, to make some collars, and he kept trying get his partner to show him the ropes, but the old vet was an expert *coop*er: He knew every spot in the precinct where you

could pull into a hidden driveway, an alley, a back parking lot . . .
He'd say, "Wake me if anything comes over the radio, sport," and
then he'd slouch back with his hat over his face. Jack felt like a kid in
the presence of the old cop, and didn't feel like he could argue. He
tried cajoling, but Flannery just told him to get out and walk
around if he was so goddamn fired up. He couldn't do that, couldn't
leave the car and the radio, so he just sat there squirming in the passenger seat, cursing his luck. What was he gonna do? Turn the old
guy in? Lose the trust of every cop in the precinct? Make it so nobody would wanna work with him? He had kept his mouth shut for
three months, until he finally got a chance to switch to a younger
and more arrest-hungry partner.

This situation was worse because it wasn't just about him and his
partner. It also involved the man's whole damn family.

Jack stood up. "I'll do the dishes."

"Really?" Michelle asked.

"Sure. You cooked." With his ex-wife, she had done all of the
household chores, but he figured that it was a new era. Michelle had
her own day job, and he ought to pull his weight on the home front.
It seemed only fair.

In the kitchen, he stacked the dishes in the sink and waited until
the water grew hot. He held his hand under the faucet, and the feel
of the water on his hands was soothing. It helped him think. He ran
the sponge over the plates as he tumbled the options. If he turned a
blind eye, his whole career could go down the tubes. On the other
hand, if he simply turned Balfa in to Internal Affairs—and if Balfa
was telling the truth about the kid—then he'd be completely ruining
the guy's family.

He turned off the water and sighed. Maybe there was a third way.
He knew a good detective, an old partner, who had been called in to
work for the IAB. Maybe the man could use Balfa undercover in
whatever mess he was involved with, break a big case. Maybe he

could help the guy turn the whole thing around . . . And maybe they could throw some kind of Department fund-raiser to help the girl . . .

First thing in the A.M., he decided, he would make a call . . .

"DO YOU WANT SOME water?" Michelle said later. She swung her legs over the edge of the bed and pushed her feet into a pair of fleecy slippers she had bought Jack as a little present when he got out of the hospital.

"What?" He lay staring at the ceiling, frowning.

"I'll get you some," she said, shaking her head.

In the kitchen, when she turned on the light, a little cockroach scurried beneath the counter, tiny legs pumping wildly. She filled a couple of glasses, but then perched on the edge of a chair for a moment. She thought of her stepfather, of a certain edgy tone in his voice, which had always seemed to be there—he didn't need much of a reason. A familiar sourness crept into her chest.

She stood and headed for the bedroom, but detoured into the bathroom on the way. She set the water glass down on the sink and stared at her reflection in the mirror. Usually, she thought of herself as she had been in her twenties. Sometimes, though, she still felt like a little girl. She had been so young, but she had had to mother her own mother, who slowly collapsed as the love of her life, Michelle's father, wasted away. Then he died, and her mother had disappeared into herself for a couple of years, and then came the stepfather. A man in the prime of his life, vigorous, but selfish and demanding. Michelle had finally escaped, gone off to college, gotten her degree, and then what was the first thing she had done? Found herself an older man. In shaky health. By the time he had proposed to her, they both knew he was on the way out. Emphysema. And she had married him anyhow. Something in her needed to protect men, to try to save them.

Jack coughed in the bedroom and she turned, startled. She had mothered him, too, in the hospital and after. What was she setting herself up for? She had read an article about it in a magazine. *Repetition compulsion.* You kept revisiting the situation, trying to make it right . . . She turned back to the mirror, which certainly did not reflect a little girl. Her skin was rough, weathered looking. Little crow's-feet in the corners of her eyes.

Nobody was getting any younger.

She shivered and returned to the bedroom.

She and Jack lay in bed for a few minutes, silent, separate, curled away from each other. And then, unexpected, she felt his warm hand on the base of her spine. He pressed it against her cool skin, then smoothed it up over her tight back muscles. He massaged them, kneaded her shoulders, brushed her hair out of the way, and firmly stroked the back of her neck. She pressed her face down into the pillow, felt the tension leaving her body with each long breath.

Suddenly she felt closer to him than she had for weeks.

Relationships were such a mysterious things.

CHAPTER *twenty-two*

Sleet peppered the roof of the car like buckshot. Several inches of snow that had fallen overnight were now rimed with ice, and Jack glanced out from his warm submarine cabin to watch passersby totter along the sidewalks, slipping occasionally and throwing their arms up like actors in some old slapstick movie.

Traffic was crawling. He glanced at his watch: He was due to meet with his old friend down at the IAB office in Manhattan in fifteen minutes, yet here he was still plodding toward the Brooklyn-Queens Expressway. He groaned; he wanted to get past this situation as soon as possible, to let someone else worry about Tommy Balfa's screwed-up life. As soon as he got downtown, it would no longer be his problem.

He finally made it up onto the highway, which rose on stilts as it neared the Brooklyn waterfront. Below and to the right slid the dark polluted worm of the Gowanus Canal; to the left stretched the warehouses and loading docks of Red Hook. Beyond them, through the sleet, the winter-dulled harbor faintly shone. The traffic was just starting to pick up when his beeper went off. He pulled out his cell phone.

"Jack? It's Mike Pacelli." Harbor Unit. "You said you wanted to hear about any unusual activity along the waterfront. Something just came in. We got a call that someone might have just broken into a boat out in Bay Ridge. I'm in the middle of a rescue in Coney Island right now, but I'm sending one of our patrol launches over. Are you anywhere near there?"

Jack swerved toward an exit ramp. There was no way he could pass up an opportunity to catch the Governors Island killer—IAB would have to wait. "I'll be there as soon as I can." He pulled his rotating beacon from beneath the seat and stuck it up on the dash. He cut around an eighteen-wheeler and felt his tires grabbing for traction as he skidded down the ramp. He clutched the wheel with one hand and his cell phone with the other. He needed backup. He had already learned his lesson about going out on a dangerous call alone—he had a bullet-shaped scar on his chest to prove it. Tommy Balfa was still point man on the case, but the thought of working with the detective this morning was hardly appealing. He tried Gary Daskivitch, but got his voice mail. He tried the Seven-six desk, got a sergeant he knew, and learned that Balfa's boss was out on a call. He thought of Raymond Hillhouse, but the man was in Manhattan. He frowned; time was slipping away.

Cursing under his breath, he punched in Balfa's cell number. Maybe this could be the detective's chance to rehabilitate his sorry ass.

Balfa didn't answer.

Jack called the Seven-six desk again. "Do you know where Detective Balfa is this morning?"

"Yeah," the sergeant answered. "He's at home. He called in sick today."

Yeah, right, Jack thought. *Sick with guilt.* He hoped the detective hadn't gone a runner. "Do you know where he lives?"

"Gimme a sec."

The sergeant came back on the line with an address in Sunset Park. Half the way toward the marina.

———————

BALFA ANSWERED THE DOOR fully dressed. He started to say something, but stopped, a look of total surprise on his face. "What are you doing here?"

Jack got the sense that the detective had been expecting someone else. He didn't bother giving him any grief about his fake sick day. "Let's go," he said brusquely. "I've got a hot lead on our Governors Island perp."

"I can't," Balfa sputtered. "I have things—"

"No. *This* is what you're doing. Get your coat and let's go."

He pushed the detective in the chest, and then—without asking— he followed the man into his modest two-story aluminum-sided house.

"I'm not really—"

"*Come on,*" Jack said. "We nail this guy and you're gonna be in a lot better shape. Do something right for once."

Balfa stared at him for a moment, nodded, and then walked down a hallway and pulled his shoulder holster and coat from a hook on the back of the kitchen door.

The thought of riding with the other man, armed, didn't make Jack happy, but if Balfa was prepared to shoot him right out on a city street, he could certainly have done it the day before. "Joe Reppi gave me your address," he said, letting Balfa know that the desk sergeant at the Seven-six knew he was here, just to be on the safe side. "Charlie Unit's gonna meet us at the scene." He glanced impatiently at his watch. "Where's your Kevlar?"

BALFA STAYED MOSTLY SILENT during the high-speed ride out to the shore, except that at one point he asked, "Have you thought about what we talked about yesterday?"

Jack shook his head. "Not now. We need to focus on what's going down here, one hundred and ten percent." The scar on his chest told him all too well what a moment's inattention could bring. And he didn't see any need to warn Balfa about his appointment with his friend at IAB. He was doing the jerk a favor.

Ten minutes later, they reached the shore. Jack peered out his side window at a small marina, where five or six small boats were docked. He couldn't see anyone, and nothing looked out of place. There was no sign of the Harbor Unit, either.

He gave them a couple of minutes, then decided that he couldn't wait. "Let's go," he said, stepping out into the cold. The sleet had stopped, but the wind was fierce; it sanded his exposed face and hands. He opened his trunk and pulled out his own Kevlar vest.

As the two detectives neared the marina, leaning into the stiff wind, Jack heard a sharp pinging noise. It took him a moment to place it over the dense flutter of the wind and slap of the waves: just a cable clinking against a boat's hollow metal mast. Nobody was visible. Motioning to Balfa to stay silent, Jack stopped and listened. *Clink, clink.* The wind whistled in from across the harbor. The sky was gray, leaden, sullen. Jack stared out across the churning gray and white water, but couldn't see any police boats.

He turned his head sharply. Had he imagined it? *Another noise, muffled* . . . Something moving inside one of the boats. He scanned them slowly. And then he spotted an inflatable Zodiac tethered to the last vessel, a sleek modern sailboat with blue covers wrapped around its furled sails. He gestured to Balfa and they moved forward carefully out onto the pier; the concrete was covered with snow and ice. *There, again*—a muffled knock from inside the last boat.

The ice crunched underfoot and he winced as he moved forward. As he came up to the boat, he reached into his coat and pulled out his gun. He was sweating now, despite the cold, envisioning another bullet slamming into his chest.

He scanned the harbor again: still no sign of backup. Next to him, Balfa reached into his coat and pulled out his own service weapon. Jack prayed for the sound of the Charlie Unit launch; it was too stressful trying to keep one eye on the boat, one eye on his own partner. Balfa, though, seemed focused on the job at hand.

Jack communicated with him through gestures. *I'll pull the boat closer; you step aboard. I'll be right behind you.* (At this point, he had no intention of stepping out in front of the man.)

Balfa nodded. Jack bent down and took hold of a mooring rope attached to the rear of the boat, some four feet away. He pulled slowly and it arced in toward the dock and thudded against some old tires strapped to the side of the pier. Balfa grabbed a cable that encircled the deck and stepped over it. Jack dropped the rope and followed suit. The deck was slick, and rocked with the waves. He reached out and grabbed hold of the blue-wrapped boom. It swung a bit, but it was tethered to the deck; it made for an unsteady support as he stepped toward the cabin. He walked on the left side of the boom, Balfa on the right. A textbook pattern—you never wanted to approach together and present a single target.

He heard footsteps down below. A wooden hatch at the rear of the cabin swung open. Jack raised his gun. A man's head emerged. He looked to be about sixty-five or older—not a vigorous young carpenter and seaman, someone who could sneak aboard an island, build a coffin, and beat a security guard to death.

"Can I help you?" the man said. He had a thick, upswept shock of wirelike gray hair; a craggy face with bright blue eyes, a sharp nose, and a thin, sour mouth. Prominent ears. He sounded low-key and polite, but he had the bristly, rather offended look of a hawk or eagle.

"We're police officers," Jack said. "Would you mind stepping up on deck?"

The man looked puzzled. "Of course not. I was just closing up my boat for the winter."

He came up carrying a big paper shopping bag. It looked to be filled with clothes. "What's going on?" the man said. As he clambered out, Jack noticed that the clothes he wore seemed wrinkled and dirty. He stared into the man's stark eyes. Something was wrong.

Balfa stepped forward. "Sir, could you set the bag—"

A shot rang out. At first Jack thought it might have come from behind him, on the waterfront somewhere, but it was so *loud*. He turned to see Tommy Balfa put his hand up to a red hole in his cheek, and then the detective fell to the deck. Jack turned back to the other man, who had dropped the paper bag he had just shot through and was raising a pistol.

Jack raised his own gun, but the boat swayed and he almost lost his footing. He grabbed at the boom; once he had a hold of it, he swung it as hard as he could to the right. It caught the man in the side; he grunted in surprise as the gun flew out of his hands and disappeared over the side of the boat.

"Don't move!" Jack shouted, doing his best to steady his aim on the man's chest. He snuck a glance down at his partner, who was writhing feebly on the deck—things didn't look good. Balfa needed medical treatment, *fast*. Jack took a step forward, which was a mistake, because he had nothing to hold on to, and he felt his feet start to go out from under him.

The man shouted something, lowered his head, and charged. He ducked under the boom and slammed into Jack's chest. Both men had lost their footing now, and they slid across the deck, wrestling furiously. Jack grabbed the man's arm and his hand closed on pure muscle. The man chopped his hand down on Jack's wrist and he was appalled to watch his gun leave his hand and skate across the deck.

He threw up an elbow and felt a satisfying *whump* as it caught the man's cheek. He was struggling to his feet when the man grabbed his pants leg and yanked. Jack slid toward the side of the boat and felt the wire lifeline catch him at mid-thigh, and then he was toppling over the cable toward the waves.

CHAPTER *twenty-three*

The cold water burned like fire.

Jack had no time to consider the strangeness of that shock, because it was immediately followed by another: He was sinking fast. His wool overcoat, which seconds ago had protected him from the cold air, had turned into a soggy shroud, and the Kevlar vest into a heavy straitjacket. Even as he tumbled down, a shard of irony pierced his consciousness: He was drowning because of a bulletproof vest. Bubbles burbled around his head like angry bees. The water was so murky that he couldn't even see which way was up. Panicked, he managed to work his frozen fingers enough to unbutton the coat. He shrugged his way out of it, and then—lungs bursting—wormed out of the vest. He saw a dim light ahead and struck out toward it, praying that it would bring him back into the life-giving air.

What seemed like minutes later, he broke the surface, gasping. The currents spun him around, and he glimpsed the sailboat, ten yards away. He saw the man gripping the wire cable, staring dispassionately down at him, and then the currents bore him away.

Even without the weight of the coat and vest, he could barely manage to keep his head above the water. He kicked his shoes off, then lashed out furiously toward the shore, but he was caught in the massive hand of the current as it pulled him out into the open water, claiming him: *MINE*. It swirled him under again, and then released him just enough so that he was able to grab another mouthful of air. He was shivering desperately, and moving faster now. His right shoulder suddenly slammed into something; he never found out what it was because the current rushed him on. He caught a view of the low mass of Staten Island far in the distance, and the leaden clouds, pierced by a slanting ray of sunlight, like some heavenly annunciation. The view of the harbor was shockingly different from the water; there was none of the lordly perspective and distance afforded by the deck of a boat.

The grip of the current suddenly released him into a pocket of less angry water, and he was able to keep his head above it, and to note how bleak his situation was. Lifting his chin, he was able to look out for the Charlie Unit boat: nowhere in sight. He could make out the orange bulk of the Staten Island ferry far in the distance, way too far for anyone to hear his shivery cries. Aside from a long dark tanker even farther off, there was not another vessel in sight. The shore was a hundred yards away now. Even if he could buck the currents, time was running out. Hypothermia was setting in—he could feel it: His hands and feet were going numb, his muscles cramping, his brain getting foggy. He was moving out toward sea now and he remembered what Mike Pacelli had told him about how floating objects in the harbor tended to wash up on the south shore of Long Island. In this cold, he wouldn't live to make it anywhere near that far. He thought of what the old sailor had told him decades before: There comes a point when you can only take in a deep lungful of water and let the ocean win.

He pictured Michelle, though; pictured his son. He wasn't ready to leave them behind. He managed to raise his head again, and spotted something light-colored, drifting, maybe twenty yards away. He splashed toward it, each stroke an agony of effort. Finally, he closed in: a wooden pallet. His hands wouldn't cooperate to grip the rough slats, but he threw an arm over the edge and managed to pull himself partway onto it. The little raft depressed under his weight, but it kept his head above the slap of the frozen waves.

He spit out a mouthful of salty water, gasped for air, and lay there, shivering uncontrollably. He was drifting toward the middle of the harbor. A wave slapped against the pallet and the spray stung his eyes; he rubbed an unfeeling hand across them. It was no good. Maybe he wouldn't drown now, but he might freeze to death before the next boat came along.

After a couple of minutes he heard a clanking.

He wondered if he was hallucinating, but there it was again.

His neck muscles strained as he raised his head above the wood.

There! Maybe thirty yards away, approaching on his right. A bright green tower, bobbing on the waves, one of the harbor markers. His only chance.

With his last bit of strength, he pushed himself away from the relative safety of the pallet, back down into the icy waves, and slapped furiously at the water.

He could barely keep his head high enough to see now, but his ears led him on. *Clank, clank.* The sound grew louder. He strained his head up one last time, corrected his trajectory, and redoubled his efforts. If he swept past the buoy, he might as well pack it in.

He needn't have worried: The current slammed him right into the metal side. The challenge was to hold on—the base was a tall cylinder encrusted with barnacles, slimed with sea moss. Desperate, he flailed up and grabbed a bar of the latticed tower. He reached up and managed to place his other hand. He stopped, groaning. Just a little more . . . He felt drowsy now—all he really wanted to do was sleep—but he clung to the buoy, and then pulled back with all of his remaining strength. The little tower swayed sharply and the bell clanged; the sound was so close that it felt as if it was cleaving his head in two. Grimly, he repeated the motion.

The bell clanged and clanged.

CHAPTER *twenty-four*

He stood on the little marina's pier the next morning, shivering, though he was bundled in layers and layers of clothes: long johns, down vest, hat, gloves... Every few minutes someone approached, offering another cup of hot coffee. They all figured he was nuts to come back so soon; that he'd never want to get near cold water again. He stood there and shivered, and didn't tell anybody the real reasons why. The sudden bark of the gunshot. The bloody hole in Tommy Balfa's face, the sight of the old man raising the gun to fire again... And there was only one reason Balfa had been on that boat in the first place.

He took another sip of coffee and watched as techs in jumpsuits swarmed up the staircase from the boat's small cabin. It seemed that they were done with their forensics work. He glanced back toward the base of the pier, where a big knot of NYPD brass conferred gravely. A cop had been killed, and this was no longer just a precinct affair. The mighty behemoth of the Department had stirred in anger and deep affront. Back on shore, a line of uniforms did their best to keep a jostling horde of press behind the Crime Scene tape. TV news vans filled the street, their tall satellite antennas broadcasting the pompous voices of on-the-spot reporters who were clearly thrilled by the previous day's events. *Vampires.*

Jack stood apart, on the end of the pier. The wind was calm today, and the water smooth. It was cold, though, damned cold.

He could have remained in his warm hospital bed. The doctors had advised it, but being back in a hospital again gave him the heebie-jeebies. After a night rendered sleepless—first by urgent official interviews about the shooting, then by an anxious visit from Michelle, finally by vicious dreams—he was glad to escape, even if it meant being caught up in this roiling drama. It was a crime scene; he was a homicide cop. This was where the action was; it was where he belonged. Most of all, he burned to catch the man who had killed a young boy, and a security guard, and messed-up Tommy Balfa, who had died—after all—in the line of duty.

He knew what the Crime Scene techs had found when they arrived the previous afternoon. One ransacked cabin, valuables still present. One NYPD detective, deceased, with the letters *G.I.* Magic Markered on his forehead.

He also knew what they hadn't found. An NYPD Glock-19 service pistol, registered to one Jack Leightner. He pictured it skidding across the deck . . . It hadn't gone overboard, though, not that he could recall. The loss of your service piece was one of the most profound embarrassments for a cop—especially when it ended up in the hands of a killer.

Thankfully, that detail had eluded the reporters. HERO COP SLAIN IN HUNT FOR SERIAL KILLER, read the cover of the *Post*. Ridiculous, of course—killing three separate people under different circumstances didn't necessarily make a perp a true serial killer. But they didn't care; they had papers to sell. As for the *hero cop* part . . . Jack rubbed a glove across his face. Through all of the turmoil of the last twenty-four hours—Balfa's killing, his own rescue, the ensuing mobilization of forces, the media frenzy—he had not mentioned the detective's little secret. It had been one thing too much.

A seagull landed a few feet away. It lifted one leg and scratched it against the other, eying Jack warily. A thin breeze ruffled its feath-ers. "If you were smart," Jack told it, "you would've flown to Florida a month ago."

A figure broke through the scrum at the base of the pier and walked out. Mike Pacelli, from the Harbor Unit.

"How ya doin'?" he asked.

Jack just shrugged.

Pacelli shook his head. "Next time you feel like taking a dip, can I suggest a membership at the Y?"

Jack smiled, weary.

Pacelli stood next to him and together they stared down at the water. "You need anything?" his old colleague asked.

Jack nodded. "The scuba unit."

Pacelli sighed. "I was afraid you were gonna say that."

THREE HOURS LATER, THE Harbor Unit man opened the door of Jack's car and slid into the passenger seat. He took his gloves off and held his hands up to a heater vent.

Jack glanced out at the Scuba Unit launch anchored next to the pier. Burly men in thick black drysuits stomped around on the deck. "They find anything yet?"

Pacelli shook his head. "Not yet. This could take a while."

"I'm sorry to send those poor bastards down on a day like this."

Cold aside, it was a tedious job, crawling around in the muck at the bottom of the river. The divers worked a pattern line, a one-hundred-foot rope stretched out and secured at both ends. Visibility was zero, so they had to reach around in the dark. When they had checked along the entire length of the line, they moved it over a few feet and started again. Finding a gun could take hours—or days.

Pacelli glanced at a cup of coffee on the dashboard. "Mind if I have a sip?"

"Take the whole thing. If I have any more, it's gonna start coming out my ears."

"Don't worry about the scubas. This is a breeze for them." Pacelli took a good slug of the warm coffee. "You know what they have to do to get into the unit in the first place?"

Jack shook his head.

"First, they take a written test, all the technical crap they need to know to keep them alive. If they fail any part of it, they're out. Next, they go to the gym for pull-ups, push-ups, and sit-ups. Then they have to run a mile in less than six thirty-eight. Then they have to go in the pool and do twenty laps in eleven minutes. If the other applicants do it in less, they're out. They have to go one length underwater without coming up. Then they have to put on a weight belt and do it again. They do a half-hour survival float, and then tread water for fifteen to twenty minutes, with their hands out of the water for the last few minutes."

"Jesus."

Pacelli shook his head. "That's the easy part. If they make it through all that, then they put some scuba gear on, and they have to swim into the deep end of the pool and get past five or six members of the team. If they come up, they're out."

"What do you mean, 'get past'?"

"They'll spin you around, and someone will rip your mask off, then pass you off to someone else, who'll yank your regulator out of your mouth. The job isn't just physical—you can't panic. You might be deep in a river, and you can't see your hand in front of your face, and the currents are ripping along . . . you never know what you might run into. Shopping carts. Cars. Bodies." He stopped when he noticed Jack's gray face. "Sorry—I guess you know something about the water, now."

Someone tapped on the window and Jack looked up, startled.

A young uniform. "Excuse me, sir," the kid said. "The scubas found something and they'd like you to take a look."

Jack and his colleague bundled up again, left the warm bubble of the car, pushed through the press throng as calmly as they could, and finally reached the end of the pier, where they met with the head of the scuba unit, a crewcut sergeant in his mid-forties who looked like he was made of pure gristle. The man presented them with a recovered gun.

"Sorry," Jack said. "This is too new. My perp had an old Smith & Wesson revolver, or a Colt."

The man shrugged. "No problem. One time, we were diving in the Hudson and we found five wrong guns in forty minutes." He signaled to his team to keep looking, then turned back to Jack. "You wouldn't believe the shit we're coming across down there. So far we've run into a washing machine, a butcher knife, and an electric guitar. Fender Stratocaster, early sixties . . ."

BY LATE AFTERNOON, THE crowd of onlookers had thinned considerably. Most of the reporters had left for other, more visually compelling scenes. The police brass had retreated to the comfort of their offices at One Police Plaza, or the Puzzle Palace, as it was sometimes known by the cops on the street.

Jack made another trip down to the end of the pier, impressed by the dedication of the scuba unit.

"Why don't you go someplace warm?" the sergeant said to him. "I'll call you as soon as we find anything."

Jack just shook his head. The hunk of metal lying somewhere beneath this frigid gray water was his best chance of catching the man who had murdered his partner. Of course, the gun might not be registered, which would leave him back at square one, but he had high hopes: Despite his success rate thus far, the killer seemed like an amateur, hopefully not street-smart enough to know how to get hold of an anonymous piece.

"Sorry about this crappy job," he told the Scuba Unit sergeant.

The man shrugged. "We'd rather be out there saving a bridge jumper or something, but this is part of what we do."

An hour later, a diver bobbed up, lifting an old revolver as if it were a trophy.

CHAPTER *twenty-five*

I brought some pretzels," Gary Daskivitch said. "On a long drive, you gotta have snacks."

Jack nodded absently, staring out the passenger window, watching the blue steel girders of the Triborough Bridge flick by in the morning sun. It was good to get out of the city, away from the press and the Department brass and the crazy memories of the past few days. Good to hit the open road, with only this over-sized cheery kid beside him for company. Maybe he'd be able to clear his head, sort some things out.

"You can lean the seat back," Daskivitch said. "Catch some Zs if you want."

Jack shook his head. "I'm fine." Off to his right, a plane swooped up from a tarmac at LaGuardia Airport, then thundered over a small stretch of water and the barb-wired fences ringing Riker's Island. He glanced down at a manila folder in his lap. They had been on the road for only a few minutes, yet he had already opened the thing three times. Stared down at the faxed copy of the New Hampshire driver's license that had accompanied the gun registration. Stared at the harsh, hawklike face of the man who had shot Tommy Balfa. *Robert Dietrich Sperry.* D.O.B. March 7, 1937. Five-foot ten. Blue eyes.

"Why do you think he did it?" Daskivitch said. "I mean, the Balfa thing is pretty obvious, and the security guard, but why kill the boy?"

"We don't know that he did for sure; we haven't proven that connection."

Daskivitch frowned earnestly. "All right, well . . . What do you think all this *G.I.* shit is about?"

Jack shrugged. "Who knows? He's a squirrel, that's all." On TV, detectives lost sleep trying to puzzle out their suspects' motivations. Maybe talking dogs had told the perp to kill; maybe he was out to kill anyone who reminded him of his grade school math classes. It wasn't Jack's concern. As long as he had evidence tying Sperry to at least one of the killings—and he did, now that the ballistics had matched up—all he had to do was catch the man and hand him over to the DA. That was the job; end of story.

He flipped past the fax and picked up a couple of news clippings. COFFIN KILLER STRIKES AGAIN, read the one from the *Post*. He set the article down. It wasn't this one that bugged him, but the other. The one that mentioned the fact that Detective First Grade Jack Leightner had taken a little harbor swim. The one that pointed out how he had barely survived a previous shooting incident, just months before.

Daskivitch took his eyes off the highway for a second and glanced down at the clipping, with its photo and everything. "How do you like that, huh? You're a star."

Jack made a sour face.

"What's the matter? You don't want your fifteen minutes of fame?"

Jack sighed. "You don't know how the other guys looked at me, after the Red Hook thing."

Daskivitch shifted uncomfortably. His big square head barely cleared the roof of the car. "Whaddaya mean?"

"What do I mean? They looked at me like I was a freaking Jonah."

Daskivitch frowned. "It wasn't your fault."

"It doesn't have to be." Jack turned and stared out the window. "Let me tell you a story. Back when I was on patrol, there was this great old cop in the house named Harry Geraghty. One day, in the middle of a tour, he stopped at a Dunkin' Donuts and walked right into a mess. This E.D.P."—Emotionally Disturbed Person—"had gotten behind the counter and was waving a knife. Harry was a great talker; people used to say he could talk a rabid dog off a meat truck. So he decides to try and calm the guy down. He's talkin' away when suddenly the perp lunges forward and stabs the girl working the register. He didn't kill her, but he did some nasty damage. And Harry had to pop the guy. It was a fucked-up situation, like that film they show you in the Academy, where the crackhead is coming at you waving a machete and carrying a baby. What do you do? There's no simple answer."

Daskivitch made a face. "Yikes."

Jack sighed. "Everybody second-guessed Harry. They said he should've drawn his piece right away and taken the guy out. They said the Department would've backed him up, called it a good shooting. People started edging away from him."

Jack fell silent, remembering the part of the story he didn't want to tell. He had come out of the station house one afternoon and bumped into the man on the steps. Harry had asked if he wanted to go out for a beer, and he had responded with a lie, saying he had to run some errands for his wife. The memory still shamed him.

"What happened to him?"

Jack shrugged. "Nothing dramatic. He didn't eat his gun, or become a drunk or anything. But he retired soon after. He was a great cop, but he just faded away."

Daskivitch considered the story. "No offense, but I don't think you're looking at this the right way. I mean, sure, you got caught up in a couple of incidents recently, but you survived. Twice. You're not a Jonah, man; you're *lucky*. And here's what's gonna happen when we catch this Sperry creep: You'll be a hero. Cops'll be lining up to work with ya."

Jack snorted. "You're a good kid, Gary." He made his seat recline a bit, and let the drive lull him. All around him on the highway sat other people in little self-contained bubbles, everything so orderly, everybody imbued with such a sense of direction, of purpose. On the road, Americans.

He chewed over what Daskivitch had said. Maybe he *was* lucky. Maybe he should be having those enjoy-every-moment-you're-alive feelings, like somebody on an afternoon talk show. Now that he had time to think about it—and the drive ahead would certainly give him that—he found that he didn't want to think about it. He was sure of one thing, though: Tommy Balfa had certainly run out of luck. He wondered about the man's wife and child, and what would become of them now. If the daughter really was sick, maybe the compensation from the City would at least pay for the new treatment . . .

He turned to Daskivitch. "Did Balfa ever talk to you about his daughter?"

The young detective spoke around a mouthful of pretzel. "Nope. The guy was only around for a couple of months, and he never discussed his private life."

Jack loosened his seat belt; the damn newfangled models always cinched him tighter and tighter. He thought about Balfa's upcoming funeral, about the inevitable pomp and circumstance, and what the hell he could manage to say to the man's wife.

There was no point in worrying about it right now. Instead, he closed his eyes, and soon he was busy imagining his upcoming proposal to Michelle. They'd share some bubbly, pull some Fred-Astaire-and-Ginger-Rogers moves out on the dance floor, enjoy the festivities. And then, at the height of the countdown, he'd drop to one knee and bust out the ring. And then would come a midnight kiss to beat the band.

RURAL NEW HAMPSHIRE WAS a surprise.

The towns looked the way Jack had expected, with their picturesque commons, quaint steeples, cheery Victorian houses, everything blanketed in snow like some Hallmark greeting card, but once they got out into the countryside an ominous note crept in. The weather had something to do with it—a gray, wintry afternoon with the threat of more snow—but some of the roads just seemed downright creepy.

After they rendezvoused with FBI man Ray Hillhouse, who had flown up to join them—feds had better discretionary budgets—and a couple of swaggering state troopers, who had secured a search warrant, their little caravan made its way out of the town of Keene and soon was winding along some serious country roads. The terrain was steeply ridged, and the houses widely separated, each with its own deep front yard and mailbox out on the road. The stark, bare woods afforded glimpses of a world that was far from picturesque. Rusting carcasses of cars up on blocks, broken-down heavy machinery, piles of trash, dilapidated trailers or humble ranch houses with little trails of smoke ribboning up from chimneys—it looked like a poverty-stricken Appalachian backwoods. A mangy dog rushed down a snow-covered hillside, barking furiously, and Jack had a premonition of what he was about to find. He had come on such scenes in his days as a patrol cop, following some anonymous tip about child abuse: filthy homes piled with junk, TVs blaring, smells of dogshit and bad cooking, half-clothed kids running around dirty in the general chaos . . .

The state troopers pulled over to the side of the road and the others followed suit. Everybody piled out and pulled armored vests and weapons out of car trunks. Jack was getting mighty tired of pulling on the Kevlar. It was brutally cold; the hairs inside his nose froze stiff within seconds of their exposure to the winter air. The staties— one young and one old—were dressed for the weather, with their lined jackets and thick boots, but the cityslicker detectives stumbled along the snowy road in their black dress shoes. They came to a driveway and the young trooper pointed up a hill, but the house was not visible.

The older trooper opened the roadside mailbox: It was stuffed full of junk mail.

"Maybe he's not home, but don't relax," Jack said grimly, his breath puffing out into the cold. "This bastard is full of surprises."

The shotgun-bearing staties led the way as the team tromped up the long driveway. They tried to maintain a quiet approach, but that was impossible; the landscape was preternaturally still and their feet crunched and squeaked in the thick snow, which looked undisturbed—another reason for everyone to breathe a touch easier. They came over a rise and looked down on a trim, dark green, two-story house, which sat in a small hollow. The yard, to Jack's surprise, was well kept, devoid of cars or junk, though a modest motorboat rested at the back of the small clearing, up on blocks and covered with a green tarp. Just as he had expected: Sperry was familiar with the water.

After a quick whispered conference, Hillhouse and the older trooper split off to go around the back of the house, and the rest of the team warily approached the front porch. The ridge behind the house blocked much of the sun, and it was colder in the gloomy late-afternoon shade. It went deep into the marrow of Jack's bones, reminding him of the freezing harbor.

Snow had drifted up onto the porch. The front windows were all shuttered. A red metal swing seat creaked in the wind; there was no other sound, save for the tense breathing of the three men as they crept up the steps and took positions at the sides of the door.

"He's not home," the young statie muttered, but he was looking considerably less cocky now. Jack was glad for Gary Daskivitch's comforting bulk.

The big young detective looked like he could use a little comforting himself. He was staring down at the doormat with a queasy look. Jack glanced down: The damn thing was printed with the New Hampshire state motto: *Live Free or Die.*

Jack reached out and slowly opened the screen door, which squeaked loudly. He winced, then knocked on the heavy wooden door. The three men waited for a moment, their breaths puffing out like nervous thought balloons. Jack knocked again, louder.

Still no answer.

"Anything back there?" he called out, his voice echoing in the stillness of the hollow.

"Nothing here," Ray Hillhouse hollered back.

The statie reached out and tried the doorknob. "Stand back," he said, and raised his shotgun.

"Whoa!" Jack said. "That's gonna ricochet and put somebody's eye out."

The statie looked like a kid whose firecrackers had just been confiscated, but he lowered the .12 gauge.

Jack edged over to a window and tried to raise it. No luck. He tried the next one, then stepped down off the porch, and tromped awkwardly into a heavy snowdrift on the side of the house. The first window there, about five feet off the ground, rose easily. "Shit," he muttered. The thought of going in first gave him the heebie-jeebies, conjuring ugly images of a bloody Red Hook basement. Michelle had been incredibly patient with him so far, but he couldn't imagine that she would put up with him taking another bullet. On the other hand, he couldn't imagine sending someone else in his place. Fuck it, he was a cop—he hadn't signed on for a lifetime of driving a desk. He looked around for something to boost himself up with.

Daskivitch and the statie lumbered into view.

"Lemme go in first," whispered the big detective from the Seven-six.

Jack snorted. "First of all, there's no way I could get you up there. Second, you wouldn't even fit through the window."

"I'll go," the statie said, visions of merit badges no doubt dancing in his head. "This is my territory."

Jack sighed. "Look, if we start arguing about turf, we're gonna freeze to death out here. I know what this guy looks like. I'll deal with it."

"I don't know . . ." the statie said.

Jack nudged Daskivitch. "Give me a boost." He turned to the trooper. "How about you go around front and make a big racket on the porch?"

He waited until the man crunched around the side of the house and started pounding on the front door. Then he stepped up into Daskivitch's cupped palms.

Next thing he knew he was sliding headfirst into a dim room. A pantry, heavily stocked. Shit—that meant the kitchen was right outside. And every patrol cop knew that with its plethora of knives, frying pans, and other potential weapons, the kitchen was the most dangerous room in a house. Of course, the man wouldn't need any of that if he had a gun.

Jack's gun.

He crouched down, breathing way too loud, and yanked its replacement out of its holster.

He listened.

CHAPTER *twenty-six*

At that same moment, one hundred and ninety miles to the south, Michelle Wilber bit into a hot cheese puff. She waved a hand in front of her mouth and did a little involuntary cool-off dance. She glanced around to see if anyone had noticed. In a couple of hours, when the open bar had done its work, no one would be noticing much of anything, but there was something about the first half hour or so of an office party that made everyone stiffen up and act all formal.

The DJ was playing "Three Times a Lady," and Michelle half-expected to look out on the floor and see a bunch of teenagers slow-dancing in pastel tuxedoes and dresses.

"You looking for the mirror ball?"

She turned to find her colleague Rose standing next to her, eating from a little plate of toothpick-pierced hors d'oeuvres.

Michelle smiled. "I know—I keep thinking about my high school prom."

Rose shrugged. "At least the place is swanky." It was true: The company had bartered some future discounts to get this party space, a ballroom on lower Fifth Avenue. It looked especially nice now, with all the holiday wreaths and twinkling Christmas lights. The catering was on the skimpy side, though: small plates, baskets of crudités, cheese platters . . .

Rose glanced anxiously around the room. Michelle knew that she was wondering if it would be okay to light up. Her friend's gravelly voice was the result of a habit that had begun in the sixth grade.

"Where's your beau?" Rose asked.

Michelle frowned. "He had to work." She didn't want to discuss it. She was already going to miss out on Christmas Eve and Day with Jack; now he had bailed out on this party and didn't seem to quite get how disappointed she was.

Rose made a face. "My cousin married a cop. They're never around when you need them." She laughed a throaty laugh.

Michelle liked her. She remembered one office party when Rose had ended up doing a limbo dance in her stocking feet at the end of the night, her dress plastered with everybody's name tags.

"Oops, there's my hubby," Rose announced. She set down her plate and rushed off toward the front door.

Michelle felt a twinge of loneliness. Just about everybody else had a date tonight. She would have enjoyed introducing Jack around. People always seemed to get a kick out of meeting a real detective. *NYPD Blue.* A waitress came by with a tray of something deep-fried. The poor girl was speckled with acne, and her tux jacket looked about six inches too long. "You're doing a great job," Michelle said, just to be nice.

The room was filling up now, and she was just considering whether she wanted to try to make it through the crowd around the bar when she had a sudden jolt of recognition. Over by the front door, handing his briefcase to the coat check girl: Steve McCleod, a sales rep for one of the biggest catering companies in town. Even across this big room, his rugged good looks were apparent. She had shared some drinks with him at the holiday party two years ago.

They had a lot in common, being in the same business, and he was her age, and funny in a self-deprecating way. He was married, but it soon became evident that the union was not happy. Michelle had felt a powerful attraction to the man, and he had—by the end of the party—gone so far as to say that he felt it, too. She had been single, but neither of them had been willing to act on their feelings at the time . . .

She flushed at the memory, and looked away. She took out her cell phone. It was early, still—not even dark outside. She considered calling Jack, but she knew that he was on an important trip and wouldn't want to be bothered.

"GIN-AND-TONIC?"

She turned to find Steve McCleod at her shoulder, looking quizzically at her drink.

"Vodka," she answered, hoping she wasn't blushing. She had spent much of the past hour in this balcony above the ballroom, trying to keep the man in sight so she wouldn't accidentally bump into him.

"How have you been?" he asked. He had one of those interesting faces that—roughened by early skin problems—somehow seemed more attractive in middle age. He was taller than Jack, with broader shoulders.

Michelle shrugged. "Pretty good. You?"

The music was loud, the latest raucous dance hit. Steve leaned in closer. "I was wondering if you were going to be here."

Now she was definitely blushing. "How's it going with your wife?" she said, wanting to put herself back on firmer ground.

He stared down at the dance floor, which was crowded now that the alcohol was kicking in. "We're legally separated. The divorce'll be final in a couple of months."

She could see the pain in his face. "I'm sorry. How are you hold-ing up?"

He sighed. "I'm doing the best I can." He glanced back at the dance floor and winced. Then he turned to her. "Listen—how about if we go into the other room where it's quiet and we can talk?"

CHAPTER *twenty-seven*

I t wasn't until the fifth photograph that Jack began to realize the significance of what he had found.

HE AND HIS COLLEAGUES had split up to search the house. The place could not have been more different than he had expected. It was the home of someone so severely orderly that even Jack Leightner was troubled by the rigidity of it all. It was a country cabin completely devoid of homey touches: no throw rugs, no knick-knacks, not a single picture on the walls. Everything that could be sorted by size or shape or color was laid out just so, including the pots and pans in the kitchen, the cans in the kitchen cupboards, even the stacked wood by the fireplace. Order, efficiency, cleanliness. The lone bookshelf held a Bible, several auto repair manuals, a number of books on woodworking, and a collection of volumes of military history.

The only exception to this fanatical neatness? In a small spare room at the back of the house, Jack found a small amount of clothing, sized about right for a ten-year-old boy. Some more comic books, a small TV, and a video game controller. No signs of forced captivity. It was not really a child's room, though: no pictures on the walls, an almost empty closet, very little accumulated *stuff*. It was a guest room, Jack decided, and the boy had probably not stayed long. Unfortunately, there was no ID lying around.

Across the hall, another small room had been made into a sparse woodworking shop: a few saws, calipers, and wrenches; a shelf of glass jars filled with nails and screws, several old power tools. Enough space to build a coffee table or a bookshelf—or a homemade coffin.

He found the photo album in Sperry's bedroom. This room looked somewhat more lived in, but again, the sparseness gave Jack the sense that the man had not lived here long. The bed, a bureau, and an armchair were the only significant pieces of furniture. He knew from long experience that the most efficient way to toss a bureau was to work from the bottom up, so that you didn't have to keep closing drawers to get to the next one. The first drawer held rows of socks, folded neatly and arranged by color. The second, stacks of age-stained T-shirts, neatly pressed. Even the boxer shorts in the third drawer had been ironed, and they were also organized by color.

The top drawer held some small change (sorted, of course, by denomination), and a little leather photo album. Jack hoped that it might contain information about the boy, but as soon as he opened it he saw that the black-and-white snapshots were too old; they were turning brown, and bore the soft focus of a cheap camera. He flipped through. Four young girls smiling shyly at the camera; hair pulled back in ponytails, they wore buttoned sweaters and pleated skirts. A little gang of adolescent boys gathered around a boy aiming what looked like a BB gun; they wore short-sleeve shirts and boxy trousers with the cuffs rolled. A group of choirboys smiling awkwardly, gathered around a plump, friendly-faced priest. An older photo, slightly more sepia: a handsome crew-cut man leading a pony while a pretty blond woman reached up to support the little boy on its back.

The time looked to be somewhere in the forties or fifties, but the photos could have been taken anywhere. Then Jack flipped to the next page. Another group of wholesome-looking boys, sitting along the barrel of a cannon. His heart sped up—*there,* in the background, barely visible, yet unmistakable: the head and upraised arm of the Statue of Liberty. He flipped to the next page and stopped still: a row of big, dignified wood-framed houses. Jack recognized the one on the right: Just days ago he had examined a dead security guard in its basement. The next photo showed a proud young man with a row of ribbons across the chest of his Army uniform. Jack turned back to the photo of the man leading the pony—he couldn't be sure, but they looked the same. Next page: a group of uniformed, helmeted soldiers standing at attention in a quadrangle.

A group of adults in clown costumes and kids in face paint playing on a lawn, with one of Governors Island's big brick barracks in the background. A boy, maybe eleven years old, with large ears that stuck out from his crew-cut head, leaning against the seat of a spiffy rocketlike bicycle while the man who had led the pony looked on, smiling. Jack held up the album: There was something familiar about the boy's narrow face. An image jumped to mind: a hawk-faced older man staring down at him from the deck of a boat.

CHAPTER *twenty-eight*

A police funeral was always a big event, with hundreds of cops lined up to show support. The fact that many of them would be total strangers to the deceased was not important, Jack mused, as he sat near the rear of the church during the service for Tommy Balfa. (If you were dead, you were dead, and it didn't matter who the hell showed up.) No, the funerals were for the living, to make the families proud, and most of all to make the other cops feel better about the risks they took every day. (If you had to take a bullet, you were damned well gonna go out a hero.) That's what all the hoopla was for: The flag-draped coffin, the flags and trumpets, the dress uniforms with the yellow piping on the pants, and the huge floral bouquets, one of them in the shape of the deceased's badge.

Such events were usually required only a couple of times a year, but there was a definite weariness on the faces of this afternoon's crowd. After the towers came down, too many funerals in one short season. Still, the Department couldn't stint. The mayor and the commish made the obligatory speeches, going on and on about Tommy Balfa's unfailing service and heroism. It was true: Balfa had died honorably, in the line of duty, but Jack sat thinking about the man's deceptions, about a gray plastic bag filled with cash. But who would want to see a hero tarnished? He glanced around, wondering if Balfa's mystery redhead would have the nerve to show, but she didn't seem to be in the crowd.

Outside, after, the Pipes and Drums corps of the Emerald Society played "Amazing Grace" as the coffin was loaded into the hearse. The music affected Jack in a way that all the speeches couldn't; he felt himself getting choked up, and he said a quick prayer for Tommy Balfa, even though he wasn't much of a believer. Ranks of cops saluted, their hands encased in white dress gloves. Two officers supported the grieving widow, a thin, frosty-looking bleached blonde.

Jack waited to say anything to her until after the interment, when the mourners adjourned to a catering hall. However, the wife spoke first. She was talking to a couple of Seven-six detectives over by the bar, and one of them nodded toward Jack, who was sitting uncomfortably at a cocktail table in the corner. The woman came toward him, clutching her pocketbook with both hands. She seemed brittle, and Jack sensed an anger under her grief. Not surprising—the Job had taken her spouse. He wished he could have reported that he had caught her husband's killer, but the trip up to New Hampshire had not provided any clues about Sperry's current whereabouts.

"They tell me you were with him when it happened."

He stood quickly. "Yes, ma'am. I'm very sorry for your loss."

He steeled himself for questions about the deadly scene on the boat, but the woman just stared. There were questions Jack wanted to ask, too, about her husband's behavior in the past couple of months, but this was obviously not the time. The silence grew awkward.

He cleared his throat. "I barely knew your husband, but we went out for dinner the night before. He told me how much he loved you. And I know that he would have done anything to help your daughter."

The woman's gaze went weird. "What are you talking about?"

Jack frowned and lowered his voice. "He told me about her condition. I'm very sorry."

The woman backed away a couple of steps, and turned toward the crowd, as if seeking some help or explanation. She turned back to Jack, voice shrill. "Is this some kind of joke?"

Jack stared at her. "No, ma'am. He said she—"

The woman cut him off. "I don't know what the hell you're talking about. Tommy and I never had any kids."

CHAPTER *twenty-nine*

I t made no sense.

Balfa had sounded fairly convincing, with all the details about stages of the disease and European cures, but the heart of the lie was so flimsy that it was sure to be discovered in short order. (And it would hardly take a detective to do so.) Was Balfa crazy? Or did he subconsciously feel guilty, and want to get caught? Sitting behind a desk in the Seven-six precinct house the next morning, Jack shook his head. The man had already *been* caught. And even the most inept street punk could have come up with a more durable story.

Several phones rang at once and Jack glanced up. The normally calm squad room had been transformed. A cop had been shot, and now the place was crackling: More desks had been moved in, new phone lines installed, extra detectives brought in from other houses. The *G.I. Killer Task Force*, the brass were calling it. Every uniform in the city had been issued a photocopy of Robert Sperry. His mug had been plastered on lampposts and bus stops all over town. Most likely it was only a matter of hours before a cab driver or bodega owner called in a good tip, hoping for the $10,000 CopShot reward.

Despite all of the publicity and manpower, though, the team was working against one significant drawback: Sperry's loner status.

Even the most violent, hardened drug dealer was part of an extensive social network of customers, suppliers, coworkers, girlfriends, and rivals, all of whom might have some financial or personal motivation to snitch. But Sperry was a stranger to the city, and even on his home turf he had kept to himself. FBI agents had interviewed the man's New Hampshire neighbors and come up with surprisingly little info. The killer had lived there for only a few months, no one knew where he had come from, and he kept fiercely to himself. The neighbors had reported seeing a boy with him in the last few weeks, a kid who matched the picture of the victim in the floating box, but nobody knew who the child was or where *he* had come from. There was no indication of kidnapping or coercion. The boy had looked glum, but he had been walking about freely and alone when someone had spotted him on the road near Sperry's house.

Jack had spent some somber time thinking about the kid since receiving those reports, but this morning his mind was fixed on Sperry's latest victim. He listened idly as a detective at the next desk phoned an informant, fishing for news of the killer—and then he froze as a new thought occurred to him. Tommy Balfa's flimsy lie made no sense unless the man was only hoping to buy a little more time for himself. Unless he had been planning to skip town.

Sure enough—it took Jack just minutes to verify his hunch. After a couple of calls, Balfa's name popped up in a passenger list at Newark airport. A 2:07 P.M. flight on the day he had been killed, one ticket to Mexico City, purchased a full three weeks before Jack discovered what his temporary partner was up to. Balfa had been planning to run for a while, and it was only a phenomenal double stroke of bad luck that had put the kibosh on his plan. Jack was not much of a believer in a universe in which everything happened for a good reason, but this series of events—the man getting caught and killed within twenty-four hours of his planned escape to enjoy his ill-gotten gains—seemed almost like a Biblical judgment.

He pictured the look on Balfa's face when they had driven out to the marina, when the detective had asked if he had thought things over. The bastard was just trying to find out if he'd still be able to bolt.

Which raised the question of why he had not simply taken off the night before.

Jack sat for a minute, sipping a lukewarm cup of coffee, considering the options. Maybe the man had been reluctant to leave his wife. Or his mistress. No, that didn't seem likely—he could always send for either one later . . . Jack thought of the money he had seen in the gray bag. It had seemed like a lot at the time, but it couldn't have been more than ten or twenty large. Not enough to compensate for leaving a good job and a home behind. But maybe there had been other payments . . . What if Balfa had been foolish enough to bank the money, or greedy enough to invest it? He would need to go back during business hours and withdraw the funds . . .

His cell phone snapped him out of his reverie. Sergeant Tanney.

"How's it going with the Balfa thing?"

For a second, the question unnerved him, as if the sergeant had been reading his mind, but he dropped the thought. Tanney wanted the murder solved; that was all. Every officer on the force was crazy eager to catch a cop-killer, and the pressure from Downtown to wrap things up was intense, but Tanney was extra fired up. He had a special interest in covering his ass for all of the ways in which he had minimized the initial investigations.

At this point, though, the sergeant reminded Jack of his main priority: catching a live killer, not worrying about Balfa's shenanigans before he got shot.

AND SO IT WAS that he found himself driving out into the heart of suburban New Jersey.

Much of the trip was ugly. First there was the huge toll plaza at the other end of the Lincoln Tunnel, with its pall of exhaust—he couldn't imagine sitting in one of those booths all day, no matter how good the pay or perks might be. Near the plaza stood several gritty by-the-hour motels, and he knew that if he worked Homicide in Jersey he would be quite familiar with those. Finally, for someone who hated shopping as much as he did, the highways themselves were a vision of hell, mile after endless mile of strip malls: mattress discounters and junk food chains and window foofiness specialists . . . He knew from prior drives that New Jersey had lots of beautiful countryside, and he expected to end up shortly in an idyllic, picturesque town, but meanwhile the state seemed determined to put its worst features on display.

IT SEEMED THAT THERE was no human experience that didn't attract its amateur historians. It didn't matter if it was trivial or terrible or just of interest to a very limited audience. The horrific World War II Death March from Bataan? Someone kept the memory alive with photos and a pen-pal club. Train schedules in rural England? Hundreds found them fascinating enough to explore every detail.

Jack had put in a call to Michael Durkin, asking who would know about the island's history. The security supervisor had called back in a couple of minutes, saying that he had found "just the man." Five seconds in Gene Hoffer's study made clear the object of his own itch to memorialize. The paneled walls were covered with framed photos of Governor Island life in the late forties and early fifties, the same self-contained world documented in Robert Sperry's little photo album.

Hoffer was a retired insurance executive; he had replaced his business attire with a green flannel shirt and khaki pants. The man's handsome head was crowned with thick white hair, and he wore thin wire-framed glasses. Behind him, a picture window gave out on a pool covered with a winter tarp, and ranks of what in summer would undoubtedly be impressive flower beds. The pool, the sleek Beemer in the driveway, the huge flat screen TV they had passed in the living room—Hoffer was clearly determined to enjoy his free time and disposable income.

The man settled down behind his desk and motioned Jack to a white wicker armchair. "What exactly is this about?"

Jack shrugged. "First off, I was hoping you could tell me a little about what the Island was like back in the old days." Long experience had shown him that if you cut too directly to the chase, you only got answers to the questions you knew to ask—and risked missing out on all sorts of unexpected material. Sometimes it was best to just let a subject ramble.

Hoffer chuckled. "Well, you've certainly asked the right person."

Jack nodded, doing his best to communicate enthusiasm. Most people would be more curious about why an NYPD detective had trekked all the way to another state, but Hoffer impressed him as the kind of man who was chiefly interested in what he himself had to say.

The man's wife, a trim, pretty brunette, came in with a tray of refreshments. The couple looked like they spent their days doing something brisk and active, hiking or skiing . . . "I thought you boys would enjoy a hot drink," the woman said as she moved aside some papers on her husband's crowded desk.

"The best coffee you're ever going to have," Hoffer said, turning to Jack. "Did you know that I met Bitsy here when we were both Army brats on the Island?"

Of course, there was no way Jack could know any such thing, but such was his host's rhetorical style. He smiled appreciatively, then made a puzzled face. "Wasn't it a Coast Guard base?"

Hoffer nodded smugly. "Of course it was, but that's only the tip of the iceberg. The island was transferred to the Coast Guard in Sixty-six, but before that the Army had it for over a hundred and fifty years. They constructed Fort Jay and Castle Clinton there between Eighteen-oh-six and Eighteen-oh-nine, and then of course during the War of Eighteen Twelve—"

"I was asking what it was like back when you were kids there," Jack said to Mrs. Hoffer, hoping to head off a detailed inventory of the island's early years.

The woman smiled. "Oh, it was a paradise for children. Both of those big forts to play in, and the movie theater, and the YMCA—"

"The Y was supposed to be for the troops," her husband interjected, "but there were hardly any. At that time the island was the headquarters for the First Army, so there were mostly just officers around."

"And parolees," his wife added.

Jack perked up. "Parolees? From what?"

Mr. Hoffer took the question. "They were Army prisoners in the fort who were allowed out to do chores. They were mostly just homesick kids themselves; they taught us kids how to throw a baseball."

"Those were innocent times," Hoffer's wife said. "And the island was a wonderful, safe place to grow up. There was no crime at all to speak of."

"*Well . . .*" Hoffer said, and he and his wife chuckled.

"Did I miss something?" Jack asked.

Hoffer grinned. "The only crime on the island was perpetuated by adolescent boys. Gosh, we had some *fun.* It would only take six or eight of us to tip one of those old cannons onto its muzzle. And there was that time with the fireworks—"

"Maybe you shouldn't tell that one to a policeman," chided Mrs. H.

Her husband smiled. "I think only an MP would have jurisdiction, and anyhow the statute of limitations has long expired."

"What happened?"

Hoffer placed both of his hands behind his head and leaned back in his chair. "One time, several boys—and I'm not saying *who*—set off some fireworks on the Fourth of July. Only problem was, we didn't realize that we were doing it right on top of the munitions storage area."

"Was there an explosion?"

Hoffer smiled. "Let's just say that we were very, very lucky."

His wife shook her head. "You boys were a *terror*. How about the things you used to put in the cannons?"

Jack turned to Mr. Hoffer. He was beginning to feel as if he was watching a Ping-Pong match.

The man smiled impishly. "The howitzer crews used to fire test rounds. They only used blanks, of course, and they never checked the bores. So we kids would put things in there and watch them get a free ride over to Manhattan. One time there was this dead cat—"

"Don't tell that one," his wife said, with considerably less humor.

Jack stood up. "Mind if I take a look at your photos?"

"Go right ahead," Hoffer said. He kept up a running commentary as Jack moved from picture to picture. "That was the time we had a little circus. That was our Friday bowling night. That was our Little League team . . ."

Jack scanned the photos, searching for the faces of one particular boy and his father. After an exhaustive catalog of every possible childhood activity and party, he came up with zilch.

He reached into his sports coat and pulled out several snapshots of his own. He held up a picture of Sperry as a boy, and another of the man in military regalia who appeared to be the child's father. "Do you recognize these people?"

Hoffer's face immediately clouded up. His wife came around and peered over his shoulder, and she also turned grim. Jack could almost sense the milk curdling in his perfect cup of coffee.

Hoffer shook his head. "Listen, officer, I don't know why you're bringing this up. Isn't it just ancient history?"

The question, coming from this compulsive recorder of past events, almost made Jack laugh, but he pressed on. "Do you know the boy in these pictures? Why don't you tell me about him?"

Hoffer stared down at his desk for a moment. When he looked up, he was scowling. "I'm going to tell you, detective, and then—and I don't mean to be rude—I'm going to have to request that you leave."

CHAPTER *thirty*

Jack reflected on Hoffer's tale as he sat in his car the next day, but other, more mundane matters kept intruding into his thoughts. He cast an envious eye on a man walking by with a cup of deli coffee; he could have used the wake-up, but he had no idea how long he'd be waiting on this quiet Cobble Hill street, and he didn't want to have to pee. He shivered; the morning sun was too weak to take the stinging chill out of the air. He turned on the engine to warm up the car for a minute, then glanced down at his watch. He'd have to be gone by afternoon, when his next tour began.

With any luck, by then he might receive a fax that would go a long way toward completing the back story of Robert Dietrich Sperry. He wasn't counting on it, though. Arlington, Virginia, was a long way from New York, both in distance and in attitude: The Pentagon's Office of the Judge Advocate General sounded like a typical bureaucratic sinkhole, and the records he was seeking were half a century old. If found, though, they might complete what Gene Hoffer had started: detailing the childhood roots of Sperry's recent penchant for homicide.

Jack reached down and made sure that his cell phone was on. He was running two investigations simultaneously, one very high profile and by-the-book, one unofficial and secret. Right now he was off the clock, freezing his balls off just for the sake of finding out what Tommy Balfa had been up to in his ill-fated final days. Which was not necessarily a smart career move. The Department was only concerned with Dead Tommy Balfa, Hero Cop. Alive, the man had presented problems, and if Jack kept tugging at those unresolved threads, who knew what was going to come unraveled, or where the strands might lead?

One definitely led to Maureen Duffy. Other residents of her brownstone-lined street were coming down off their stoops, heading toward the subway and their day jobs, but Duffy worked just a few blocks away, as a night nurse at the local hospital. Jack glanced down at the seat next to him at a photocopy he had run off earlier in the Midwood precinct house. Judging by her driver's license photo, Duffy didn't look much like the femme fatale he had been imagining for the past few days, after he had glimpsed her driving away from the side street where she had dropped Tommy Balfa. She was an attractive redhead, but she was only twenty-three, with the healthy, freckled wholesomeness of a girl who had grown up in a big, happy Irish family. It was easy to picture her babysitting nieces and nephews, or tending to some elderly patient; harder to imagine her having a fling with a married man. Jack frowned. Who knew? . . . Maybe they weren't having an affair at all. Maybe he had jumped to conclusions. Hopefully soon, she would walk out of that heavy front door and he'd find out for sure.

The day before, when he got back to the office, it had occurred to him that maybe Tommy Balfa had not planned to leave town alone. The man had bought only one plane ticket, but that didn't mean that his female friend had not booked a seat, too. Balfa, unexpectedly deceased, had never boarded the plane; Jack called the airline and asked who else had not shown up for the flight. Only two other names popped: a businessman from Kansas City who had missed his connecting leg, and one Maureen Duffy from Brooklyn, New York. Jack called the DMV and got her driver's license photo—*bingo.*

He shifted around in his seat, trying to get comfortable. Anybody who thought detective work was nonstop excitement should be forced to participate in a long stakeout. It would make a hell of a reality TV show: a bunch of cops sit in cars for hours; they get booted off the show one by one as they succumb to the need to doze or to pee. He glanced in his rearview mirror, wondering if the young woman was already out of the house, maybe on her way back, but a large van obscured his view. He heard a high-pitched yapping. On the sidewalk a few houses down an elderly woman was walking a little sculpted poodle.

Some other motion caught the corner of Jack's eye. His body tightened. No mistaking that red hair, it was Duffy and she was already halfway down the front stoop. He swung his door open, got out, and began crossing the street. Duffy had stopped on the sidewalk and was staring his way. There was something odd about her gaze, though, and it took him a moment to figure it out. She was staring in his direction, but not at *him.*

He looked over his shoulder: Two men were walking quickly down the middle of the street, toward Duffy. He took in quick impressions: One was big as a soda machine, the other just very large. They shared the meaty, disgruntled look of men who threatened other people for a living.

"Tipsy, *no!*"

He swiveled back. The neighbor with the poodle had returned, and was trying to remove something from the animal's mouth. Jack looked over his shoulder again: The two strangers had paused at the sight of the old woman, but they were moving forward again, and opening their jackets.

Duffy stared at them like a mouse hypnotized by a snake.

Jack reached into his own coat. Not for his gun—he wasn't about to instigate a shootout on a Cobble Hill street—but for his badge. He pulled out the leather case, flipped it open, and held it up high so everyone could see.

"Miss Duffy," he called out. "I'm with the NYPD. I need to speak with you."

He looked over his shoulder: Thankfully, the two men had stopped. The badge seemed to work on them like a cross on vampires. They stared at it, stared at Jack, stared at each other, confused and clearly pissed off, and then—without a word—they turned and strode away.

Jack turned back. Maureen Duffy had slumped down on her stoop, and as he came near he could see that she was trembling. He sat down next to her, then lifted up a bit to tuck the back of his coat between his ass and the cold brown concrete.

He nodded at the street. "Do you know those charming individuals?"

The young woman shifted away from him until she was backed up against the curlicued stair rail. She wasn't sultry, or beautiful— she was *cute*. "How do I know you're a cop?" she said. "You can buy a fake badge in Times Square."

Jack shook his head somewhat ruefully. "Those days are gone. It's all Disney now." He took out his business card and his cell phone. "Here. You can dial my office number, or get the NYPD number from Information."

She took the card and stared at it dully.

Jack stood up. "It's freezing out here. Can we talk inside? Or in a coffee shop somewhere?"

She stared up at him. Green eyes, freckles, rounded cheeks. A quirky mouth that under brighter circumstances might curve up into a mischievous grin.

She wasn't smiling now.

"Who *are* you? What do you want from me?"

Jack shrugged. "If you ask me, your real worry is what those two meatheads want."

Maureen Duffy tried to look defiant, but couldn't hide the fact that she was scared stiff.

"I'M NOT HUNGRY," SHE said, pushing away the menu. They were in the back of a Greek coffee shop, which didn't fit in with the neighborhood's new program of trendy bistros and swank bars.

The waiter, a doleful little man with stringy hair that looked coated with black shoe polish, shrugged sadly, then turned to Jack.

"I'll just have a cup of coffee."

A little sign on the table said that there was a five-dollar minimum, but the waiter looked too resigned to the general injustice of life to attempt to enforce it.

"I'll have a corn muffin, too," Jack added, mostly for the old guy's benefit. "Toasted." He shook his head at Maureen as the man trudged away. "I can never believe how long the menus are at these places. There's no way they could keep all this stuff around fresh." Bullshit small talk, to put the girl at ease.

It wasn't working. She had her paper napkin in her hands and was twisting it as if it were some kind of abdominal exerciser.

"Did Tommy treat you well?"

That got her attention. She looked frightened all over again.

Jack reached into his pocket and pulled out a roll of antacids. "Here—take one of these. I'm a bit of a worrier myself . . ."

"I know it's wrong," she blurted, "but I didn't think it was an actual *crime*."

Jack did his best to keep his eyes from widening at this shift into confessional mode. "Whoa. Slow down a minute. You didn't think *what* was a crime?"

She slumped back into the booth's padded seat. "I knew he was married. I'm not stupid."

Jack raised his hands in mock surrender. "Okay. Nobody's saying you are. But *what* wasn't a crime?"

She looked at him as if he was stupid. "Having an affair. It's not illegal, is it?"

The waiter swung by with Jack's cup of coffee and he waited until the old man was out of hearing distance before he continued. "Why don't you tell me about those two creeps?"

She returned a look of wide-eyed innocence. "I don't know. I've never seen them before. Maybe they were sent by Tommy's wife?"

Her ditziness sounded convincing, but Jack wasn't quite buying it. A changeup, to throw her off balance: "Where did he get the money?"

She frowned. "What money?"

"Come on, Maureen. I already know about it."

She just stared. "I don't what you're talking about."

"Then why were you running away with him?"

She looked confused. "Running? What do you mean? He said he wanted to take me on a vacation."

"With less than twenty-four hours notice?"

She nodded. "He's . . . he was a very spontaneous kind of person." She paused a moment to snuffle back a tear. "He was a lot of fun. And I work a flexible schedule. I got some of the other girls to cover my shifts."

Jack frowned. This description of a freewheeling, joyous Tommy Balfa didn't exactly accord with his own experience. But then, he wasn't a cute twenty-three-year-old . . . "Why did you buy a one-way ticket?"

She shrugged. "That's what he told me to get."

"And you didn't think that was strange?"

She looked down at the table and sighed. In a softer, more tentative voice: "I was hoping he was going to tell me he was leaving his wife. And that he was going to propose to me. I thought maybe he had booked tickets for some sort of trip to celebrate from there. That's just the kind of thing he would do."

Jack blinked at this mention of proposals, a subject much on his mind of late. He stirred some sugar into his coffee, taking a moment to think. The girl's story was getting convoluted, but that didn't mean it wasn't true. He would need to follow up, to probe for holes, maybe talk to her supervisor at the hospital . . . His beeper went off. He glanced down. "Excuse me a sec." He pulled out his cell phone and called Stephen Tanney.

"I want you to get over to the Seven-six house right away," the sergeant said. "Your fax from the Pentagon came in."

Jack's eyes widened at this unexpected bureaucratic efficiency. He pinched his lower lip; he desperately needed to see the fax, yet he wanted to finish this interview. "I'm not on until four," he said.

"A cop's been shot," his boss replied. "You have something more important to do?"

Jack winced at this uncomfortable echo of his own comments to a distracted Tommy Balfa. "I'll be right there."

He flipped the phone closed, then looked at the girl. "Listen, Maureen: Those gorillas are gonna be back for you. There's only one way for you to be safe here, and that's to tell me exactly what Tommy was up to."

She just stared at him with those guileless green eyes. "I don't know. I don't know anything."

Jack groaned, glanced at his watch. "You can't go back to your apartment. Do you have a friend or somebody you can stay with?"

She thought about it, looking like a worried little kid.

He stood and reached into his pocket for his card. "Let me

know where you end up. And call me. I can't help you if you don't help me."

As he rushed out, he passed the old waiter, bearing his corn muffin. The man raised his arm and was about to say something. Too late: Jack was gone.

CHAPTER *thirty-one*

The Seven-six squad room was packed and loud, but all the noise and commotion faded from Jack's awareness as he funneled down into the stack of Pentagon records on the desk in front of him. The dense military and legal terminology mixed in his mind with a series of old snapshots, and the sound of Gene Hoffer's begrudging voice, and family memories of his own, and soon the squad room disappeared altogether, replaced by a series of grainy imagined scenes running through a Super-8 film projector in his head.

A group of crew-cut boys in plaid shirts and wool pants push down on the black barrel of a cannon. Behind them, across the harbor, the gray stone towers of lower Manhattan rise up in the dusk. "Somebody keep an eye out for MPs," says one of the boys. "Not you," he adds, pointing to ten-year-old Bobby Dietrich Sperry. "We don't trust German spies."

(Gene Hoffer: "We used to tease him a little, because his ears stuck out so much, and because of his middle name. Just boys, you know, kidding around . . .) *Just kidding*, Jack thinks bitterly. He knows this teasing all too well: His parents came to the United States from the Ukraine, and the Red Hook bullies loved to make fun of their accents, and to call him "Commie" and "Pinko."

Young Bobby and his mother and father are seated at a dinner table.

The boy asks his father about an upcoming training exercise. He loves the way Lieutenant Colonel Ted Sperry is at the center of such plans, loves his father's uniforms and medals and the way everyone salutes him, loves his dad, his hero. Unlike Jack's father, the bitter drinker, wielder of a strap. *Like Jack's father, Lieutenant Colonel Sperry is tormented by an inner demon, but unlike Jack's old man, he never speaks of it, never takes it out on his family. He's a model father, a model husband, a model soldier, a model man.*

New scene. *A parolee on work detail paints a house in Nolan Park. He brushes white trim around the yellow exterior walls he painted the day before. His name is Lowell Cates and his shirt is off because it's a sweltering August day. He is a small young man with a bit of the swagger of movie star John Garfield, though he is hardly a gangster—he has been put in the stockade for the crime of coming back to the island late from weekend leaves.*

What happened next was pure speculation. *Maybe the lieutenant colonel's wife had taken the ferry into the city. Maybe the boy had gone with her. Maybe the screen door opened and the officer came out with two glasses of lemonade. "Thank you, Lieutenant," the parolee said. The officer handed him a glass. "Enough with the lieutenant stuff. You can just call me Ted." Maybe they chatted for a while on the porch.*

Jack moved from speculation into the cold hard facts of the Army's court-martial report. Seven weeks later a neighbor, a Colonel from Fort Wayne, Indiana, happened to wander into the house and find Sperry and Cates engaged in an act severely frowned on by members of that man's army. The legalese of the records did little to disguise the disgust of the other officers involved in the court-martial, especially after Lieutenant Colonel Sperry stood up and made a brave but suicidal speech to the effect that his love for Lowell Cates was no one's business but God's and his own.

Jack was well into his second reading of the minutes before the full significance of the verdict caught his eye. Lieutenant Theodore

Sperry and Corporal Lowell Cates had been summarily, dishonor-
ably discharged from the Army for conduct unbecoming to an officer or enlisted man. For "gross indecency."

And there it was: **G.I.**

Gene Hoffer had reluctantly filled in the rest of the tale. Young
Bobby Sperry had seen his father stripped of all dignity and respect,
kicked out of the Army, divorced from his family, sent reeling in dis-
grace. And the other kids' casual ribbing had turned to fierce, full-
throated jeers. It only took six or eight of them to get together and
finish destroying Bobby's world, to tip it until his small heart fell
out, and then to stuff that heart into a cannon and hurl it spinning
(along with a significant, never-to-be-recovered part of his mind)
toward the distant moon.

CHAPTER *thirty-two*

T he problem was what to do with all his keys.

Jack stood in the jogging lane of the Prospect Park roadway staring down at his baggy new sweatpants. They had pockets, but when he put his house keys and car keys in there, they slapped against his leg with every step, and he jingled like one of Santa's reindeer.

He clutched the keys in his fist and set off around the park in the early morning light. Well, not *around* the park—he would have been happy to make it a quarter of the way. He prided himself on having a pretty trim physique for a middle-aged man, but he was still not entirely recovered from his gunshot wound, and this jogging business was turning out to be surprisingly hard work.

He reached down and patted his stomach. Three or four pounds off would do it. He was breathing heavily now, only three hundred yards down the road, but he pressed on, determined. This exercising was not just for him; it was for Michelle, too. His fiancée, just hours from now, if all went well. Tonight was New Year's Eve, and he had the ring and the dinner reservations, and a woman who loved him, and the sun was shining, sparkling on the park's little lake, and he could see his breath in the crisp December air, and he felt good despite the complaints from his knees and the crick in his side. He felt even better after he breezed past a little old geezer in a fancy running outfit, but then was brought down to earth as a couple of pastel-suited girls bounced past him, chatting merrily without even pausing for breath.

He smiled at himself. Okay, so he'd have to keep at this for a while to get his wind up. Not a problem. Maybe he wasn't a great runner, but he was a damn good detective. He was moving forward inexorably on the Sperry case, and he had a strong hunch that something was going to pop very soon on his private investigation. Balfa's girlfriend was holding something back, and either she'd give it up voluntarily or he would pry it out of her. He shrugged off these thoughts, rolling his head like a boxer warming up. He had the day off; for once he was going to have a personal life, and to hell with work.

He was loosening up, despite the cold, and wondered if he was hitting some kind of stride. If those things were kicking in—what were they called? *Endorphins.* Life was a lot different here in the park when you weren't zipping by in a sealed-off car. He listened to the steady shuffle of his footsteps on the asphalt and to the jagged rhythm of his breath. He started noticing the different kinds of trees, and the way a goose waddled down to the water's edge, and then he was pondering why the goose hadn't flown farther south for the winter, and where its comrades were, and soon—pleasantly, and for the first time since he had looked down at the boy in the box—he wasn't thinking about much of anything at all.

HE DIDN'T BAT AN eye at the prices on the dinner menu, even though they were so high they would have made both of his parents faint. He didn't bother hiding the ring in any desserts. He didn't even wonder which knee to get down on. That morning he had had a major realization—an epiphany, really—and it had come from the most unlikely source.

He had come back from a run—he liked the way that sounded, even though it had been more of a *plod*—and taken a hot bath. He came out feeling good and sporty, as if he were in a locker room. He went into the kitchen in search of breakfast, turned on the little TV over the microwave, and there was Regis Philbin with some pert blonde, and they were chatting jovially with some singer Jack didn't know, a handsome young guy wearing a cowboy hat and boots.

"How did you pop the question?" Regis was saying. "Did you take her for a carriage ride around Central Park and open a bottle of champagne?"

The singer shook his handsome head and leaned forward, resting his elbows on his knees. He had a shy, modest manner that clearly drove the women in the studio audience wild. "I didn't do any of that," he said. "No violin players, no hidin' the ring, no pretendin' or foolin' around. I just wanted it to be a really simple moment, you know. *Authentic.*" The camera cut to several middle-aged women in the audience, nodding their heads, mesmerized. "I took her hand and told her that I loved her and that I hoped she would spend the rest of her life letting me make her happy." A number of women in the studio audience wiped their eyes.

And that was it. Jack stood there in his kitchen, open-mouthed, holding two eggs he was about to crack over a frying pan. *Keep it simple.* What a fool he had been, thinking that the moment should be about some clever trick or elaborate setup, when all he needed to do was speak from his heart.

Now here he was in this too-fancy Midtown restaurant, with red leather booths and subdued lighting glowing from behind polished wood panels on the walls, but it was okay, it still felt *right*. Michelle was wearing a dress that he loved, and she looked gorgeous. (He noticed several model-like women sitting with rich older men, and they looked glamorous in a superficial way, but he was proud to be here with his date.) He didn't fidget, didn't check to see if he had remembered the ring. He didn't for one second wonder if he was do-ing the right thing. He just felt it, in his heart, like he was floating, like he was in the *zone*, Michael Jordan swooping serenely up for a three-point half-court *swish*.

A waiter went around with a silver tray handing out noisemakers and party hats. The countdown to midnight was coming up, but suddenly Jack didn't want to wait anymore—he didn't want the mo-ment swallowed up in a crowd of shouting revelers.

He raised his champagne glass. "To the most beautiful woman in the room."

Michelle clinked glasses with him. She hadn't eaten much this evening, said she was saving up for the post-midnight snacks, but that was okay. This wasn't about having some kind of perfect meal—this was about starting their future together, and he didn't care if it happened over a couple of Big Macs.

He pushed aside the votive candle in the middle of the table and reached out and took Michelle's hand. "You know what?" he said, brushing aside the cowboy's words, which were still bouncing around in his head. "I know this has been a crazy year, what with my time in the hospital, and . . . you know . . ." He didn't want to mention Sep-tember 11, not now . . . "And then there was my little swim, and everything. But even so, I wanna tell you that these have been the best few months of my life. Because of you." He looked down for a moment, embarrassed to find himself choking up. Still holding on to her hand, he reached into his pocket, pulled out the little velvet ring box, and set it on the table. "Will you marry me?"

Michelle's eyes widened. "Oh my God," she said. She pulled out of his grasp and knocked over her water glass as her hand flew up to cover her mouth. "Oh my God," she repeated, and her eyes crin-kled up.

A nice couple at the next table realized what was going on and they smiled encouragingly. Jack grinned back. As he mopped at the table, Michelle began to cry. He reached out to offer his napkin, but then realized that it was wet.

Michelle cried, and cried.

After a minute, Jack's grin faltered.

She couldn't seem to stop.

He reached out for her hand again, but she just shook her head and blubbered something through her tears.

"What's this?" he said gently.

"I've been seeing someone."

He stared at her, bewildered, a foolish grin still plastered on his face. "You've been going to a shrink?"

She shook her head, weeping. "I've been *seeing* someone."

He sat there, frozen. After a minute, he heard words coming out of his mouth. "I know I've been busy at work and all . . ."

She shook her head again. "It's nothing to do with you. I didn't plan it. It just happened."

"Michelle . . ." He reached out for her, but she stood abruptly, knocking her silverware off the edge of her plate. It clattered to the floor, causing several nearby diners to look over.

She grabbed her purse and fled.

CHAPTER *thirty-three*

W e just got a report that he's been sighted out at Rye Playland."

"Huh?" Jack looked up, and then up higher, at Gary Daskivitch's big frame planted in front of his desk in the Seven-six squad room.

"Sperry," Daskivitch said. "Somebody called and said they spotted him on the water slide." The detective shook his head. "This guy really gets around. So far he's been spotted at Katz's Deli, the top of the Empire State Building, and the ice skating rink in Central Park. What's next: The stage of a Broadway show?" Daskivitch grinned, waiting for Jack to share his appreciation of all these nutty phone tips, but he just nodded absently.

"Okay," he murmured. "Put somebody on that."

Daskivitch's eyes widened. "The *water slide*? Are you kidding?"

Jack frowned. "Sorry—I wasn't paying attention."

"You okay?"

"I'm fine."

The young detective stared down at him, dubious, but then his phone rang and he turned away to his desk.

Jack sat gripping the metal arms of his chair. *Fine*. He shouldn't have come in to work this morning, he knew that, but what was the alternative? To sit home wondering if Michelle was ever going to call him back?

Last night he had settled the bill at the restaurant, then gone out looking for her, but she wasn't waiting by his car. And she wouldn't answer her cell phone. She wasn't waiting for him when he finally gave up and went home. He had thought of going by her place, but then he realized that if she wasn't there, he didn't want to know. He didn't want to know anything more about what had just happened. It was impossible to believe; his mind just couldn't accept it.

He had lain down on his bed, fully clothed, with all the lights off. *I've been seeing someone*: The words kept clanging in his head. He thought of old cartoons he had laughed at when he was a kid, Wile E. Coyote suddenly finding himself suspended in midair after running off a cliff, or Elmer Fudd coated in ashes, staring at the stub of an exploded cigar. All he wanted, all he really wanted, was to just wind back time a few minutes, a few frames, before he had lit the cigar, before he had gone over the cliff, before Michelle had dropped her sudden, utterly mystifying bomb. Before he had taken the little ring box out and set it on the table. He thought of that and was deeply embarrassed, and then hurt in a primal way, like a dog that has been hit by a car, and then a flare of anger snapped open inside of him, a raw liquid lava of fury. His fists clenched, and he felt a pain in the back of his head, and for a moment he thought he might be having a stroke.

Eventually his blood pressure dropped, but he was unable to sleep. At some point he had rolled over and glanced at the glowing green numbers of the digital clock: 3:27 A.M. He knew he had to go to work the next morning, and he was angry all over again, pissed that Michelle was keeping him up so late on a work night, and he narrowed his focus to this small problem so that he wouldn't have to think about the big one.

———————

FOR A PARTY RENTAL company, New Year's Day was busy, but Michelle wasn't at work this morning. He hated himself for doing it, but the first thing he had done when he reached the squad room was call her office. They said she'd called in sick.

Now he sat at his desk in the middle of the task force's buzz of activity and forced himself to plod through a few small tasks, as if nothing had happened, but a strange torpor was sliding down over him. He pictured the face of the woman in Park Slope, the doctor's wife, after he and Vargas had informed her of her husband's death. He recalled the odd, inscrutable expressions that had slipped across her face, and her plaintive voice: "No, he'll be back in a few minutes. He just went for a jog."

HE WENT FOR A jog, too.

At four o'clock, after his tour was over, he went home, but the silence and hollowness of the apartment were so overwhelming that he fled. Jumped into his sweats, grabbed his keys and cell phone, drove off to the park.

Once he hit the loop road, he moved forward grimly, hunching his shoulders, with keys clenched in one fist and cell phone in the other. He had called her ten times already, and he wasn't going to call anymore—he had pledged himself that, not even if the world was about to end, because that small point of pride seemed to be all that he had left.

Seeing someone? he thought as he set off down the road. Who? For how long? Where had they met? How had she kept it a secret? He considered himself a damn good judge of character—he had to be, in his line of work. How had he misjudged her so profoundly? It was impossible.

He moved on and he didn't stop, even when his breath grew ragged and he developed a crick in his side. He didn't want to ever stop, because then he would have to notice how shaky the world had suddenly grown under his feet.

A car horn bleated behind him and he looked up, startled. He was out in the middle of the road and a Parks Department pickup was trying to get by. Chastened, he veered back into the jogging lane. Overhead, the wind sifted harshly through brittle leaves. To his left, the late afternoon sun slanted across the surface of the little lake and filled it with a cold orange fire.

Jack ran.

LATER, WHEN HE WAS filling up his post-run bath, he stopped the water because he thought he heard the front door open. He stopped breathing, too, and listened for a moment, then unclenched his body and turned the tap back on. She might still walk in any second, though, and he steeled himself for that, trying to anticipate what he might say or do. Maybe he would present her with an elaborate show of indifference. Or punch a hole through a wall.

In the hot bath, he lay back, playing their last conversation over and over in his mind. Had she even said she was sorry? He didn't think so, but he couldn't be sure. She certainly hadn't made any effort to explain. And didn't he at least deserve that much?

After his bath, he fixed himself dinner, making a production of it. He opened a bottle of wine, which had always seemed a waste during his solo days. He even made a salad, with lettuce she had bought, because he never would have bought it for himself. (She was always telling him he should eat more greens.) Grimly he chopped some carrots, then stopped because he thought he heard the door open again, but it wasn't the door, and he slammed the cutting board on the floor in a fit of self-disgust. He left the chopped carrots on the linoleum because *fuck the carrots. And fuck health.* He had no appetite.

He carried his glass of wine into the front room. He glanced out the windows at the front walk, then took his cell phone out to make sure it was on. *I'm seeing someone.* Clang, clang, clang. He clenched his fists in another gust of rage. *Fuck her. I'll change the locks. I'll put her clothes on the cutting board and chop them into little pieces and throw them on the lawn.*

He thought of the Park Slope doctor's widow again, of watching her face as she saw her whole future disappear. Bridge out.

He couldn't believe it. It was unbelievable. Michelle would never do something like this. She wasn't that type of person. And he loved her with all his heart, even—remarkably—now. It was a mistake, a fluke, and she'd be back, pleading for forgiveness. And he *would* forgive her, because he loved her, still.

The apartment was quiet as a tomb.

CHAPTER *thirty-four*

"What are you doing here? I thought this was your day off."

Nancy Amerulo, one of the Seven-six detectives assigned to the Governors Island task force, glanced up as he strode into that precinct's squad room armed with an extra-large coffee the next morning. Amerulo was a handsome blonde, big-boned, well-liked. She looked tired, though—this high-pressure, no-results investigation was wearing everybody down.

Jack shrugged. "Justice never rests."

The detective stared at him, then shrugged back. She didn't know him well enough to pry.

He moved away, and took a big slug of coffee. Time to buckle down. For the past few weeks he had been working at less than his true capacity, because—whether Michelle believed it or not—he had made an effort to get home for her. She had walked anyway. He made a sour face. It happened every day, to cops all over the world. The divorce rate for members of service was insane. *So what?* To hell with her. People were getting killed here. What was he supposed to do, not give a damn?

Over in a far corner, he dropped into a chair next to Anita Tam, a very tall, very skinny young black detective attached to the Medical

Examiner's office. Tam was a computer whiz; she brought her own high-tech laptop to the task force office, scorning the dinosaur desktops of the precinct house.

"Don't those get in the way?" Jack asked, nodding down at her long fingernails poised over the keyboard.

"I like the clacking sound," she replied.

"Really?"

She just grinned. Long stints of overtime research had given them a relaxed familiarity.

"Anything new?" Jack asked. While the rest of the task force was focused on the present whereabouts of Robert Dietrich Sperry, he was still determined to discover the identity of the boy in the box. He had a hunch that this was how the killer would be found.

Detective Tam nodded toward the computer screen: yet another list of missing persons. "You wouldn't believe what a mess it is out there."

Jack frowned—he would believe it all too well.

"What's the plan for today?"

Jack shrugged. "I don't know. I'm wondering if maybe we should look at Canadian missing persons. After all, that's not so far from New Hampshire . . ."

Tam sighed and hunkered down.

After a couple of hours of staring at the computer screen, Jack grew bleary-eyed; he found himself imagining some strange alternate universe peopled by all the might-be-alives and the insufficiently remembereds, a twilight world of putty faces and eerie smiles.

Just before lunch, the other detective's phone rang.

Tam picked up; her eyes widened. "DNA results," she whispered to Jack.

At the Governors Island crime scene, the M.E.'s crew had taken hair samples from the bedding of Robert Sperry and the deceased boy. On TV, Crime Scene wizards would plug such samples into some high-tech gizmo and get instant results; in real life, it sometimes took weeks or months.

"Mm-hm," the detective said. Her face fell. "That's okay, we expected that." Then her face brightened. "Really? Are you sure? It's a definite match? All right, thanks a lot."

Jack was sitting up now, leaning forward. "What? What did they say?"

Tam frowned. "First of all, the boy's DNA didn't match anything from the missing person databases. No surprise there, but check this out: His DNA and Sperry's are a definite match. They were related."

Jack sat back, clasped his hands behind his head, and thought for a minute. "All right, let's try to put this together . . . I doubt that Sperry was the kid's father, because we would have seen that name pop among the New Hampshire school rolls. If the man was his grandfather, the kid might have had a different last name. But if that's the case, why didn't his parents report him missing?"

The two detectives sat in silence for a minute, thinking and thinking and not getting anywhere.

AT HOME THAT AFTERNOON, Jack made a beeline for the answering machine, but the goddamn red light didn't blink once.

"Bitch," he muttered, then felt guilty because he was talking about the woman he still loved. At least, he still loved her in the part of his heart that wasn't hating her right now.

The thought of spending any more time in the apartment was oppressive, and he considered putting on his sweats and going for another run, but gravity and fatigue won out and he sank down into the couch in the front room. Michelle's departure still had an air of unreality to it, as if she might still come home and point to a hidden camera and tell him that the whole thing had been a gag.

It wasn't even five, but the room was already growing dark. He lay back and closed his eyes. After a few minutes, he rolled over, to make himself more comfortable for a nap, and felt something press into his side. He dug into his jacket pocket and winced.

The little ring box.

That made him too agitated to sleep. He went into the kitchen and fixed himself a bowl of cereal and then he returned to the couch and half-watched several hours of TV. He didn't care what was on, as long as the noise covered up the apartment's silence, and helped drive bad thoughts from his head.

He had finally dozed off when—over the racket of a commercial— he barely heard his cell phone ring. Scrambling, heart pumping, he found the remote and killed the TV.

When he flipped his phone open, a woman's voice came on the line and he was flooded with relief.

"Michelle?" he said. "Are you okay?"

But it wasn't Michelle.

It was Maureen Duffy.

CHAPTER *thirty-five*

I'm on the corner," he said into his cell phone half an hour later. "Are you standing by?"

When the girl replied in the affirmative, he set off jogging down the block, still holding the phone up to his ear. He wanted to scan the street, but forced himself to keep his head down, tucked inside the hood of his sweatshirt. He pushed a pair of non-prescription eyeglasses higher on his nose and hoped that the getup would serve to fool the two meatballs he had met in front of Duffy's apartment, if they were waiting outside her friend's place now. (When he bought his exercise outfit, he had been concerned with Linda Vargas's comments about the embarrassing nature of Spandex; he had never considered its suitability as a disguise. Thankfully, the baggy clothes concealed his shoulder holster as well as his private parts.)

The street was lined with three- or four-story brick apartment buildings. Out of the corner of his eye, he noted an address, then counted down to Duffy's hideout. Without pausing, he jogged briskly up the stoop, took out his keys, and pretended to insert them into the front door. "Buzz me in," he said into the cell phone. With a little luck, he would look like some resident returning from an exercise break.

Duffy was on the third floor.

"Why all this secrecy?" she asked as soon as she opened the door, but he ignored her; the doorway opened into a front room, and the lights were on, and he headed straight for the switch. He turned it off, then made for the windows, cursing as his shin barked a coffee table. Carefully he opened a space between two blinds. The street was dark, save for pools of light under the well-spaced streetlamps, and it was impossible to see into all of the parked cars. No one was out in front of the building, though.

Jack turned back to the girl. "I could've shown up with a lot of noise and flashing lights, and that would have just scared off your friends, and then where would we be? I want a chance to find out what's going on." He didn't mention that he was handling this case strictly off duty, and that bringing in the troops would have given him a lot of explaining to do. "Let's talk in the back," he said. They made their way down a narrow hallway, and she turned on a light in the kitchen, a space barely big enough for a little table and a couple of potted plants. Jack noted a bunch of bright children's drawings plastered on the fridge. *Hapy Birdy!*, one of them said.

Duffy sat down. She was wearing a tight Hunter College T-shirt and a pair of basketball shorts, white satin with blue trim. Hardly January attire, but the apartment was hot and stuffy. The girl's outfit left little to the imagination; Tommy Balfa had risked his marriage for this. Was this all it had taken with Michelle, some moment of opportunity like this, some momentary excitement that could justify ruining months of a deep relationship?

"Who owns this place?" Jack said.

Maureen pushed a lock of red hair out of her eyes. "It's a friend's. She's out of town."

He leaned back against the sink. "Did you actually see someone coming after you?"

Maureen frowned. "Yes. There were two of them. I didn't get a good look so I don't know if it was the same ones, but they were definitely following."

"What did you do?"

"I know the man at the deli around the corner from my place, this nice Egyptian guy, and he let me go out the back way. I didn't want to go home again, but luckily I had these keys with me."

"Did you see anybody after that?"

She shook her head. "No, but I had a *feeling*, when I was on my way over here."

"Why didn't you just call the cops?"

She stared. "That's what I did. *You're* a cop, right?"

He ignored the question. "Are you sure there isn't something you want to tell me? Like why these guys might be after you?"

She shook her head again. "I swear. I don't know why anybody would be interested."

Jack didn't say anything for a minute, hoping the awkward silence might prompt her to open up, but she stayed mum. "Well," he finally said, "it looks like there's a good lock downstairs, and a decent one on the front door here, so you should be all right."

The girl grabbed the bottom of her T-shirt and twisted it nervously. "There aren't any bars on the windows, and there's a fire escape in the back."

Jack sighed.

He thought of the empty apartment waiting for him at home.

THE SOFA BED IN the front room had a bar in the middle that jabbed into his back, and the radiator was so hot that the place was stuffy even with the front windows cracked, but Jack barely noticed.

Every few minutes he pushed the rumpled sheets off his body, got up, and padded to the front window. Nothing to see, for now . . . His thoughts inevitably returned to Michelle, and they were so painful that he started to actually welcome the idea of an attack on the apartment, as a diversion.

He lay back down, settling onto the creaky bed and trying to avoid the middle bar. After a while, he drifted into a weird fantasy. There'd be sirens. Another terrorist attack, something big, and he would call Michelle, and go and fight through traffic and find her, on foot if he had to, and even though the event would be terrible, catastrophic, he would hold her and they'd be close again . . .

In the middle of the night, sleep finally put him out of his misery.

A HAND ON HIS shoulder jolted him awake.

"*Detective.*"

He rolled over, groggy. At first he thought it was Michelle, and he almost reached out for her, but then he remembered that he wasn't at home, and it was only the girl, her form indistinct in the dark.

"I think they're out there."

He rubbed his face. "Who? Where?" He swung his legs over the side of the bed.

"Out front."

He got up and moved to the window, skirting the coffee table this time. He stood in the dark corner, then pulled apart two of the metal blinds. There was a car across the street, parked, but with taillights bright. (Engine on for heat?) He sat watching for a minute. The taillights went off, but nobody got out. There was no way a person would sit out in that cold without a damned good reason.

"Shit," Jack grumbled. He returned to the bedside. At least he didn't have to get dressed; the sweats served as pajamas and street gear, rolled into one. He slipped his feet into his running shoes and picked up his shoulder holster.

"I'M GETTING TOO OLD for this crap," he muttered to himself as he knelt on the back fire escape and lowered its heavy iron ladder. One small security light shone over the back door below, and there were a couple of lights over some of the garages along the alley, but things were still good and dark. He clambered over the side and down the ladder, the rungs freezing his bare hands. The late night had a chill, cathedral hush.

He came out of the alley, turned the corner, walked fifteen yards, and peered around the next corner: Nobody around. The street-lights were ringed by rainbow halos. He took a deep breath, then darted across the street and slipped along behind the parked cars.

Ten yards away, he pulled his new service piece out of its holster. He was sweating now, despite the cold, and once again he couldn't help envisioning a cold, dank basement in Red Hook. After his shooting he had promised himself that he would stay out of trouble. It wasn't just that he had a son to think of—there was Michelle, and his oath that he would never put her through something like that again. What did that oath mean now?

He wiped his gun hand against his leg and took a few deep breaths—and noticed that his exhalations were puffing out white into the air. Easy to spot in a rearview mirror? While he waited for his breathing to calm down, he suddenly wondered if he had turned his cell phone off. He slapped at his thigh, then realized that he had left the phone in the apartment. What if Michelle tried to call him right now? But she wouldn't . . . The thought of her refusal to talk sent another bolt of rage through him, and he wanted to take it out on whoever was in the dark car ahead. As he came closer, its engine suddenly revved up. Jack flinched, but he stayed back in the shadows for a few seconds and the car didn't go anywhere. *The heater.*

Closer. He only saw one silhouette, from behind, in the driver's seat. As he crept forward, he peered down into the back to make sure. He stopped a couple feet behind the driver so the center post would give him a little cover and he wouldn't get caught by a rammed-open door. He rapped against the front window and held up his shield and service weapon. The man turned, startled.

Jack steadied his grip as he pointed his gun.

CHAPTER *thirty-six*

Outside a certain Carroll Gardens social club later that same morning, Jack saw—remarkably—young hipsters passing by, the same sort he had noticed in the nearby Thai restaurant where he had shared dinner with Michelle. These were not the sort of kids you could find on Manhattan's Lower East Side, not punk rockers or impoverished NYU students dressed in Salvation Army castoffs—no, these were comfortable-looking young professionals wearing expensive designer sneakers and smugly ironic trucker caps. *Hipsters*, on *Smith Street*.

The thoroughfare ran just a block away from the Gowanus Houses, for chrissakes, *the projects*, a group of huge redbrick hives that had long provided fresh cases for Brooklyn Homicide. The Heights had gotten gentrified, yeah, and Park Slope and Cobble Hill, too, but Jack never thought he'd see the day when real estate brokers could charge a million dollars for a humble brick row house around the corner from the projects. Now *there* was a mystery. And every week it seemed like another local business got forced out: a little bodega with its red-and-yellow awning, a botanica with statues of saints, a Chinese take-out place with Plexiglas windows in front of the cashier. *Good-bye, mom-and-pop*. In their places sprang French bistros and those kind of snooty boutiques that seemed to have only one rack of clothing in the entire joint.

He parked across the street and stepped out of his car. The club was a little nondescript brick storefront, no windows, no sign above. It was almost comforting to see that places like this still existed, some small tie to his past, before the area got fancied up with the name Carroll Gardens. Back in the day, this had all been brawling Red Hook, and such clubs were a dime a dozen. Inside sat some of the most powerful men in New York. There had been lots of them then, and they ruled the docks. Albert "The Mad Hatter" Anastasia, head of Murder Inc.; Crazy Joe Gallo and his gang; Joseph Profaci; Carmine "The Snake" Persico; the list went on and on. When Jack was a kid, such thugs had been dark powers in the neighborhood, the kind of men people didn't even dare talk about behind closed doors.

Now it wasn't just the old businesses that were on the way out; the waterfront kingdoms were waning, too. Not just because of the efforts of eager, career-building prosecutors like Rudy Giuliani, or the invasions of yuppies, but inescapable shifts of time and tide. The shipping industry had drifted away from Brooklyn. Gone were the days of infinite swag, when the mob and the longshoremen's union had diverted mountains of goods from the holds of vessels into local basements and the trunks of cars.

Which was not to say that the day of the dons was over for good. There were other lucrative businesses to infiltrate, and when the feds busted one they moved on to another. Gravel and concrete. Trash hauling. The Fulton Fish Market. And construction projects, the specialty of the man who owned this particular club, one John Carpsio Jr.

Last night, the man outside Maureen Duffy's had played dumb, but a computer check of his license revealed that he was a known associate of Carpsio, and the car had been registered to a Carpsio-owned business. Carpsio himself had been indicted twice, though never convicted. The first time, back in the nineties, had been for dealing narcotics. In the second case, he had been allegedly involved in a common type of labor scam in which contractors charged for providing union labor for a City project, though they actually hired illegal immigrants who were too scared to complain about their appallingly low pay.

Jack crossed the street. The social club was in the middle of the block, not far from a store window full of trendy baby clothes and a restaurant advertising "French-Asian fusion." The old metal door had a diamond-shaped little window cut in the center, blocked by a faded red curtain. When Jack knocked, the curtain slid aside. He held up his tin. Someone inside gave him the hairy eyeball, then the curtain slipped back into place. The door didn't open for another thirty seconds.

An old geezer wearing a beige leather sports jacket finally invited him in. Jack glanced around the tiny club, which resembled a basement rec room. Cheap wood paneling, an ancient jukebox, a bottom-shelf wet bar—everything overhung with a pall of cigar smoke. It was a dump. Jack knew the old-school mobsters didn't like to flash their money, and lived in modest neighborhood row houses instead of suburban McMansions, but still, it was depressing. Cops had to work out of cruddy precinct houses, crammed with drab furniture, glommed with institutional paint, but that was due to lack of funds. What was the point of making big money if you still had to surround yourself with *this?*

Three middle-aged men in athletic clothes sat around a card table in the middle of the room, and several other men, older, stood looking over their shoulders. A game of dominoes. The older men wore sporty tweed caps, jackets that might once have seemed sporty (epaulets, lots of zippers . . . *Member's Only*). They looked like the kind of old-timers who hung out at the OTB over on Court Street, cheering on the ponies. The twilight of the gods.

One of the men at the table stood up, walked over to the bar, and sat on a stool. He gazed up at a big-screen TV, which was playing one of those cheesy courtroom shows where ex-roommates duked it out over unpaid bills.

The geezer who had opened the door led Jack over for an audience. John Carpsio Jr. was a small man, trim, maybe mid-fifties, wearing bleached jeans and a blue sweatshirt. With his brushy gray crew-cut, wire-rimmed spectacles, and nondescript face, he looked, Jack thought, more like an unfriendly pharmacist than a gangster. (The kind of pharmacist who might boost his profits by substituting sugar pills for cancer prescriptions.)

The man barely acknowledged Jack's presence. His cronies over by the domino game studiously maintained their casual postures, but Jack could sense a tension in the air.

He shifted on his feet. Normally, standing while an interview subject was seated would give him a psychological edge, but not now. He was the odd man out. He glanced over Carpsio's shoulder. Up on the TV screen, a sour, unhappy-looking plaintiff hugged herself as she got smacked down, loudly, by the judge.

Jack frowned. "Why don't you turn that off for a minute?"

Carpsio, in the middle of lighting a cigarette, turned and stared; he clearly wasn't used to being told what to do in his own club. After a tense moment, he shrugged. His voice was gritty. "The noise'll give us privacy."

It was hard to argue with that. Round one: Carpsio.

The man reached over the bar and picked up a big bottle of Diet Coke. He seemed very calm. He was so calm, in fact, that Jack began to wonder if maybe he was mistaken about Carpsio's connection to the Balfa case.

No point in wasting time. "I bet you miss Tommy Balfa," he said, just to see if the man would twitch.

Carpsio didn't blink. "Never heard of him."

"I'm not here because of that," Jack said. "I know you didn't have anything to do with what happened to him."

Carpsio just glanced at the dominoes table, as if he was impatient to get back to it, then returned his gaze to Jack. "Who are you supposed to be, exactly?"

Jack took out one of his business cards and laid it on the bar.

Carpsio picked it up, then pushed his glasses higher on his nose. "I heard of you. You're that cop took the swim in the harbor."

Jack did his best not to react.

Carpsio squinted at the card again, then handed it back. "Leightner," he said, pronouncing it correctly, like *light.* "I know that name. You go to P.S. 27?"

Jack frowned. He *had* gone to that Red Hook elementary school, but the last thing he wanted was to discuss old times with this neighborhood blight. He felt a familiar tightness in his stomach: He realized what was coming next.

Carpsio blew a puff of smoke toward the ceiling. "I knew I remembered the name. I must've been two, three grades ahead of you. I'll tell you one thing: I sure as hell remember what happened to your brother. *Petey,* right? Terrible thing. They ever catch who did it? Couple'a niggers, as I recall . . ."

Jack couldn't help scowling. His brother's murder was something he never talked about, and certainly not with scum like this. Back when he was growing up, his father had always warned him away from such men. His father had been no prince—he had been, in fact, an abusive alcoholic—but at least he had been a hard worker. Exactly what these bastards were not, with their goddamn leisure outfits designed to show how they never had to lift a pinkie. They were just leeches, draining the livelihood of working families . . . He took a deep breath and rubbed the sides of his mouth; he needed to take charge of the situation, but he was coming perilously close to playing defense.

Carpsio shook his head. "Your old man should've reached out. There was plenty of people in the neighborhood who would've been glad to help. They would've caught those *mulignans*"—Italian for "eggplants"—"and taken care of them that same fuckin' day." The man suddenly squinted again. "What's this?" He was looking down, at Jack's shoulder. He reached out, and Jack forced himself not to flinch. The man picked something microscopic off Jack's sport coat. "Looks like a piece of lint, or something." He grinned.

Jack frowned. He wasn't about to be intimidated by some little two-bit gangster. This was no Joe Profaci, no Carmine Persico. Carpsio was just a neighborhood asshole running small-time contracting scams.

"I'm not here to shoot the shit. I want you to lay off Maureen Duffy. She's just a kid—a goddamn *nurse*, for chrissakes—and she needs to be left out of whatever's going on here."

Carpsio shrugged. "I don't know where you're getting your information, but somebody's been yanking your chain."

Jack was about to protest when the front door of the club swung open and in walked a beefy man who looked like a football linebacker gone to seed. One of the two thugs who had tried to come up on Maureen Duffy the other day. The punk pulled up short when he noticed the detective.

"Nice to see you again," Jack said.

The man colored, then hurried across the room and ducked out through a door behind the bar.

Funny how the tide of an interview could turn in a second. Jack looked at Carpsio and shook his head. "Now—what were you saying?"

Carpsio didn't say anything for a moment. He glanced up at the TV, took another deliberate sip of his soda. He turned back to Jack with a new businesslike air. He patted his chest. "You mind if we check you out a little?"

Jack shrugged. "Go ahead."

Carpsio called over one of the men from the card table, who gave Jack the most thorough frisking he had ever received, checking for a transmitter under his shirt, all through his jacket lining, even inside the cuffs of his slacks. "He's clean," the man concluded, and returned to his seat.

Carpsio nodded. He pointed at Jack with his cigarette. "I'm gonna spell a few things out for you. This Duffy cooze is no angel. She was in cahoots with your dirty cop from the get-go, tryin'a shake me down." Jack started to say something, but the man raised a hand. "Even so, I don't have anything against her. There's just one little problem: She's got something that isn't hers. She gives it back, we're done. You wanna do a good deed, maybe you could talk to her, help her figure things out . . ."

Jack scoffed. "I'm not here to run errands for you."

Carpsio just shrugged. "Don't be so touchy. One hand washes the other. Maybe I could help *you* with something. Like this nutjob you've got running loose around the waterfront, whackin' people right and left . . . I know things aren't what they used to be, but I still got some eyes and ears down the docks."

Jack snorted. "I don't need any help. Leave the girl alone, or the NYPD is gonna drop on you like a ton of bricks."

Carpsio made a sour face of his own. "I already told you. She gives back what isn't hers, she goes her way, nobody touches her. You got my word."

"And if she doesn't?"

Carpsio let an unpleasant silence fill the room.

CHAPTER *thirty-seven*

I only have a minute," Maureen Duffy said, looking around nervously as other nurses and doctors bustled in and out of the front entrance of Long Island College Hospital. She wore her red hair up in a bun, and looked cute as ever in her green scrubs.

"Let's take a little walk," Jack said.

The nurse hugged herself. "It's cold out here."

Jack removed his coat, draped it around her shoulders, then led her around the corner. To the left, an ambulance zoomed up to the Emergency entrance. To the right, a couple of blocks away, the street ended at the waterfront, where a red tugboat was pushing a long black barge. Jack turned toward the water. The girl followed, reluctantly.

As they came closer to the harbor, a vista opened up of the lower Manhattan skyline. Always now, that stupendous absence . . . Jack pressed his elbows against his sides, trying to keep warm. He turned toward the girl. "You need to know something: I can't be around to protect you every night. And I can't call for a patrol watch unless you tell me what's going on."

Duffy chewed her lower lip, but remained silent.

Jack felt a band of pressure building up between his eyes. Tommy

Balfa had been a pain in the ass when alive, and he was proving to be a bigger pain now. Whatever the detective and Carpsio had cooked up, unless it somehow involved a homicide, it was outside his official purview. He considered taking what he knew to the boys over in the Organized Crime Division, but things would likely rebound in some unfortunate way, seeing as how he would be tainting the Dead Hero Cop. He rubbed his forehead, suddenly weary as hell. He didn't want to let Carpsio get away with whatever bad business he was up to, but he already had enough crap to deal with. Right then, he made a resolution: He'd make an end run around the NYPD and gift his information to Ray Hillhouse, ask the FBI man to keep his name out of it. Then he'd get back to focusing on his own goddamned job.

Meanwhile, though, there was this reckless young woman to worry about. "I just had a little talk with John Carpsio," Jack told her.

Duffy stayed quiet, but her somber green eyes opened wider.

"He says you've got something that belongs to him. My guess is it's just cash, or he wouldn't have let me know about it." He crossed his arms over his chest. "You have three options here. You can cooperate with me, tell me what's going on. Or you can cooperate with Carpsio. The third option is not very pretty."

Duffy still wouldn't talk, but he had her full attention.

"These guys will get to you eventually, Maureen. Don't doubt it. They'll hurt you really bad, or worse. You could try running, but I have to tell you that the track record of people who've done that is not very good. They'll catch up with you, and by then they'll be *really* pissed off."

He stopped. Duffy walked on for a few steps, then stopped, too. She turned away from him, stood facing the harbor, thinking.

After a minute, she turned back. "I don't know anything."

Jack sighed. "Then I hope you pick option two, or else one of these nights I'm gonna get a call and I'm going to have to come look at your corpse."

———

THE CHILL JANUARY WIND sent dead leaves skittering across the sidewalk, swirling after Maureen Duffy. Jack just stood and watched her walk away. He didn't know what game she was playing, but he knew she was in over her head. A man like John Carpsio would have no compunction about stuffing her battered body in a car trunk and dropping it off somewhere along the Belt Parkway.

The nurse turned the corner and disappeared. He glanced at his watch, though it was another day off and he didn't have anywhere he needed to be. The Seven-six house was only a few blocks away, but he knew that he wouldn't be able to focus on work. He turned toward the waterfront and suddenly a massive wave of loneliness swept all thoughts of Maureen Duffy from his mind.

Michelle, he wanted to shout into the breeze. He wanted to reach out and grab her shoulders and shake her. He wanted to strike her, or pull her close. He took out his cell phone and glanced hungrily at its little screen, wondering if he might have missed her call. He couldn't believe the business about an affair. Maybe that was just a smokescreen; maybe she had gotten cold feet, scared off by his sudden proposal. Maybe she was nervous about marrying someone who was so clearly already married to his job. Maybe she was worried he would never want to have kids. He felt a rush of sympathy. Maybe she was scared and lonely, too. Maybe he could help her.

Then he remembered what she had actually said. *I'm seeing someone. It just happened. It's nothing to do with you.* His fists tightened. She had betrayed him, plain and simple. How could he have been so incredibly, stupidly blind?

CHAPTER *thirty-eight*

Some bars had regulars; Tony B's had irregulars. Give me your poor, your huddled masses, your toothless, gimpy, weak of liver. A sign over the garish jukebox summed up the clientele: WE'RE ALL HERE BECAUSE WE'RE NOT ALL THERE.

The old dive was down near the East River, stuck like a barnacle to the edge of swanky Brooklyn Heights. Jack had always joked to himself that if he was ever searching for Popeye, this was where he'd start. The old sailor would feel at home here, with the life preservers hanging overhead, models of ships on the walls, dusty semaphore flags. Old photos and newspaper clippings recalled the waterfront's World War Two heyday, when hundreds of craftsmen built great navy ships and thousands of sailors roamed this shore.

Normally he came here only when he needed to consult one of his neighborhood informants. The snitch, a scrappy little bantam who went by the nickname *T*, was sitting under the fog bank that enveloped the bar, accompanied as always by his true love, Janelle, who looked like a bobby-soxer ravaged by crack. The little guy straightened up expectantly, but Jack just shook his head.

He had eaten some crappy lasagna at a pizza joint a few blocks away. After, he hadn't been able to face the thought of returning to his empty apartment, so he had just driven around aimlessly for a while, killing time, trying to keep his mind off his troubles. Now here he was, Tony B's . . . The bar was crowded. He took one of two remaining seats, over by the front window, which was made of glass blocks heavy enough to deflect a wandering punch or a tossed barstool. He ordered a Rolling Rock. Wrapped his hand around the cool green bottle, took a swig. He had never been much of a drinker, but tonight he was considering putting a dent in that reputation. It was hereditary, after all. He thought of his father on paydays, spinning like a tornado through Red Hook's waterfront bars.

The Old Man would certainly have appreciated Tony B's. For years he had made his living as a stevedore in Red Hook, hauling cargo out of ships. And then some bright mind came up with the idea of *containerization*: instead of using muscle to lift boxes from the holds, the shipping companies could stack their cargo in huge metal containers, which could be hoisted out by cranes and set directly onto railroad cars. For every twenty men who had worked the docks before, only one was needed now. Most of the work had moved to New Jersey, where trains could roll right up to the shore. The Old Man lost his job, and then he started drinking in earnest. He'd always been a scrapper, but how could he fight something as abstract as technology? He became a walking mourner of his own ruined life.

Jack had always sworn he would never end up like that.

He glanced at the other people huddled around the bar and—as if his own suffering had lifted a veil—he noticed the pain and loneliness in their faces.

Midway through his fourth beer, he started thinking about the night he had been shot. He pictured the other man who had lain dying on the basement floor with a bullet-torn mouth. This was the sort of thing he was supposed to come upon later, when he'd arrive with a group of fellow detectives and Crime Scene guys and everything was quiet and safe. Somebody would make a gruesome joke about the victim—"This guy must've drank like a fish"—and they'd all chuckle and be very calm and clinical about the whole thing. And he wouldn't have to think about how much pain that man must have been in before he died.

A woman took the stool next to him and leaned into the smoky yellow light. She was middle-aged. At first glance she seemed out of place in her businesswoman's suit. Jack glanced again. She was pretty attractive, but a touch the worse for wear. Her silk blouse was unbuttoned enough to reveal the edge of a satiny black bra. And deep, freckled cleavage. She reminded him of some star of the seventies, Joan Collins maybe, or that one who got famous for the scene where she went swimming in a T-shirt . . .

She ordered a gin-and-tonic. From her purse she removed a pack of cigarettes, tapped the end, and set it neatly along the bar's scarred edge. There was a precision to the gesture that spoke of many nights in many bars.

She turned to Jack. "Do you have a light?" Husky voice.

One look in her eyes and he could see that she wasn't so out of place after all. They said *There's something broken deep inside me, but I could fuck you all night long.*

He thought of Michelle again, and got angry at himself. Michelle was with someone else. Her choice. He didn't have to take her goddamn feelings into account anymore. Besides, wasn't it better not to depend on anyone?

The woman was waiting for an answer. He supposed he should say something smooth, something witty, but he'd never had the knack. He reached down the bar and scooped up a book of matches. She touched his hand as he lit her cigarette and it occurred to him that he might not have to say much at all.

"My name's Natalie," she said, her speech slightly slurred. Evidently Tony B's had not been her first stop this evening.

"Jack."

She held up her pack of smokes. "Would you like one?"

He hesitated. He imagined the nicotine reaching out to him, swelling into his lungs. He shook his head.

The woman took a deep drag of her cigarette. "So, Jack, what do you do?"

"I'm a detective. NYPD."

She sipped her gin. Smoothed her lipstick with a long-nailed finger. "That sounds like fun."

Some women had a thing for cops.

A Johnny Mathis song came on, "Chances Are." It was that kind of juke. Barry White was probably next.

They shot the breeze. She worked in a real estate office in the Heights—she gave him her business card, in case he was ever "looking." (Looking for what, she didn't say.) He bought her another drink. She drank it. Then she stood up and rested her hand on his for a pulse-quickening second. "I'll be right back. Don't go away."

He remembered a sign over the bathroom door: ONLY ONE PERSON AT A TIME. Natalie made him think about why the sign was needed. He thought about unbuttoning that blouse all the way, watching sweat run down between those heavy freckled breasts . . . A guy next to him laughed loudly, turned, and spilled his drink—some of it splashed on Jack's hand. He jumped up. All of a sudden, he wanted to punch somebody.

The man raised his hands. "Sorry, buddy. No problem, okay?"

"I'll tell *you* if there's a problem," Jack muttered. But he sat down, breathing heavily. He could feel the adrenaline cycling through his system like a red, live thing. How many times had he seen the aftermath of a moment like this? Too much booze, an unintended slight, a concealed weapon no longer concealed. A star-flash; a body splayed on a grubby floor. He gulped down the last half of his beer.

His father would have thrown the punch. He thought of the Old Man's rages, the way he'd come trudging back from the bars, seemingly calm, only to flare up like a gas-soaked rag at the slightest provocation. A piece of undercooked chicken on the dinner table. A giggle from Jack or his brother Petey. The anger had always seemed incomprehensible, but Jack understood it better tonight. It wasn't one little match that caused the fire—it was the heat of many matches, building . . .

Natalie came back from the ladies room. He could have sworn that she had undone another button on her blouse.

He threw some cash on the bar, stood up, and laid a hand on her shoulder. "Why don't we go somewhere?"

CHAPTER *thirty-nine*

ichelle Wilber turned the TV down so as not to wake Steve McCleod, who had retired to his bedroom early. (He liked to get up at five A.M. so he could visit the gym before work. She liked the results on his lean body, but didn't enjoy waking in an empty bed.) She sat there on his expensive leather couch, and dug down into the bowl she held on her lap, seeking the last few little clouds of popcorn buried amidst the hard, unpopped kernels.

She licked her fingertips, savoring the last taste of butter and salt. Steve's living room was dark, except for the big flat-screen TV over by the wet bar. (A true bachelor pad.) The airwaves tonight seemed dominated by so-called reality shows: people forcing themselves to eat disgusting things; people racing through airports and across foreign landscapes; housefuls of fake-titted bimbos and male models and second-string celebrities loudly failing to get along. Michelle's attention wandered.

She looked around the room, noticing piles of things in the dim blue light: clothes, junk mail, rental videotapes, CDs. Steve was certainly not a neat freak like one Jack Leightner. She winced at the thought, and then glanced toward the hallway that led toward Steve's room. In a little while she'd head back there, slip into his bed.

"Six-hundred-thread-count," he'd told her proudly about his bed sheets, an observation that was a little too metrosexual for her taste. There was nothing wimpy about him in bed, though. Maybe, when she came in now, he would wake up bearing the hardness he seemed perpetually graced with. Younger men. Maybe it was just the first flush of romance, though; maybe—if this kept going—things would slow down and get that usual relationshippy over-familiarity in the bedroom, like she'd started to feel with Jack.

There he was, intruding into her thoughts again. He'd been no sexual gymnast most of the time, but she *had* felt more comfortable with him, never self-conscious about her thighs or her un-plastic-surgeried breasts ... She frowned; just the other night she'd gone out for dinner with Eileen Leonard, a friend from work, and Eileen had warned her about getting moony about the past. Eileen had walked out on her own mate the year before, and now all she talked about was how great it was to have her freedom, to be away from that unsupportive, boring lump. They were sitting in a Thai restaurant—unlike someone else, Eileen knew her way around the menu—and she had caught Michelle glancing at her cell phone. "*No,*" she'd said, as if reading Michelle's thoughts. "*Don't even think about it.* What's the point? If you call him, he'll just be angry and mean, or he'll make you feel guilty, and the next thing you know you'll go running back. Listen—you made the break; you did what you had to do. Don't *engage* with him. Just let it go. He was never going to have a kid with you. Trust me. *Cops.* My sister was married to one and I know all about it." She rolled her eyes. "All they want is to go out drinking after work and be all secretive about their little cowboy-and-Indian games." Eileen's face gleamed in the restaurant's candlelight, fervent as if she were preaching. The thing was, sometimes it seemed as if she were really trying to convince herself. For all her vaunted "freedom," she hadn't actually seemed all that blissful the past year. Maybe there was something faulty with the notion that you could just leave all your unhappiness behind . . .

Michelle clicked off the TV and sat in the dark. As the night grew colder, Steve's radiators began to hiss; the apartment was dry and stuffy, pulling the moisture from her lips. Eileen had been right: She had escaped a trap. Jack would never have agreed to have kids. And now she didn't have to worry about growing old with an older man, someone so set in his ways, who never wanted to go out dancing, or do anything spontaneous. But he *had* been kind. And—when Jack wasn't totally absorbed by some difficult case—he had been more aware of her somehow than Steve McCleod, he of the six-pack abs and youthful libido . . .

She wondered if Jack and his colleagues might figure that she had really bailed out due to simple cowardice—to fears about becoming a cop's wife. (Especially, the wife of a cop who seemed prone to getting shot, dunked, etc.) She wished she could explain: That wasn't it at all. The fact was, it would have been all too easy for her to slip into that familiar role, the supportive wife. And it wasn't about Steve McCleod; not really. No, the reason she couldn't talk to Jack was that she simply didn't know what to say. There was no single obvious reason why she had done what she'd done. Things just hadn't felt right. Life was messy sometimes; you couldn't always put everything into words.

She pushed herself back into the sofa cushions and hugged herself, picturing Jack's stunned face in the restaurant, the last she'd seen of him. Her own face contorted, thinking of it now.

No. She had done the right thing, the only thing she *could* do. She was sure of it. Ninety-nine percent sure.

Ninety percent . . .

CHAPTER *forty*

J ack drove. A few blocks from the bar, he stopped for a red light on Henry Street, dense trees obscuring the street-lights above, nobody else around except a late-night dog walker disappearing down a block of elegant Cobble Hill brownstones. Casually, Natalie rested her hand on his thigh. There was nothing coy about it: They knew where they were going and what would happen when they got there. Jack glanced up: The light was still red. He glanced over: Natalie's half-open shirt gave him a view of her firm breasts.

A memory: his second date with Michelle. They were sitting on a picnic bench in his backyard, after lots of food and wine, and she leaned back against him. He inhaled her soft scent, slid his hands over her blouse . . .

Natalie shifted in the car seat, opening her legs; she wore dark, silky stockings. Her nipples pressed against her blouse like ripe berries. Jack was flooded with brilliant desire—it pushed everything else out of his mind, all his memories, all his worries. This was what he wanted: to be right here, right now, drowning in something sweet. To hell with Michelle; maybe *she* didn't want him, but *this* woman did. The light on the dashboard shifted and he looked up: green. Natalie kicked off her shoes, leaned back, legs open wide, one of her hands busy down below. He had to work hard to keep his eyes on the road.

Two minutes later, the woman directed him into the parking lot of what looked like an old factory. Judging by the careful renovation job and the expensive cars in the lot, he guessed that it had gone co-op. Natalie stepped out of the car in her stocking feet, carrying her high-heeled shoes with two fingers. Before he got out, Jack took off his pager and threw it, along with his cell phone, into the glove compartment. To hell with it: He was off duty and tonight he didn't want to be bothered.

There was a bright chrome elevator inside. Even before the door closed, Natalie pressed up against him and stuck her tongue in his mouth. She tasted gritty of cigarettes and booze, but he was too worked up to care. He reached down, lifted her skirt, grabbed her silky ass, pulled her close.

"How about a little nightcap?" she said as soon as they got inside her apartment.

Jack nodded. He needed the drink. She probably didn't, but that was her business. He watched her zigzag over to a glass sideboard covered with bottles.

He sat down on a big expensive-looking sofa in the middle of her big loft living room, but then he got up and walked over to the picture window that dominated the back wall. Three stories down, the Brooklyn Queens Expressway channeled through south Brooklyn, separating this fancy brownstone neighborhood from working-class Red Hook; the highway was a river of streaming lights. The Seven-six house was just a few blocks away, with all of those detectives scrambling around their desks. Even closer was the hospital, where Maureen Duffy was probably in the middle of a shift. Farther west, over the dark rooftops, he could see New York Harbor, with the tiny lights of Jersey shimmering on the far shore. The apartment probably cost a fortune, but then he remembered that this woman was in real estate: She must have held on to a sweet deal. It was twice the size of his own apartment but it reminded him of the way his place had looked before Michelle came into his life: neat and sparse. The brick walls were almost bare and there was little furniture, as if the woman had just ordered the basics from a catalog and then called it a day. It was a workaholic's crash pad, not a home. A framed photo stood on a side table next to the couch; he bent down for a look. A smiling young man in a black graduation gown. Did Natalie have a son, too?

"Here we go," she said, coming at him across the white shag carpet. She leaned down to square a coaster against the edge of the glass coffee table. As she set down his drink, her freckled breasts almost spilled out of her top.

Another memory: how gentle Michelle had been with him that first time when he had just gotten out of the hospital . . .

Natalie planted her hands on his knees, leaned in closer and gave him a big sloppy kiss. She stood, unsteady on her feet, and went over to a stereo in the corner. Put on an old Motown record. The Supremes: "Where Did Our Love Go?"

"Come on," she said, coming back and grabbing his hands. "Let's dance."

He resisted, thinking of Michelle again. He scowled at himself. He could do any damned thing he pleased, and who was Michelle to say boo?

"Come *on*," Natalie said, pouting in a way that was supposed to be cute.

He let her tug him to his feet and he halfheartedly pulled out some old ballroom moves. As soon as the song ended, he sat down and picked up his drink. Natalie scooted in next to him. Her skirt was half open. She hoisted her gin-and-tonic and drained half of it.

She leaned over to kiss him again, and then she nuzzled his neck. Her hand slipped down between his legs.

All he could think about was Michelle. What the hell was he doing? Did he believe that this woman could be a substitute for her, that any other body would do?

"What's the matter?" Natalie said. "Are you married or something?"

"No. It's just . . . I'm kind of tired."

She was clearly let down, but did her best to cover it up. She didn't look so wild anymore, just tired and lonely, hoping for a little human contact at the end of the day.

"I'm sorry," Jack said, and he meant it. He leaned back into the soft cushions and closed his eyes. He heard ice cubes clinking in her drink. He wanted to get up and head out, but didn't know how to make a graceful exit. He kept his eyes shut, embarrassed to find himself playing possum.

"Thanks a lot, tiger," he heard Natalie mutter. Her breathing grew slow.

Jack lay there in her apartment, still feeling the terrible weight of Michelle's disappearance in his chest, strong as ever despite the alcohol, despite this stranger's desire. For some reason, he thought of the little nun at the Tibetan center, of the way she had kept calm even after hearing of her friend's sudden death. Was it just some callous malarkey, or did she actually know something about how to deal with pain?

A minute later, Natalie began to snore.

CHAPTER *forty-one*

Don't take your coat off," was the first thing Gary Daskivitch said when Jack walked into the Seven-six squad room early the next morning.

"Why not?" he asked, glancing toward the coffee maker in the far corner.

Daskivitch frowned like a bear whose porridge had just been eaten. "It's our *G.I.* head case—he struck again. I tried calling you last night, and I paged you twice."

Jack felt a jolt of adrenaline, and then he winced as he thought of his pager buzzing away in the glove compartment of his car.

UN-FREAKING-BELIEVABLE.

He shook his head, then shook it some more. Half a block—that's how close he had come to the hideout of Robert Dietrich Sperry, just the night before. Life was so weird sometimes. If he had known, he might have prevented the latest attack. He might have caught the *G.I.* killer.

If.

The narrow, lopsided old row house was just down the street from Tony B's. The latest victim, one of the tenants, had the great good fortune to still be upright and breathing. Jack badged the uniforms who had cordoned off the front of the house, and then he and Daskivitch went inside to interview Jerome Konetz.

The first thing Jack noticed was a red smudge on the old man's forehead. Konetz had a belly the shape of a beach ball, with an ancient plaid wool shirt stretched over it. He also wore a pair of grubby khaki pants and some battered leather slippers. He squinted at the bright winter light like a nocturnal animal peeping out of its burrow. Jack sensed that he didn't get visitors very often. He seemed cheerful, though, you had to give him that, despite the blood-stained compress bandaged to the side of his head.

Jack rubbed his hands together as he stood in the tiny vestibule. He had been hoping for some heat inside, but was disappointed. He frowned at Konetz. "Are you sure you should be up and about?"

The old man shrugged. "I took worse than this in WW Two. And I'm not stayin' in no hospital. I could buy a car for what it costs for one day in there."

You could afford some heat, too, Jack thought, but he kept the observation to himself.

Daskivitch stepped forward, his bulk taking up most of the entryway. "Would you feel up to showing us where the attack took place?"

"It's back this way." Konetz led them down a poorly lit hallway, his slippers scuffing on the cracked linoleum floor. From a side table he picked up a black metal flashlight the size of his forearm. "Watch your step," he said. "I don't wanna get sued, especially by the goddamned City."

Jack and Daskivitch followed him down a steep staircase. A strong musty smell hit them and Jack thought of another basement, in Red Hook . . . and yet another one, on Governors Island. He was tired of basements.

Konetz's flashlight swung circles ahead, and then the old man reached up and tugged a chain. A dim bulb went on overhead, barely illuminating a narrow, wood-paneled hallway, floored by a moth-eaten white carpet. Jack sneezed; the place was thick with dust, compounded by plenty of fingerprint powder brushed on by the Crime Scene techs. He noticed a faint smell of urine.

"You own the house?"

Konetz turned. "I already told those cops last night. Don't you guys put your information on a computer? My grandson is a real whiz at that crap." He snorted. "The kid's got one of those little metal pegs in his tongue. I can't believe my daughter let him get away with it. You can get diseases from that crap, you know, some dirty biker tattoo joint . . ." He shook his head, then winced in pain and pressed his hand against his bandage.

The old man's rambling talk made Jack wonder if he was suffering some residual shock. He tried again. "Are you the owner?"

Konetz snorted. "Who, me? Not goddamned likely. I just rent the top floor. And I look after the place—the owner lives in Jersey." He shuffled halfway down the hall and stopped again. "You understand that this is not an apartment down here, right? I was just doin' the guy a favor."

"Don't worry about it," Jack said. He figured the tenant was pulling in a little cash on the side, renting out a basement room with no *Certificate of Occupancy*. No taxes, either. He noticed a red stain on the carpet. "This is where the man attacked you?"

Konetz nodded. He looked pale, all of a sudden, and Jack worried about his ability to stay upright.

"How did you meet him?"

The little man frowned. "It was a few days ago. I was at the bar down the street. Tony B's."

Jack's eyes widened. Sperry had the nerve to appear in public?

What if he had sat down next to the man by accident last night, when every cop in the five boroughs was hot on his trail? "Did you talk to him much?"

Konetz squinted. "He said he was new in town, lookin' for work and a place to kip. He told me his name was Rogers. Bruce Rogers." He made a face. "Jesus, if I had known he was some kind of *psycho killer...*"

Daskivitch held a pen poised over a notepad. "You didn't recognize his face from the newspapers?"

"I don't read much; my eyesight isn't so hot. They could invade the country or somethin', and I wouldn't find out about it till three weeks later..."

"Why did you come down to the basement last night?"

Konetz gestured toward a closed door. "I was gonna look for a sled in the boiler room here. A Flexible Flyer. You remember those?" He brightened. "They made a great old sled. You ever see that movie, black and white, with Orson Welles? What did he call that thing? *Rosebush,* or somethin'?"

"You were looking for a *sled?*" Jack asked, steering the little man back on track.

Konetz nodded. "Yeah. For my grandkid. My daughter says he's too old, wouldn't be interested in something like that, no batteries, no computer screen. I say to hell with it—if I wanna give him a sled, I'll give him a goddamned sled."

Over the old man's shoulder, Daskivitch smiled.

"So you came down here. Then what?"

Konetz shivered. "It was quiet, and I didn't call out or nothin', 'cause I didn't think the guy was around. That's his room, down at the end there. I was just about to open this door, and *Bam!* Next thing I know, I'm seein' stars. When my eyes cleared up, there he was, holdin' a chair leg or somethin'. He had this crazy look, like he didn't even recognize me." He grimaced. "I was about to ask why the hell he hit me, when he clocked me again."

"Did you fight back?"

The old man raised the big metal flashlight. "I got in one good lick, with this. I think I caught him on the arm. Then he hit me again, and I passed out."

"When you came to, he was gone?"

Konetz put a hand against a wall to steady himself. "No. I woke up because I felt somethin' on my face. I didn't know what the hell he was doin', so I kept my eyes shut." He reached up and touched his forehead. "It wasn't till they brung me to the hospital that I found out that he had *written* on me. Creepy bastard."

Jack nodded, picturing the two red letters. And he thought of the way he himself had played possum the same night, over at Natalie's place. Weird. "Why did you wait until one in the morning to call nine-one-one?"

Konetz shook his head, winced. "I passed out again. Didn't come to for a while . . ."

"Did you hear anything while you were still conscious? Did he say anything?"

Konetz grimaced. "He didn't say anything, but I heard somethin'. I'm not sure, but I think the guy was *crying*." He shook his head, and trembled. "I'm just glad I kept my eyes shut. If he saw I was still alive, I think for sure he would've killed me."

THE ROOM DOWN THE hall, the one where Sperry had been staying for the past several days, was dismal. It was stuffed with crap: a bed frame, cardboard boxes, a cane chair with a ruptured seat, piles of faded newspapers. This jumble had been shoved aside just enough to make room for an old cot. The source of the urine smell was revealed: a pail in the corner. (Evidently the nonapartment had a nonbathroom.)

Jack shook his head. "This doesn't make sense."

Daskivitch was poking around by the cot, nose wrinkled against the smell. "What?"

Jack eyed the grubby hideout. "I understand why Sperry wouldn't go back to his place in New Hampshire, since that's been in the papers. But he could have gone anywhere in the whole country to hide out, in a lot more comfort than this. New York is an incredibly risky place for him to be. Why in the hell would he stick around?"

The answer came in just nine hours.

CHAPTER *forty-two*

The fact was, Jack was sick and tired of Robert Sperry. The man wasn't some diabolical serial killer. He had really only killed once in premeditation, and that was possibly a quote-unquote mercy killing. The other times, Sperry had felt threatened and cornered, and he had lashed out. He wasn't an active murderer, seeking victims out; he was more like a hidden rattlesnake, or a human land mine. He was a sad mess, and he needed to be stopped, but Jack wished he had never been called onto the case. He had his own problems to worry about.

After leaving the latest crime scene, he and Gary Daskivitch stopped at a local deli for coffee. Jack had just settled into the passenger seat of the young detective's car when Daskivitch said, "Hey, do you and Michelle wanna go out to Sheepshead Bay with me and Jeannie next week? We were thinking about checking out one of those Italian restaurants on the water." The big kid set his drink in a cup holder, put the car in gear, and swung out onto Atlantic Avenue.

Jack sat in silence. Daskivitch's wife was the one who had originally set him up with Michelle. The women were friends. Evidently Michelle had not told her about what had just happened. Was she embarrassed? Was she ashamed?

"Jack? You in there?"

He roused himself. "Sorry. I was still thinking about Sperry."

"So whadda you think? A double date?"

Jack sipped his coffee, scrambling for words. "I'll talk to Michelle about it. We'll get back to you."

He flushed and looked away, out the window, at a woman in a bright knit cap pushing a baby stroller down the sidewalk.

FOR THE REST OF the tour, a blot of shame and dismay spread through his chest. The afternoon went by in a daze; typewriters clacked in the background of the Seven-six squad room, phones rang, reports came in of the canvassing effort up and down Jerome Konetz's block, but Jack couldn't focus.

After work he went home and lay down, but couldn't sleep. He was wired, uneasy, as if he had drunk a gallon of coffee. For the first time, he peered around his stubborn secret hope and saw that Michelle might be gone for good. Unwanted feelings writhed in him like cats in a bag. It wasn't just that he missed her, their time together. His future had disappeared. For fifteen years after his first marriage, he had grown used to his return to bachelorhood, thought he was comfortable with it—and then Michelle had shown him how much he was missing.

He needed to escape, but he didn't know where or how. He thought of Natalie. He could return to Tony B's, pretend he was there to interview the patrons. Maybe she'd be sitting there at the bar, tapping her cigarettes against the scarred wood. Maybe he could drink enough to ask for a second chance. He shifted in his bed, knowing how little that would relieve his torment. He thought of calling his son, but again, he didn't want to have to admit that Michelle was gone. He thought of going back to work, maybe scanning the Missing Persons lists again, but knew he wasn't up to it. He considered going for a run in the park, but realized that he could run around the whole thing a hundred times and never outpace the darkness creeping up on him. A mean red notion blossomed: Michelle's new lover was taking a hell of a risk, cuckolding a man who carried a loaded gun . . . One little trigger pull and the source of his new troubles would be gone . . .

He lay back, shaking his head. Too many cops had gone down that terrible dark road.

He remembered something he had seen in an arcade in Chinatown. WORLD FAMOUS DANCING CHICKEN, a sign had read, over a glass booth with a scrawny live rooster inside. You put your money in, and some music came on, and after a moment the chicken launched into a jerky, hectic dance. Tourists gathered, and they laughed and laughed. They didn't know the secret of the thing: that the bird stood on a metal plate that heated up, burning its wiry feet.

He lay in the dark for another half hour, tossing and turning, until a surprising calm face rose into his mind.

"THERE'S A POLICEMAN HERE to see you," the young woman said. She left Jack standing in the doorway of Tenzin Pemo's little office.

The nun looked up, face placid as ever. "Hello. Detective Leightner, is that right?" That British accent, again.

He nodded, standing there awkward, like a kid called to the principal's office. "I wanted to tell you that we're going to be moving forward soon with the prosecution of the youths who committed the crime against your, um, coworker."

The woman nodded. "I know. Someone from the district attorney's office called the other day."

"Oh." Jack's face fell.

"Did you come all the way over here to tell me that? That's very kind of you."

He cleared his throat. "I wanted to apologize, too. For what I said the last time I was here."

"That's quite all right." The nun smiled.

Jack didn't smile back. He just stood in the doorway.

The nun stared at him, and he felt that she was looking straight into his miserable soul.

"Tell me something," she said. "Did you drive? I hate to trouble you, but I'd be grateful if you could give me a lift."

"I guess I could do that," he said stiffly. "I'm not actually on duty right now."

She gathered her scarlet-and-yellow robes and stood up. "Thank you. I just need to grab something and I'll be right back."

Jack stepped aside. While she was gone, he contemplated the sign on the office wall. EITHER WAY, YOU DON'T HAVE TO WORRY. He scowled. It made less sense than ever.

A few seconds later the nun reappeared, wearing a pink wool coat—surprisingly un-nun-like—and carrying a Tupperware container. "I need to drop this off for a sick friend down near the Manhattan Bridge. It's matzoh ball soup. That's an ancient Tibetan remedy." When Jack didn't reply, she smiled and shrugged. "Perhaps my delivery could be improved upon, detective, but that was something of a joke."

THE EVENING WAS SURPRISINGLY warm and the air was dense, foretelling rain. The avenues shone with a special richness, streams of headlights, splashes of neon. Jack didn't say much on the drive to the waterfront. The nun questioned him a bit about the details of the prosecution, with a special concern about what would happen to the attackers if they were convicted, but eventually she, too, fell silent.

Soon they found themselves in DUMBO, the odd, near-empty old neighborhood between the Brooklyn and Manhattan bridges. A few of the streets were still cobbled; they floored dark canyons between warehouses and industrial buildings. Some artists had moved in, taking over factory lofts, and now developers were starting to capitalize on the neighborhood's new hipness; they were gutting buildings and installing high-ceilinged condos with river views. On a night like tonight, though, it was hard to believe that these desolate, shadowy blocks would ever really come alive.

"Right over there," the nun said, pointing to a brick apartment building tucked between two colossal warehouses. She lifted her soup container. "If you wouldn't mind waiting, I'll just run this up."

Jack nodded, and settled back in his seat. A memory rose: He and Michelle had come down here one weekend afternoon because she had read about a fancy new chocolate shop in some magazine. He'd laughed at the orgasmic look on her face as she bit into some delicate, pricey little concoction ... He sighed and closed his eyes. Was this what he was condemned to now, running into her ghost all over town? His love for her was like a terrible worm, burrowing into his chest—he wished he could dig in with his bare hands and rip it out.

A few minutes later, he was startled when the nun suddenly appeared at his window.

"It's a lovely night, detective. Would you have time to take a short walk down to the river?"

Jack stared at his hands on the steering wheel. The nun had not asked him what he wanted, but she seemed to sense that he had some hidden agenda. And what was it? What was he doing, a homicide cop from Red Hook hanging around with a freaking Buddhist nun? He was tempted to say that he had somewhere to go—but then the worm would just keep churning away inside. *Hell*, he thought— he asked people for advice every day, experts on ballistics, organized crime, medical pathologies ... Why not her? Who else did he have to turn to?

He sighed. "I guess I don't have anywhere I need to be."

When he shut the car door, the sound echoed in the narrow street. There wasn't another soul about. High above, the massive blue base of the Manhattan Bridge arced into the night like some awesome prehistoric monument. Jack and the nun set off toward the river. A thunderous shuttling overhead, a subway train rocketing toward Manhattan, obviated the need to talk. When the sound died down, the nun broke the resulting hollow silence.

"What's on your mind, detective? Is it something about my colleague's death?"

He didn't look at her. "Not really. I was just thinking about what you were saying the other day. About not having to suffer and all."

She kept her own face pointed neutrally ahead. "What made you think of that?"

He flushed, and was glad of the dark. He walked another half block before he finally answered. "I guess my interest is not just professional."

She looked at him with concern. "Did something happen?"

He shrugged, awkward. "Nobody died, or anything. It's nothing major."

"A personal matter?"

He lowered his head. He didn't want to talk about it. He *needed* to talk about it. He almost had to reach in and pull the words out of his throat. "It's just . . . my, ah, my girlfriend walked out on me. She said she's been seeing someone else."

The nun stopped. "I'm very sorry to hear that. When did this happen?"

Jack shrank into himself. "Just a few days ago. New Year's Eve, actually." He managed a sickly grin. "She did it right after I proposed."

The nun winced. "Not very good timing, I must say." She sighed. "That's quite fresh. To be honest, I don't know if there's anything an old woman can say right now that would provide much consolation." She gestured forward. "Shall we walk?"

He nodded and they continued on, strolling with hands in pockets through the moist night air. When the nun spoke again, Jack thought she might launch into some religious platitude, but she surprised him.

"I was a rather unattractive girl."

He tried to think of something diplomatic to say, but she cut him off.

"Such were the facts. Boys never paid much attention to me. I'm afraid, though, that I grew up on a steady diet of books about romance. You know how it is. The heroine is kind, but rather plain. The hero falls in love with a prettier girl, but at the end he realizes his mistake and comes back for the ugly duckling. He swears he'll love her unto death." She scoffed. "My husband made the same promise."

Jack nodded. "You mentioned something about being married."

"Indeed. I was twenty-one, and I thought all my days of loneliness were miraculously over. He was a young engineer in my father's office, and he came along and swept me off my feet, just like in the fairy tales. And we were happy, for a number of years. At least, I thought so."

An SUV came rumbling down the cobbled street, blasting heavy dance music. Jack watched it go, then turned back to the nun. "What happened?"

She made a sour face. "One day I discovered that my husband had been having an affair with my father's secretary. For over a year. Very attractive little swan, that one." She looked at Jack. "I suppose you know what that feels like."

He grimaced. "Damn right I do. It's like she yanked the rug right out from under me."

"And now you have no place to stand?"

He nodded.

"You probably think that's a very bad place to be. You wish you could get back into your relationship, or find a new one, or find something that would take away this groundless feeling. Am I right?"

He thought it over, then nodded again.

"Do you remember that story I told you about the problem on the subway? About how you can think of it as an opportunity?"

He made a face. "What, you're going to tell me that suffering will make me a better person? No offense, but that doesn't feel like a lotta help right now."

They came upon a busy little bar, stuck between two buildings like some sudden desert outpost. Two young men stumbled out the door, lighting up cigarettes. Jack and the nun walked on in silence for a moment.

"Let's back up a bit," she finally said. "My husband ran off with his secretary. Why don't you tell me where the problem is?"

He snorted. "That's no toughie. Your husband was a louse."

She smiled. "Despite my spiritual perspective, I'm tempted to agree. But he wasn't really the problem."

Jack's eyebrows went up. "How do you figure?"

She pulled the collar of her coat tighter against her neck. "Let me tell you what I was angriest about. Among many things . . . I kept thinking about our wedding day. It was hugely romantic. We were married out of doors, on the coast near Brighton." She smiled. "In England, that is, not near Coney Island. It was a beautiful sunny day. Over there, that's worth a lot. I marched up the aisle, and I looked at my new husband-to-be, and I thought, *Now my unhappiness is over. Now my life can finally begin.*" She shook her head ruefully. "After he left, I kept looking back at that moment, when he uttered those vows. *To love and cherish; for better and worse; as long as ye both shall live* . . . I took that commitment very seriously. It was supposed to be so permanent." She sighed. "There we were, both *alive*, and he just walked away. I felt terribly betrayed."

Jack threw up his hands. "That's what I'm saying: The jerk left you."

The nun looked at him calmly. "Yes, but where was my anger coming from?"

Jack looked at her in utter mystification. "He was *cheating* on you. You had every right to be angry."

She shook her head. "The anger only comes from *inside*. And the sadness, and the loneliness, and all the rest of it. If I had seen that more clearly, I might have suffered a great deal less." She looked off down the street as though she were looking into her past. "It took me a long time to understand that I was not just angry at my husband. I was angry at the world, because it wasn't working the way I wanted it to. I wanted guarantees. I wanted permanence. True love, forever."

Jack frowned. "So how is that an opportunity?"

The nun considered him calmly. "Maybe your friend has given you a chance to open your eyes. To see the world more clearly. What lasts forever, detective? That's not the nature of things."

Jack remained silent.

The nun continued. "Everything changes, all the time, and everything that rises eventually falls away. In little more than a hundred years, everyone alive on this planet right now will have passed on. Is that a tragedy, or simply how things are?" She looked at him quizzically. "You must see this in your work all the time. I would imagine that you and your colleagues would get rather philosophical, no?"

Jack shrugged, sheepish. "Everyone thinks that, but talking about death actually grows old pretty fast. The fact is, mostly we sit around and jaw about what to get for lunch, or where to buy a good cigar. Anyhow, what's your point?"

The nun shrugged. "We can be like salmon, always struggling against the current, always fighting, always suffering because the world isn't the way we wish it was. Or we can accept the way the current flows."

Jack frowned. "You know, this is sounding kinda *dark*. I keep thinking about my father. He was the kind of man who would put a

little kid up on the mantelpiece and hold out his arms and say *Jump!*
And you'd jump, and then he'd pull his arms away and say *Tough
beans, kid—now you know how life works.*"

The nun shook her head. "What I'm saying is not nihilistic. Not
at all. We can work to increase happiness and to relieve suffering.
But first we have to understand where suffering comes from." She
brushed her hands together. "I've been blathering enough. I'm not
saying that some sort of intellectual insight will suddenly end your
pain. It's something you have to learn to feel, deep in your bones.
When you don't struggle against the way things are, you can discover that peace is here, all the time, waiting for you."

They rounded a corner and found a walkway into a waterfront
park. The view opened up, spectacular: the Brooklyn Bridge to the
south; the Manhattan Bridge overhead; the dark, gleaming river;
Manhattan's glowing honeycombs of light. And always, always now,
that terrible dark hole in the sky where the towers had so recently
stood. They stared across the river, neither of them saying anything.
Just a few months ago, Jack was thinking, he and Michelle had made
a terribly sad pilgrimage to nearby Brooklyn Heights, where somber
citizens had huddled along the riverside promenade to light candles
in front of impromptu shrines. Dripping wax, bouquets of flowers,
faces of lost loved ones blooming out of faded photographs . . .

He was ashamed. All of those people in the towers, all those girlfriends and boyfriends, fiancées and spouses, fathers and mothers,
suddenly wrenched out of their loved ones' lives far more brutally
than Michelle had ever left his. How could those left behind ever
deal with *that*?

Suddenly he felt a flare of anger. He turned to the nun and
pointed across the river. "What about that? What about what happened there? You don't think that's a tragedy? Like, *all those people
were gonna die someday anyhow*?"

The nun went silent, so quiet that he wondered if she would even answer his question. When she did speak, her voice was low. "That's not what I think at all, detective. I think about the men who did this terrible thing, and how they acted out of the most horrible delusions of ignorance, and anger. I think about how immense those delusions are in our world today. To be honest, I worry about how much we can do to fight them, to help people free themselves from such dark thoughts."

Jack turned back toward the water. He didn't feel angry anymore, just sad.

They strolled down to a rocky little beach at the water's edge. An occasional passing boat or barge sent wakes surfing toward it, their crests rippling silver as they caught the light.

After a couple of minutes of deep silence, the nun glanced at her watch. "I'm sorry, but I should get back to the center. I don't know if any of this has been helpful to you. It takes a great deal of time and effort to heal such wounds, and I don't expect that one short talk will make much difference. You might venture one little exercise, though: When angry or terribly sad thoughts come upon you, as I'm sure they must, don't fight them. Take a breath and look at them for what they are: just thoughts. Like everything else, they rise up; they fall away. You can just let them go."

Surprised by a surge of bitterness, Jack almost spit. "I wish I had never met her!"

The nun had started to walk away, but she stopped. "Do you think that your love brought you this pain?"

He picked up a stone and chucked it fiercely out into the water. "If I hadn't met her, I can't say I'd be dancing with joy right now, but I definitely wouldn't be going through this bullshit. Pardon my French."

The nun shook her head. "The pain comes from attachment."

He stared at her. "What, you're not supposed to be attached to people you love?"

"We use the word differently. *Attachment* is when you believe that something external will bring you happiness. It's when you say *I need you to make me happy. I need you to love me.* But love is something else. It's *I want to make* you *happy.*" She tucked her hands in her coat pockets. "I'll just say one last thing, detective: True love is *never* the cause of pain."

JACK MULLED OVER THE nun's words as they walked back to the car. He didn't know what to make of them, really. All this talk about things fading away—his own pain certainly didn't seem like it might disappear anytime soon. But there *was* something comforting about the woman, maybe just her calm presence . . .

Half an hour later, just after he had dropped her back at her office, his cell phone buzzed. Unfamiliar number, New Jersey area code.

"Detective Leightner? This is Gene Hoffer."

Jack stopped at a red light. "What is it?"

The Governors Island historian cleared his throat. "I've been talking with my wife. We'd like to apologize for the way we treated you the other day. And we feel that we may have given you a bad impression about our little group. If we can, we'd appreciate the opportunity to correct it."

Jack waited, puzzled, for the man to get to the point.

"We'd like to extend an invitation," Hoffer continued. "We're having a reunion of Governors Island alumni this weekend, and it's going to be a special one, the fiftieth anniversary of the group. We're holding two days of events out on the island."

Jack's blood went cold. "Is this something you've publicized much?"

CHAPTER *forty-three*

I know exactly how this plays out," said Gary Daskivitch. "We're all waiting for him to show up by sea, but he already knocked out a ferry worker or a maintenance guy and stole his uniform, and he tries to take us by surprise on land."

"Nah," said the young NYPD S.W.A.T. sniper sitting next to him, his black fatigues making him almost invisible in the dark room. "He takes the ferry with the other people in the reunion. He's dressed like a priest, and it looks like he's only got one leg, and he's on crutches, so nobody wants to give him a hard time about who he is. And then he gets on the island, and he unscrews a crutch, and he's got a rifle hidden inside it."

Daskivitch chuckled. "*Day of the Jackal*, right?"

"Both of you are wrong," said the fourth man in the room, a young FBI field agent. "He's got one of those folding kayaks, and he sneaks up to the island in the middle of the night. He's just about to land, when one of you S.W.A.T. bozos moves around and clinks your rifle against a wall or something, and the perp takes off."

The S.W.A.T. scoffed. "That Michael Mann flick. *Heat.* Yeah, I got a VCR, too." Jack heard him zipping up his collar in the dark; the minimally heated building offered little protection against the January cold. "So—who do you think kicks more ass: Pacino or De Niro?"

Daskivitch cracked his massive knuckles. "I don't know, but I like the fight card: Montana versus LaMotta."

Jack stirred in his chair in the corner. "Keep it down." The men were perched on the third floor of a brick building called Pershing Hall, on the northeast coast of Governors Island. The windows offered broad nighttime views. The southern tip of Manhattan, its skyscrapers crossword patchworks of light and dark, even though it was after midnight (late-shift office cleaners, hard at work). The piers of Brooklyn Heights and Red Hook across the way, with sparsely spaced security lights hanging over their long blue sheds. And the water itself, a black plain surrounding the islands.

"Ya know what I think?" the S.W.A.T. said. "I think he's gonna swim over in a scuba suit, and then he's gonna peel it off, and—"

"He'll have a tuxedo underneath," said the Feeb.

"James Bond," said Daskivitch. "*Dr. No.*"

"Actually, I think it was *Goldfinger.*"

Jack frowned. He had heard this sort of jocularity on stakeouts for years, and he knew it helped to cover nerves, but still—he wasn't in the mood. His young colleagues had never had to watch a partner get shot in the face. And they had never taken bullets of their own. This was definitely not a game. Tomorrow sixty Governors Island army alumni would land here on the island, many of them with wives and children in tow, and he hated to think what Robert Sperry might have in mind. If revenge—as somebody once said—was a dish best served cold, the man had had a good fifty years to brood. So much for the notion that he was just a passive reactor . . .

The Feeb took his turn in front of a night vision scope, scanning the water for small craft. Another contingent of task force members was camped out in the next room, and a Harbor Unit launch waited around the southern tip of the island. If Sperry showed up, he wouldn't be the one to spring the surprise.

A cell phone trilled in the dark. The Feeb fumbled it out of his pocket and turned it off.

"Jesus Christ," Jack muttered. "Put it on vibrate." He didn't like being the guy to put a damper on the festivities, but it had been a long twenty-four hours. He'd had to scramble to alert the task force and to arrange the logistics for their island trap. They'd had to plan it out carefully in case Sperry was watching. In the early morning, they'd sent a number of Canine Unit teams to scour the island in case he was already there, and then—when they'd ascertained that the grounds were clear—they'd brought the task force in under cover of night. Everything had to be set in place, hidden away for the next day's reunion, because they wouldn't be able to move about in daylight.

Jack sighed. Things would have been a lot easier if Hoffer had given him more notice of the reunion, but then he had never explained exactly why he was interested in Sperry. He had been in New Jersey to get information, not to give it, and his visit had been cut short by Hoffer and his wife. The historian, amazingly, still didn't seem aware of Sperry's recent notoriety. Maybe his ignorance wasn't so surprising: The man lived out of state, and even in New York the story had slipped to the newspapers' back pages. All anybody wanted to talk about these days was terrorists in turbans.

Jack took a turn at the night scope. A bright moving light caught his attention as it slid across the water, but he soon saw that it was attached to a barge, and moving toward Staten Island. He scanned the rest of the dark harbor, and sighed again. Opinion had been divided over the wisdom of allowing the reunion to proceed in the first place. He had voted for forcing the group to cancel, but Sergeant Tanney and Ray Hillhouse's Feeb bosses were so eager to catch their target that they had overridden any objections. And they had decided not to inform the reunion alumni of the risk. Tanney was in full John Wayne mode. "Don't sweat it," he'd said. "If Sperry is going to come over, he'll do it in the middle of the night, before any alumni even arrive. And we'll be more than ready for him."

BY MORNING, THOUGH, THEIR quarry had still not shown up, and all the members of the task force were on edge. Jack had managed to catch only a few hours of rough sleep on a cot set up in the other room. First thing in the morning, he found Sergeant Tanney in the improvised command center, an office on the second floor, looking similarly sleep-deprived. Jack didn't bother reminding his boss of his assurances that Sperry would have been caught by now; Tanney looked jittery and insecure enough as it was. (For the hundredth time, Jack wondered how the man had managed to get his current job. Undoubtedly, he had some kind of hook down at One Police Plaza: a relative, a favor owed . . .)

The reunion ferry arrived at 10 A.M., bearing sixty adults and thirty kids. Jack stood on the landing watching the excited families pour off the boat in their down jackets and knitted caps, with their fanny packs and comfortable sneakers. They were already holding up cameras and clicking away. As they tromped en mass up the road toward Pershing Hall, he heard them exclaim about how little the island had changed. (For some, this was their first visit back in almost fifty years.)

Jack found Gene Hoffer in the middle of the crowd. The man did not look happy.

"I need to talk to you." He pulled Jack aside, but waited until the crowd had moved on past the fort's heavy earthen embankment before he spoke. "Since I retired, I don't read the newspapers anymore. But I happened to mention Robert Sperry to some of the folks on the boat just now, and a couple of them informed me that he's been in the news recently." He frowned. "Which is more than *you* took the trouble to do."

Jack scratched his cheek. "As I remember, our conversation at your house ended rather abruptly."

Hoffer, forced to concede the truth of the remark, stared sourly out at the harbor. "I've already apologized for that. Let's focus on the issue here. Unless you people have already taken Sperry into custody, I don't imagine anyone knows where he is. I'd like to know if you can guarantee the safety of our group."

Jack did his best to keep a poker face. "We haven't caught up with him yet, but I can give you some good news. Since September, the government has headquartered a special anti-terrorist task force here. They're actually in the same building you're meeting in. Their job is to watch the harbor, but I've instructed them to keep a special eye out for Sperry." He patted Hoffer reassuringly on the shoulder. "I would say that Governors Island is probably the safest place your group could be right now."

Hoffer looked somewhat mollified. "And you'll be here?"

Jack nodded. "I'll be with you the whole time." Hoffer moved to rejoin his group, but Jack called him back. "Mister Hoffer—I want your people to be able to relax and enjoy themselves, so let's just keep this information to ourselves."

THE LIFE OF A rookie cop was 2 percent terror and 90 percent boredom. Most of the time, you stood around on corners trying not to think about how tired your feet were. You looked forward to meal breaks, kept an eye out for unexpected visits from your superiors, tried not to drink too much coffee. On rare occasions, you might suddenly find yourself chasing some perp down an alley and then everything narrowed into a jagged, adrenaline-fueled rush, but much of the job was pretty dull.

Today, the potential for sudden mayhem meant that Jack could never relax, but his time on the island still offered a heaping helping of banality. He was not much of a social animal. He had avoided his high school reunion, and had to force himself to get through parties and other social occasions. Now he was dropped into a crowd of complete strangers, all busy reliving memories he didn't share.

First they had filed up a staircase in front of Pershing Hall. Jack glanced to the right: The channel between the island and Red Hook was just a stone's throw away, its water reflecting back the dull silver of the winter sky.

Inside the Hall, everyone crowded into a Colonial foyer lined with time-darkened murals of scenes from various American wars. The adults proceeded to a registration table while their children ran around underfoot, excited by this unfamiliar new place. Then everybody filed into a mustard-colored lecture hall and sat under brass chandeliers while the organizers of the event welcomed them. They made speeches of reminiscence, packed with local references that meant nothing to Jack but got big laughs from the crowd. The group was middle-aged, gray-haired, bespectacled, but someone dimmed the lights and a slide show began; suddenly they were all kids again, riding ponies and bowling strikes, marching in parades and doing swing dances. Jack scanned the old photos for Robert Dietrich Sperry. He thought he saw that hawkish little face in a couple of group photos, but it was hard to be sure.

More recollections followed. He wandered back out into the foyer and flipped through a guestbook. Almost all of the alumni lived out of town; time had scattered them to Haverton, Pennsylvania, and Colorado Springs; Corvallis, Oregon, and South Bend, Indiana. He pulled out his cell phone and checked in with the team upstairs: no sign of Sperry. Behind him, the door to the outside opened and he swung around, instinctively reaching for his service weapon.

"Don't shoot," Ray Hillhouse said calmly. "It's only me."

Jack smiled. "If you're Robert Sperry, I must say that your disguise is very convincing."

"Sorry I couldn't make it here till now." The FBI agent had been down in Baltimore, working an anti-terrorism case. "Anything interesting happen yet?"

Jack sighed. "It's been slow. If I have to listen to one more story about kids tipping a cannon or throwing snowballs at a general, I'm gonna scream."

Hillhouse smiled. "I don't quite see you as the screaming type."

Jack smiled back. "You should see me when I look at my paychecks."

The FBI agent perched on a corner of the registration table. "So—you think Sperry's gonna make an appearance?"

Jack winced. "Just between you and me, I'm not sure. I'm starting to wonder if I might have sounded the alarm a little prematurely."

Hillhouse shrugged. "Everybody's been searching for this bastard for weeks now. This is the best chance we've had. I would've done the same thing."

Jack scratched his cheek. "I guess. Hey, listen—" He was about to start telling the FBI agent about Tommy Balfa and John Carpsio, but a sudden babble of voices from the lecture hall indicated that the morning's activities had come to an end.

"I better make myself scarce," Hillhouse said. "I'll see you later."

AFTER A QUICK BOX lunch, the alumni set off on a walking tour of the island. Jack had worried that they might want to spread out and explore on their own, creating a nightmare for the team assigned to protect them, but he might have guessed that his anxiety was groundless; they set off en masse, like tour groups everywhere.

Despite Jack's colleagues' jokes about mysterious strangers wearing priest's collars or other disguises, Gene Hoffer assured him that all present were well known and accounted for. In fact, the only stranger was Jack himself. He stayed on the fringes of the group, walking with Michael Durkin, the security supervisor.

"How have you been?" Jack asked.

Durkin shrugged. "Okay, I guess. I miss the old man. And it's been a bit creepy working here since that happened." He lowered his voice; he had been sworn to secrecy about the current operation. "I'll feel a lot better if you catch this guy."

The first stop was Nolan Park and its yellow officers' quarters. The alumni chatted blithely about old times as they strolled past the house where the security guard had been bludgeoned to death. Jack felt something cold on his forehead and looked up. A few snowflakes were drifting down, but they were hard to see against the dull white background of the winter sky. A chill wind picked up, but the weather did nothing to diminish the enthusiasm of the group. They were relentlessly cheery: Their kids were fantastic, their careers profitable, their retirements fun. It was like reunions everywhere, Jack supposed: These were the valedictorians, the club presidents, the joiners, and the family newsletter senders. The grumpier types like himself simply stayed home.

As the group walked farther south, snow started coming down a little heavier, swirling in the wind, whitening the view. Jack glanced back. A couple members of the team had disguised themselves as part of the island's grounds crew and were following at a discreet distance. He turned; another member was staying ahead of the alumni, a hundred yards away. The advantage of the island as a setting for this operation was clear: Anyone approaching the group would stand out immediately because there were no random passersby. For the same reason, though, maintaining an inconspicuous presence was difficult. Likewise, the snow made it easier for the team to trail the group, but it could also provide cover for a more sinister follower . . .

"What years were you here?"

Jack turned to discover a plump white-haired woman in a thick down coat walking at his elbow. "I'm not actually part of the group."

She looked puzzled.

"It's a federal regulation," he said. "Any visitors have to be accompanied by island security."

She bought this explanation without any trouble. "It must be very quiet, working here without all of the hustle and bustle of the old days. Like a ghost town, I would think."

"I'm just hired for the weekend," Jack said quickly. He didn't want to get caught up in small talk; he needed to stay focused on the bigger picture. He glanced down at his pager and pretended to read its little screen. "I'm sorry, I have to make a call."

She smiled. "It was nice to meet you."

He watched her move away in her puffy coat and he suddenly pictured the dead teenager in Prospect Park, the one Linda Vargas had called the Michelin Tire Man. The one with a blood-soaked hole in his down jacket. The image led to disquieting visions of bullets ripping into this friendly woman, and he looked around nervously, imagining Sperry running up one of these empty lanes, or popping up in a window of a long-abandoned barracks, firing wildly at the crowd . . .

"WE WERE *HERE*, MAN," said the S.W.A.T. to the young FBI. agent. "We did our jobs that day. And where were you guys, when that shit was being planned?"

"Keep it down," Jack said for the third time, looking across the dark room at the shapes huddled in front of their third-floor observation post. Having run out of jokes and the desire to tell them, the team was squabbling now, a bitter spat about who had failed on September 11. They were like kids grown cranky on a long car trip. It was inevitable—there was only so long you could keep it together with nerves stretched so tight. It certainly didn't help that conditions on the island were not conducive to overnight stays: heating provided by crappy generators, no running water . . .

"I hope one of you is keeping an eye on the harbor," Jack added. Nobody had expected that they would still be camped here. The reunion group had gone back to Manhattan for the evening, and Jack had arranged for as many security tails as he could, but there was no way to keep track of so many people dispersed all over the larger island, running off to Broadway shows, restaurants, bars. He just had to hope that Sperry's disturbed mind would seek out revenge on the site of his former humiliation. The group had one more day on Governors Island, and tonight was the last logical time for Sperry to show up.

Jack glanced at the faint glow of his watch. "Okay, let's start breaking this down into shifts. I'll go first; you guys get some shut-eye."

Nobody argued; the others made their way out of the dark office.

Alone, finally, Jack settled down in front of the night vision scope. Looking through its dark eye at ghostly liquid green outlines, it was impossible not to think of TV images of the recent raids on Afghanistan. Everyone was spouting off about the War on Terror, worrying about some massive new attack on New York. In comparison, the past efforts of one deranged individual seemed pretty marginal, but if Sperry succeeded in doing something bad to the whole reunion, even the most shell-shocked, dazed New Yorkers would sit up and take notice.

He did a complete scan of the dark harbor water, then turned toward the east. In contrast to the sleek glass-and-metal skyscrapers lining the southern tip of Manhattan, the Brooklyn skyline was caught in a time warp, most of its buildings still made of stone, their crenellated roofs providing a much lower, more modest line against the night sky. Jack played the scope over their facades, slipping into a bitter fantasy of catching Michelle and her new lover highlighted in green in some bedroom window, moving in unison in the dark.

There was no way for his mind to grasp what she had done. It was crazy. She had stuck with him through his long hospital stay, after he had explicitly told her that he didn't expect her to, that they hadn't known each other long enough, that it was okay to go. She had stuck with him through that horrible second Tuesday in September, when it had seemed that the whole world was falling apart. Why remain through those hard times, then bail out when everything was going well? What was she thinking? Her refusal to answer her phone, much less call him back, left him feeling as if he were dropping stones into a bottomless well; he couldn't even hear a distant splash. Maybe she simply didn't love him; maybe she was frightened of commitment; maybe she was having better sex with her new lover; maybe, the whole time he had known her, she had hidden a malicious streak; maybe it was his fault—maybe *he* had let *her* down . . . Without any response from her, there was no way for him to know.

He realized that all of the stress and tension of the past forty-eight hours had been a blessing, allowing him to escape from these tormenting questions. Now everything was quiet, and here he was again, running them over and over, like a mouse on a treadmill. He thought of the little Buddhist nun, and tried to share in her sense of acceptance and calm.

When his shift was over, he retired exhausted to a cot in the other room, but it still took him a while to find his way into sleep, made restless not by Robert Sperry, but the mystery of one woman's distant heart.

———

HOURS LATER, THE BUZZ of his cell phone jerked him out of sleep. (He had stuck the thing in his breast pocket so he wouldn't miss any emergency calls.) He raised his head, disoriented at first in the unfamiliar dark room, and then he pulled out the phone. An unfamiliar number scrolled across its bright blue face. He flipped it open.

"Leightner? How ya doin'?"

He frowned. "Who is this?"

"A friend from the old neighborhood."

Jack's heart rate picked up. In his sleepy state, it had taken him a moment to recognize John Carpsio Jr.'s gritty voice.

"What the hell do you want?"

He listened impatiently as the man took a drag from a cigarette. "You know," Carpsio replied, "my mother taught me that a little politeness goes a long way."

Jack growled.

"Relax," Carpsio said. "You did me a good turn, talking some sense into that stupid girl. Now I'm gonna do you one. That nutjob who's been giving you so much trouble? I know where he is."

Jack snapped awake. "Let me make sure I've got this straight: You're talking about Robert Sperry?"

"The one and only."

Jack grimaced. "Did you, uh, did you already 'take care' of him?"

Carpsio snorted. "*Please.* I'm a professional contractor and developer. You want *The Sopranos*, watch HBO." The man laughed at his own joke. "Besides," he added, "I know how much you cops love the glory. He's all yours."

"How do you know where he is?"

"I heard it from a friend. Very reliable."

Jack swung his legs over the edge of his cot. "You know where he is right now? At this moment?"

"That's what I said."

Jack thought for a few seconds. The last time he had answered a late-night tip like this, he had taken a bullet in the chest. "How do I know this isn't a trap?"

Carpsio scoffed. "Trap, schmap. Bring the Marines and the Air Force, see if I care."

"Just tell me two things," Jack said. "Where can I find him, and is he awake?"

CHAPTER *forty-four*

I t was before sunrise on a chill winter's night, but in The City
That Never Sleeps, cars were already making their way
across the Brooklyn Bridge toward Manhattan's sparsely lit
office spires. As the Harbor Unit launch plowed north below
it, Jack glanced back: The harbor was dark and misty. He saw the
Staten Island Ferry making a lonely trip out to the southwest, its
decks probably populated only by a few late-night drunks and night-
shift workers slogging home.

Ahead, strings of lights above the Manhattan and Williamsburg
bridges stood sentinel like rows of ghostly flares. They reflected on
the dark surface of the river in shimmering neon, rippling above the
muscular water currents. Currents Jack knew only too well; he shivered in the little cabin, crowded in with Mike Pacelli at the wheel,
Ray Hillhouse, one of the S.W.A.T. team members, and Gary Daskivitch.

In the middle of his call with John Carpsio, he had realized his
mistake: He had done an excellent job of bringing a team onto Governors Island, twenty-five of the area's finest law enforcement officers, but what he had not foreseen was a need to suddenly get them
off. (During the day, it would have been easy: They could have com-
mandeered the ferry over to the Brooklyn side. But that vessel was

docked across the harbor now, its crew sleeping comfortably wherever the hell they lived, and the only transport was Pacelli's small Charlie Unit boat.)

He peered up at the rapidly looming span of the Manhattan Bridge and shrugged. Maybe things would work out for the best. If Sperry had been sleeping, they might have had time to draw a big net around him, with boats and helicopters, armored units, the whole shebang, but the man was reportedly awake, and he would have been easily spooked. Jack was not familiar with the place, but he knew that the Navy Yard covered many acres. Like Red Hook, during World War II it had bustled with tens of thousands of maritime workers, but then suffered a major decline. The City had turned it into an industrial park, and was doing its best to revive it, but the Yard was still a sprawling complex of largely abandoned buildings, rusting machinery, derelict cranes, watery cul de sacs. So many hiding places, so many ways for one lone man to slip away. No—it was better to approach like this, by stealth, no thropping of helicopters or blare of sirens. On land, unmarked cars were already speeding toward the Yard to seal off the street side, and other harbor units were running north to close off the mouth of the basin.

"Can't you turn up the heat?" asked the S.W.A.T., speaking loudly over the throbbing of the engine.

Mike Pacelli frowned. "You think this is bad? I've been in here all night freezing my balls off 'cause I couldn't risk any noise."

Jack stepped out of the little boathouse and gripped the bow rail. The wind cut through the armholes of his Kevlar vest, and his face was occasionally slapped by icy spray as the launch bounced over a wave, but he wanted a clearer view (and a more settled stomach). Various images rose up—Michelle's stricken look in the restaurant on New Year's Eve, John Carpsio's smug face in the social club—but they whipped away like streamers in the wind. There was something to be said for rushing into a situation in which you might get killed: It freed the mind from other concerns.

The Manhattan Bridge slipped by far overhead and then, on the right-hand shore, four huge smokestacks from the power plant loomed up out of the mist, red aircraft beacons blinking at their peaks. The launch sped past, moving faster than Jack would have imagined possible, and then they were careening toward the Navy Yard. Pacelli slowed the engines to reduce the noise, and they slid into the shipping basin. Behind them, the skyline of Manhattan was growing faintly brighter, its glass and steel towers reflecting the first rose of the approaching dawn, but the launch might have been veering into a time warp. A number of long piers jutted out from the land, separated by narrow inlets; it was like sailing toward a big outstretched hand. The bright sodium vapor lights around the base of the power plant gave way to spotty single lights along the piers, and stark shapes loomed up along their edges: latticed gantries of loading cranes, topped by little high-perched cabins; hulking old warehouses; an ancient barge lying on the water like a huge beveled slab of rust. The era might have been World War II, or the Civil War, or some more primordial time. Way overhead, in the vaguely brightening sky, a jet struggled through the clouds, searchlights sweeping, like a lost bird.

A pyramid of gravel rose up on the far left pier; a row of squat white fuel tanks sat along the right. Dead ahead, on the end of one of the middle piers, two lights blinked on and off. Car headlights. As they came close, Jack saw a jeep with security markings. Mike Pacelli swung the launch around sideways and eased it against a row of old tires. One by one, the team clambered up over the edge of the pier, passing weapons—a shotgun and a semiautomatic rifle—up to their colleagues on shore, where a nervous Navy Yard security officer stood waiting. He had the soft look of an ex-cop with a cushy job.

Mike Pacelli started to clamber up, but Jack shook his head. "I think you should stay here."

Pacelli tried to argue, but Jack shook his head. "You'll see him if he runs for the water, and you can tell the other units where to go when they get here." He turned to the security guard. "How close are we to Building One-forty-two?"

The man pointed. "It's that way, a few buildings over. Maybe a quarter mile. You want to tell me what's going on?"

"We've got a report that a suspect might be holed up there. We need to get there fast." Jack frowned at the little vehicle.

"I can take a couple guys over and then come back," the security man said.

Jack shook his head. "We should stick together. We'll hoof it."

They set off along the edge of the pier, which ran beside a narrow inlet, their breath puffing out into the chill air. The day was breaking now, forms appearing more clearly in the swelling light: a round blue fuel tank, a jumbled pile of discarded machinery, a couple of old truck trailers up on blocks next to a warehouse loading dock. The next warehouse looked to be abandoned; its side was a checkerboard of dusty windows that gaped open in places, like missing teeth.

The men rounded a corner and came out onto a wider artery, a cobbled road lined with train or trolley tracks, which led past rows of factory buildings. Everything was eerily still in the dawn light; the place was like some radioactive ghost town. Breathing harder now, they came around the edge of a warehouse and skirted an odd feature, like a great stone bathtub set below the ground. Jack recognized it from his childhood days in Red Hook: a graving dock. Its walls were tiered stone, and they stepped down to the long rectangular pool, which was frozen over. As they jogged along the edge, he noted immobile waterfalls cascading down the sides, bundled ropes of milky ice. A row of wooden stumps rose out of the center of the pool, where—when the water was drained out—ship hulls had once come to rest.

The little team veered left, away from the dock, into an alley between two warehouses. The security man held up a hand and they paused, panting. Jack's T-shirt was damp with sweat beneath his winter layers and heavy Kevlar, but catching a cold was by far the least of his present worries.

"Okay," the security man whispered. "It's right around that corner."

"Do you know what's inside?"

The man shrugged. "It's an old abandoned shed. There's a bunch of heavy machinery in there, but I don't know the layout. No reason to go in, you know?"

Jack considered the man. "Why don't you stay here? You can keep an eye out in case he bolts, and radio for assistance if we need it."

The security man nodded, embarrassed but clearly relieved.

Jack peered around the corner. He was hoping for a small contained space, but the "shed" was a football field long, sided with more of those checkerboard windows, so dirty that they offered no view inside, at least not at this distance. Hopefully, they didn't offer much of a view out. It was hard to be sure in the thin dawn light, but it looked like there was some kind of loading dock about halfway down.

"What do you think?" Jack whispered to the S.W.A.T., who had more experience with this kind of sudden assault.

"I think Daskivitch should wait at this end. You and FBI there"— he nodded at Ray Hillhouse—"go see if there's an entrance in the middle. I'll hit the far end. When we're in position, I'll give you guys a high sign and we'll all go in at once."

Above the far end of the shed, a metal crane was already catching the first real rays of morning light. Jack pulled out his service revolver. "We better go in before it gets too bright out here. If we can, let's take him alive—I wanna know who that kid was in the box."

"Ready?" the S.W.A.T. said.

The others nodded, and then began to run.

CHAPTER *forty-five*

The S.W.A.T. went first, scuttling like a crab, below the banks of windows. Jack followed, trying to keep his head down, wincing at the thought of taking a bullet from his own captured gun. He glanced left as he ran, rewarded by an occasional glimpse through a missing pane: quick impressions of a huge open interior crowded with rusting machines. Ahead, he saw that the loading dock's big sliding door was down, but a regular door beside it was slightly ajar. A rusty tin sign hung above it: SAFETY GLASSES MUST BE WORN.

He reached the loading dock and slumped down beneath the edge. He thanked his recent park jogging for preparing him for the sudden sprint; when Hillhouse, the heavier man, dove down beside him, the FBI agent held his stomach and gasped for air. Jack glanced back at Gary Daskivitch, crouched at the corner of the shed, as hard to hide as a grizzly bear. Down at the other end of the shed, the S.W.A.T. had taken up a position behind the base of the old crane.

Hillhouse was wheezing. "You okay?" Jack asked.

The FBI man nodded, and released the safety on his shotgun.

The team exchanged thumbs-ups.

Jack took a deep breath, darted up a little staircase at the edge of the loading dock, ran across it, and paused outside the smaller door.

He listened carefully: *silence*. Maintaining a firm grip on his pistol, he reached out with his left hand and pushed very lightly on the door. *Squeak*. Jack gritted his teeth. He transferred the gun to his left hand, gripped the doorknob tightly, and lifted up on the frame, hoping the hinges would swing more freely. And they did, enough to admit him and his colleague without further complaint.

They found themselves in a narrow hallway. The air inside was musty, and probably ten degrees colder. From his glimpses in during his headlong rush outside, Jack had gathered the impression that the shed had one long open interior, but such was clearly not the case. The hallway was murky, but ten yards down light spilled in through open doorways on both sides. Just before they reached them, Ray Hillhouse tugged on Jack's sleeve. He pointed to himself, then the right doorway, then to Jack and the left.

Jack nodded. Carefully, he peered around through his designated entrance. A relatively small room, softly illuminated by light coming through a dusty skylight. Old green metal lockers knocked over and scattered as if by a giant's hand. A floor so deteriorated that scraps of linoleum were jumbled in piles that somehow made him think of raw tobacco.

Gingerly, he stepped out across the locker room floor and found another door, half open. He peered through, holding up his pistol. A big hollow skylit space, the machine floor. In one corner, a pile of red metal canisters (for acetylene torches?). In the center of the floor, a monumental piece of heavy machinery, its green paint peeling back to reveal a yellow undercoating, topped by a set of massive gears. (He had no idea what it might be for.) He heard a sudden fluttering. Startled, he pointed his gun up, only to discover a couple of disgruntled pigeons settling on a metal rafter.

Slowly, Jack stepped out across the gritty concrete, moving his gun from side to side. He peered around a pile of giant broken metal ducts. *No one*. He paused to wipe sweat off his forehead with the back of his nongun hand. He figured he must be halfway to Daskivitch now. On the right far side of the room, another open doorway . . .

Coming closer, he smelled smoke. And then he heard something, a low humming sound. *Human.*

Moving as quickly as he dared, he traversed the rest of the floor, feeling hugely vulnerable in the open space. He reached the side of the door frame and paused. The smell of smoke was stronger. He peered around. A big employee lunch room. Several long tables ran across the left side, and a bank of dusty checkerboard windows made up the right wall, brightening in the early sun. Several pigeons highstepped across the grimy green linoleum floor. One of them looked up and contemplated Jack, its little black watermelon pit eyes fixed on his face. He held his breath, praying that it wouldn't provide a warning to the white-haired man who stood in a far corner, holding out a hand to a trash-can fire. The other arm was bound in a sling—evidently Jerome Konetz had gotten in a pretty good shot with his flashlight before he had passed out in that Atlantic Avenue basement. Maybe this was why Sperry hadn't shown up at the reunion: Lifting a small craft into the water and navigating the channel's swift currents would be hugely difficult with just one functioning arm.

Sperry seemed to be singing to himself. Slowly, Jack raised his gun. He was about to shout at the man to get down on the floor when another door at the back of the room swung open and all hell broke loose. Gary Daskivitch began to come through. The pigeons flapped up toward the ceiling's water-stained acoustic tiles, squawking loudly, distracting the big detective. And Sperry didn't waste a second in surprise. He charged toward the door and slammed into a big metal shelving unit next to it, which crashed down, pinning Daskivitch on the floor. Sperry picked himself up and reached for something on a side table. Something that looked very much like a Glock-19 service weapon.

Jack lunged forward. "Freeze, goddamnit! NYPD!"

Sperry whirled around, wide-eyed, but again he didn't waste a second in acknowledgment. Abandoning the gun, he dodged around his flaming trash can and hurled himself against the bank of windows, which gave way with a crash. And then he was gone.

Cursing, Jack sprinted across the room. He paused to glance at his former partner, who lay groaning on the floor, but Daskivitch waved him on. "Go! Get the bastard!"

Jack ran over to the windows. Shark fins of broken glass still clung to the edges of the hole Sperry had made. Jack tucked his gun in its holster, picked up a chair, and smashed the opening wider. He ducked through and then he was outside, squinting in the early sun. A parking area, weeds pushing up through the broken concrete. He looked left: *nothing.* He looked right and saw Sperry limping around the far edge of the shed, clutching his damaged arm. Jack sprinted after, shouting for Ray Hillhouse and the S.W.A.T.

He ran around the end of the shed, veered around an old gray Dumpster, and saw the basin to his left, sparkling now in the light. His footsteps slapped on the concrete and echoed against the wall of the shed. His breath sounded very loud in his own ears, and ragged. He turned right again, which brought him back to the graving dock. The scene was oddly beautiful, everything tinged with morning light, all orange and rose.

Sperry was staggering along the edge of the dock, the long way, grunting in pain. Jack followed. "Stop!" he called out, between gulps of air, but the man hobbled on.

A distant shout. Jack made out the figure of the S.W.A.T. at the far end of the dock. Raising his rifle.

"Don't shoot!" Jack cried.

With his customary decisiveness, Sperry skidded to a halt and started to lower himself down the stone tiers at the side of the graving dock. By the time Jack reached the spot where he had clambered down, the man was already skidding out across the ice. The dock was perhaps two hundred feet wide. Cursing, Jack lowered himself down, tier by freezing tier. Down at the end of the dock, the S.W.A.T. was running around to the far side.

The ice was treacherous. Sperry slipped, fell on his side, and slid a few yards, but he picked himself up and scrambled on. Jack almost felt sorry for the man; he was unarmed, and injured, and nearly cornered. Then he thought of all the people Sperry had killed or wounded, and his sympathy dried up. He set out, almost skating across the ice.

"Sperry!" he called, but the fugitive ignored him. He tried another tack. "Bobby!"

This time, hearing his childhood nickname, the man paused in his flight and looked over his shoulder. And that was when the ice groaned. With a sharp, gunlike report, deep cracks appeared. Sperry looked down, finally overwhelmed by surprise and confusion, and then the broken ice dipped sideways beneath him and he dropped into the frigid water. And disappeared.

After a shockingly still moment, he bobbed back up, spluttering, arms flailing, until they found the edge of the hole.

"Hold on!" Jack shouted. He thought of something he had heard when he was a kid, about how you were supposed to lie down to spread out your weight across fragile ice, and that's what he did. Unfortunately, he was at least ten yards away.

Sperry went under again. Then he bobbed back up, spit out a mouthful of water, and cried out like a panicked child.

Jack looked up across the ice: The S.W.A.T. was directly across from him now, and he had been joined by a couple of squad cars, lights flashing. "Don't move," the S.W.A.T. shouted. "Help is on the way."

Jack wriggled out of his wool coat, held on to one arm, and tried to throw the garment out across the ice. Not even close.

Sperry's grip on the ice weakened and he plunged out of sight again. Jack winced. When the man's head popped up again, Jack called out to him.

"Bobby! Tell me: Who was the boy in the coffin? Please, Bobby, tell me . . ."

There was a terrible pleading in Sperry's eyes. And then the ice cracked some more and he was gone.

CHAPTER *forty-six*

F our days later, Jack finally discovered the identity of the floating boy.

It was no great feat of deductive reasoning, no brainstorm or exceptional piecing together of clues. It was just basic detective work, just slogging on and refusing to give up. It took many hours, but Jack had them. He didn't have to be home now at any special time, and he took vacation days so he could work without a budget-conscious Sergeant Tanney telling him that the case was already finished. He did it with a computer, a fax machine, a phone, and a little luck.

In the late afternoon, he got a call from a doctor in Michigan, a response to a photo he had faxed out hundreds of times, to hospitals across the country. Young Steven Eastlund had not stayed around for treatment, but the doctor clearly remembered diagnosing the ten-year-old's illness, and meeting his parents, and the white-haired, hawk-faced man they all called Grandpa.

After a little more legwork, Jack learned that the parents, residents of Mancellus, Michigan, had been killed soon thereafter, on September 3, 2001, by a drunk driver, on a county highway in broad daylight.

A week later, the towers came down. First the diagnosis of his grandchild's illness, then the death of his daughter and son-in-law, then September 11. Who knew if the latter event had fully unhinged Robert Sperry? It certainly could not have helped.

THREE DAYS LATER, JACK and Gary Daskivitch and Linda Vargas and some other detectives from the task force and the Seventy-sixth precinct took a trip out to Long Island, where somebody had a cousin who worked for a cemetery, and they gave the boy a proper burial, with a modest little headstone that everybody had kicked in to buy.

Jack had ordered the inscription, highly unoriginal:

Rest in peace.

CHAPTER *forty-seven*

The next morning, Jack slept late. When he finally got out of bed, he discovered that he was out of coffee, so he threw on some clothes and walked down to the corner deli. When he got back, the answering machine in the front hall caught his eye. The red message light, blinking.

He ran a hand over his mouth. He wasn't due in to work until four. He was sick of reporters and lawyers and Department brass. He just wanted to sit in his kitchen and drink his coffee, maybe go up and shoot the shit for a while with Mr. Gardner, but it was hard to ignore the machine. What if it was his son, with some emergency? Or some work thing that needed his immediate attention?

He tilted his head back, groaned, and pressed Play. And froze.

Michelle's voice, tentative. "Jack? It's me. I, uh . . . can you call me?" And then she hung up. He replayed the message immediately, then a third time, trying to tease out any hidden meanings. Did she sound sad, or upset? He thought so, but couldn't be sure. He leaned against the wall and wrapped his arms around himself. What did she want? Was she having regrets? Did she want to come back? Or did she just want to find a safe time when she could come and take back her stuff?

He returned to his bedroom and sat on the edge of his bed for five minutes, thinking. Then he stood up. He didn't reach for his cell phone. He went over to the bureau and dug into a drawer for his newest, thickest pair of athletic socks. He changed into his sweatpants, and pulled on his sneakers. Then he went out to the hall closet and pulled out his sweatshirt. He picked up his car keys, and his house keys, and he locked up, and went out and got into his car.

HE FOUND A LIGHT pole on the edge of the park and pushed against it with both hands while he stretched his Achilles tendons, and then he grabbed one foot at a time and stretched his hamstrings. Then he entered the park, got on the loop road, and started running. This was what he needed right now, this steady slapping of his feet on the asphalt, the sound of his breath huffing into the winter air.

It was a weekday, so the park was sparsely populated. He glanced over at the edge of the lake, where some fat geese were waddling along. He looked up into the trees sliding past overhead, into their bare, bristly branches. He passed a couple of heavyset women helping each other work off some extra weight, and then he was passed by a Park Slope dad pushing a toddler in an expensive jogging stroller. He thought of his son, Ben, and how that was what you did, really—you pushed your kid along in front of you, huffing and sweating, until he was able to run on his own, pick up speed, and leave you panting far behind.

He was breathing harder now, and his muscles were sore, but he pressed on. He replayed Michelle's phone message in his mind a few times, but it was opaque as ever, and he resolved not to think about it for the next three quarters of an hour.

After a while, he passed the turnoff for the Center Drive. He could see farther into the woods now, could see the outlines of the mulchy earth as it rose and fell. He was just a few hundred yards from where the dead doctor had lain, and Vargas's Michelin Tire kid. He thought of the crumpled look on the doctor's wife's face, and the stricken look on the son-in-law of the Governors Island security guard. He thought of Tommy Balfa, falling to the deck of the boat, and he thought of the cocaine addict who had drowned her children, and he thought of the other dead, the hundreds of bodies he had seen pass before him in years and years on the job.

What had the little Buddhist nun called it? *Impermanence.* Everything changes. Everything that rises falls away.

One of his hamstrings was cramping a little. He thought of Robert Dietrich Sperry, disappearing beneath the ice. And he thought of Steven Eastlund's memorial voyage from Governors Island to the shores of Red Hook. At least the kid wasn't floating nameless anymore.

Three minutes later, he came to the Boathouse and the little lagoon where he had tried to propose to Michelle. He saw a Chinese bride sitting like an open white flower at the water's edge, and then another one up on the little stone bridge, and a third one on the water's far shore, and he had to smile, despite himself.

He jogged on, sweating even in the new year's cold, and then he was pounding up a steep hill on the park's northeast corner. He saw a few scraps of autumn leaves clinging to a bare winter tree, and he thought of something else the nun had said to him: that the trees didn't try to hold on to the falling leaves, and the leaves didn't hold on either; when their time came, they just fell.

He made it to the top of the hill, where he passed a runner coming down, an elfin old man jogging with his head tilted to one side, and he felt a rush of warmth—*a fellow runner*—and almost reached out to give the man a high-five.

On the other side of the park, he came upon the concrete bandshell, site of his first date with Michelle. She had actually got him up and dancing; it had been a happy night. They had had some good times together, and those times were still alive, in his heart. Funny how the nun's words kept echoing in his head: *True love is never the cause of pain.*

He thought of Michelle's phone message. In just a few minutes, he would call her, and find out what she wanted, and maybe he'd be plunged back into despair. Maybe not. Somehow, he was not in a rush to find out.

He ran and he thought, and he ran and he thought, and he stared out at the wintry landscape, and he passed a few other runners on the loop road, and felt that same little flush of human solidarity. Oxygen passed through his lungs, and he listened to the slap of his feet on the asphalt. By the time he started down the big long hill on the southwest side of the park, he wasn't thinking about much of anything anymore. He had found his stride, and the blue lake came into view, and the morning sun shone on it, highlighting hundreds of floating white seagulls, and as he came closer they suddenly lifted into the sky, and his heart rose with them.

ACKNOWLEDGMENTS

I would like to thank Reed Farrel Coleman for the last-minute backup and longtime support, and a number of other writer friends who have helped me keep my fingers on the keyboard, including Peter Blauner, S. J. Rozan, Blake Nelson, Katy Munger, Lise Mc-Clendon, Tim Sultan, Jonathan Green, Lisa Selin Davis, Virginia Vitzthum, Meeghan Truelove, Stefan Forbes, Patrick Jennings, Ulrich Baer, Jim Fusilli, Ivor Hanson, Rob Reuland, Bill Gordon, and Tim Cockey.

For firsthand info about the work of Brooklyn homicide detectives, thanks to NYPD Lieutenant John Cornicello (check out his excellent Web site, The Squad Room at www.brooklynnorth.blogspot.com). *Street Stories: The World of Police Detectives* by Robert Jackall was also a valuable resource. For forensic info, thanks to D. P. Lyle, M.D. (www.dplylemd.com). For matters nautical, thanks to Carolina Salguero (www.portsidenewyork.org), Roberta Weisbrod (www.sustainableports.com), and the Metropolitan Waterfront Alliance (www. waterwire.net). Any technical errors are my own.

Loving thanks to Sunny Balzano and Tone Johansen.

Thanks to Roxanne Aubrey for her excellent Web site design.

For support of my writing and that of many, many other authors, grateful thanks to Bonnie Claeson and Joe Guglielmelli and the

Black Orchid Bookshop; all the kind crew at Partners & Crime; Mary Gannett, Henry Zook, and Zack Zook of BookCourt bookstore; Barbara Peters and The Poisoned Pen; and Otto Penzler and The Mysterious Bookshop.

I thank my editor, Ruth Cavin, for her kind faith in me, and her assistant, Toni Plummer, for exceptional follow-through. Last, but certainly not least, thanks to my agent, Anna Ghosh.

2/08